A STORY TO STRANGLE FOR

A HOPGOOD HALL MYSTERY

E.V. HUNTER

Boldwood

First published in Great Britain in 2023 by Boldwood Books Ltd.

Cover Photography: Shutterstock and iStock

A CIP catalogue record for this book is available from the British Library.

Paperback ISBN 978-1-80483-596-8

Large Print ISBN 978-1-80483-595-1

Hardback ISBN 978-1-80483-597-5

Ebook ISBN 978-1-80483-593-7

Kindle ISBN 978-1-80483-594-4

Audio CD ISBN 978-1-80483-602-6

MP3 CD ISBN 978-1-80483-601-9

Digital audio download ISBN 978-1-80483-600-2

Boldwood Books Ltd
23 Bowerdean Street
London SW6 3TN
www.boldwoodbooks.com

1

'It's a pleasure to welcome you all to Hopgood Hall and our inaugural journalistic awareness course. For those of you who don't know me, my name is Alexi Ellis, and I was until a year ago an investigative journalist on the *Sentinel*.'

Alexi had never had a problem with public speaking, or with poking her nose into places where it wasn't always welcome. Self-assurance was a necessary requirement in her chosen profession, along with a thick skin and a determination to get to the story ahead of the opposition, no matter what impediments were placed in her path. Today though, in a situation that she ought to be able to handle with her eyes closed, she felt inexplicably nervous.

And there was a good reason for that. She was laying her reputation on the line in an effort to make the course a resounding success. She had called in favours from her old colleagues to make it so, especially from her former boss and ex-lover, Patrick Vaughan. If all went according to plan then the publicity would go a long way to cementing the reputation of the boutique hotel in Lambourn in which Alexi held a minority

shareholding. In the wake of the questionable publicity the estab-
lishment had garnered following recent unfortunate events, it *had*
to be.

Seated round an oval table in Hopgood Hall's annex, a table
covered with a crisp white cloth bearing refreshments that no one
had yet touched, the six faces of her delegates stared back at her
with friendly curiosity. The people who had gained places on a
course that could have been filled ten times over were an eclectic
mix of ages and backgrounds. Deliberately so. They all looked at
Alexi with rapt attention, hanging on her every word, putting her
in mind of a bunch of students on the first day of term, nervous
but keen to impress. Their ages ranged from mid-twenties to mid-
seventies and as far as Alexi was aware, none of them had met
before.

They all had note-taking equipment in front of them. One of
the older people had a tablet and hit the keypad with agile fingers;
the youngest had an old-fashioned pen and paper. So much for
stereotyping, Alexi thought with an ironic twist of her lips.

'We'd all be sorry excuses for amateur journalists if we didn't
recognise you,' a voice said. Alexi glanced at her notes. He was
Peter Foreman, a civil servant with rugged features, piercing blue
eyes and a thick thatch of salt-and-pepper hair. He oozed confi-
dence and clearly looked upon himself as a leader. He also, Alexi
knew, had her firmly in his sights. He'd been coming on to her at
every opportunity, even though they'd only just met, and seemed
to think that she'd be grateful for his attention.

Pompous arse!

'Thanks.' Alexi inclined her head in recognition of the compli-
ment. 'As you're aware, you are here for five days because, as Peter
just pointed out, you all have an interest in the journalistic
process. We'll be covering the manner in which the profession has
had to adapt in order to survive in the light of the social media

explosion, *instant* news and trial by public opinion, made possible by the aforementioned social media.'

'You must know all there is to know,' a woman said, nodding as though Alexi's words were gospel.

'If I thought that then I wouldn't have lasted five minutes,' Alexi replied, watching the woman's face fall. She was Emily Bairstow, forty something, Alexi reminded herself by checking her notes. A divorcee with grown children who wanted to make a fresh start now that she had the freedom to please herself. Alexi could write the book on fresh starts and took an instinctive liking to the woman, who had intelligent, expressive eyes and under-stated style. 'I did promise that I wouldn't sugar coat,' Alexi added, smiling at Emily, 'and if anyone thinks that being a journalist is glamorous then I'm afraid you're in for a rude awakening.'

'Nothing glamorous about standing outside in all weathers, waiting for some minor celebrity that no one's heard of or cares about to emerge from a night club. Take it from one who knows.'

A thickset younger man said his piece and then crossed massive arms over his chest, as though defying anyone to repute his words. His application had intrigued Alexi. A bouncer from the east end of London was the last person she'd have expected to show an interest in her course, which was one of the reasons why he'd made the shortlist.

'Thanks, Archie,' Alexi said. 'Your comment brings me nicely on to the number one golden rule for this course. What is that golden rule in the world of journalism?' she asked. 'Can anyone tell me?'

A young Indian girl's hand shot up. 'Get the story before the opposition does,' she said.

'That's important, Ranya, but not quite what I was after. Anyone else?'

Several more suggestions were made. Alexi reminded herself

that none of these people, as far as she was aware, seriously wanted a career in journalism. They were taking a layman's interest for a variety of reasons. Some wanted to write short stories; others wanted to contribute articles to local papers and magazines; one wanted to write an investigative novel about an unsolved crime; several, like Emily, the divorcee, were simply interested.

As the ice was broken and the residents exchanged more or more unlikely suggestions between themselves, Alexi let them run on. But when she raised a hand, she was immediately rewarded with silence.

'The story,' she said simply. 'Nothing is more important than the story. And getting the facts straight. What Mrs Housewife at number seven said about the man who regularly knocked his wife about until he killed her simply won't wash. If, on the other hand, a witness actually saw the man behaving violently towards his nearest-and-dearest, that's another matter. The witness has to be able to back up his assertion with evidence, otherwise you'll be reduced to using the words *allegedly* and *accused of* and so forth, which isn't news at all. It's merely repeating what's already in the public domain and is likely to bore your readers rigid.'

'That's what the reporters on TV do all the time,' a woman called Grace Western remarked. 'They simply repeat what the anchor's already said.'

'Very true.' Alexi replied, nodding. Grace – she with the tablet computer – was the oldest person on the course. In her early seventies, she looked at least ten years younger. Her hair was shoulder length, without any grey to give her age away, and her face was surprisingly wrinkle-free. She was tall, with a figure that women half her age would likely give their right arms to possess, and there was a natural elegance about her that Alexi admired. 'And one of the reasons why I became an investigative journalist rather than one of the pack reporting on breaking news. As Archie pointed out just now, standing about for hours waiting for a soundbite becomes... well, restrictive.'

'But in-depth investigation enables you to triple check facts and brings its own rewards,' Peter said, nodding as though he knew what he was talking about. Alexi didn't like the voracious civil servant, nor did she like the way he undressed her with his eyes, but she tried not to let it show. It was early days, everyone was nervous. She would withhold judgement.

For now.

'The purpose of this course is for you to flex your own investigative muscles,' Alexi said. 'For the next five days, you are encouraged to search Lambourn for an interesting story that can be expanded into a public interest piece for the *Newbury Post*. The editor, Bill Naylor, will be here to meet you all at dinner time and has promised to publish at least a part of the most promising contributions.'

A mutter of excitement rippled through the room. Alexi hadn't told them that their purple prose might see the light of publication, mainly because she'd only just managed to twist the editor's arm.

'Think outside the box,' she added, 'and remember the second rule of good journalism, which I referred to a moment ago.' She allowed a significant pause, confident of her audience's complete attention. 'Thou shalt not bore thy reader. For instance, Mrs Potts winning the best in show for her runner beans three years in succession is hardly ground-breaking journalism. What's her secret? How does she eclipse fierce opposition to win the coveted prize year after year? Does she read her veg bedtime stories? Readers love quirky things like that.'

Peter sniffed. 'Hardly Booker Prize stuff,' he said.

'Where in a local paper, not known for its world-wide coverage, would the piece be published?' Alexi asked. 'Who would be your target readership?'

'The gardening section,' Grace responded, sharing a collusive smile with Alexi. 'Horticulturalists would actively seek it out. Locals are the readers, obviously.'

Alexi nodded. 'Think big but start small and get recognised.'

There was a pause as Diana Horton, a middle-aged, frumpy travel agent who'd taken an active interest but had yet to speak a word, reached for the coffee pot and volunteered to pour for everyone. Diana, Alexi noticed, was the first to reach for the biscuits once the cups had been handed round. Her gaze lingered pensively on Peter's face for a prolonged moment, and she looked conflicted. Alexi was about to ask her if they knew one another but Archie spoke, diverting her attention.

'We don't have to write about vegetables, do we?' he asked, dunking a biscuit in his coffee.

'Absolutely not. Use your imagination. Wander about the village, visit local businesses and wait for inspiration to strike.'

Please patronise local businesses, she silently pleaded. Alexi had visited pubs and shops, promising that her aspiring journalists would raise their profile. She was attempting to manage the damage done to the village's reputation in general and Hopgood Hall's in particular following three murders that had occurred in the past year, all with connections to Alexi and the hotel.

'Well, it's obvious what's of interest,' Peter said. 'The murders.'

'Already done.' Alexi fixed him with a challenging look. She had expected the question and wasn't surprised that Peter had been the one to voice it. Best to get the elephant in the room – the bait that had probably attracted at least some of her attendees – out in the open. 'By me. Of course, if you think you can find a different angle then feel free to give it your best shot.'

'One imagines that the village wants to play the murders down so the local paper is hardly likely to print anything about them.'

Alexi flashed a grateful smile towards Grace, impressed by her insight.

'Cosmo then,' Peter said, folding his arms defensively.

He was referring to the feral cat that Alexi had come across beneath Waterloo arches when she'd once visited the area to do a piece about the people living rough there. For reasons she had never understood, the wild cat had decided to adopt Alexi. Taciturn, and sometimes downright aggressive if he took a dislike to a person, he'd proven to be a surprisingly good judge of character. He'd also stolen the show by posing for Alexi's former colleagues during recent murder investigations.

Alexi laughed, on safer ground now. 'You'll have the dubious pleasure of meeting Cosmo later, Peter, so I'll make a deal with you. If he lets you approach him, then write what you like about him, *if* you can think of an angle that hasn't already been done to death. My cat does *not* shy away from publicity.'

Alexi would bet her bank balance on Cosmo taking a dislike against Peter.

'Deal,' Peter replied, rubbing his hands together and winking at her.

'I would suggest delving into the cases that come before the local magistrates, if any of you have a desire to report on crime. The verdicts will have been handed down but perhaps there will be an opportunity to speak to the person who's been convicted. Find out what made them do it, especially if the person was of previous good character.'

Several heads nodded and notes were scribbled.

'This is, of course, horse country and local trainers' successes are widely reported. But how about the grooms who care for the pampered equines and seldom get to share in the glory? What are their stories? What got them into the horsy world?' Alexi spread her hands. 'Think local interest.'

Ranya tugged a long plait over her shoulder. 'Horses petrify me,' she said. 'I think I'll steer well clear of them.'

'Then you, Ranya, might turn your thoughts to the time of year. We're coming up to Halloween, which is now a big deal for adults and kids alike in this country, but never used to be. What's changed? Is it a US trend that's made its way across the pond? Is there any foundation in the spiritual myth of Samhain?'

'That's not local stuff,' Peter objected.

'What, people don't celebrate Halloween in Lambourn?' Archie asked before Alexi could.

'A quicker path to national fame, if one can explode the myth,' Grace pointed out with quiet dignity.

'What did I miss?'

All heads turned as the door opened and Jack Maddox strolled through it, looking like he'd just stepped off the cover of a gent's magazine. Although he and Alexi were an item and cohabiting, her heart still stalled when she saw him unexpectedly. And even when she didn't. He appeared to have caught the attention of every woman in the room, who undoubtedly appreciated his physical attributes as much as Alexi did. Predictably, Peter scowled at him. The civil servant seemed to have an inflated opinion of his own attractiveness and didn't appreciate the competition from a man who had nothing to prove in that regard.

'This is Jack Maddox,' Alexi said. 'Ex Met police, now local private investigator.'

'Hi,' Jack said, giving the gathering a little wave as he took a seat beside Alexi. 'And welcome one and all.'

'Jack will be on hand to offer help and advice on any police procedural queries you might have before writing your piece. Or pieces. You have five days and can write as many as you like in that period. I will be here to offer guidance, if you want me to. If you'd prefer to keep it to yourself until the final full stop then feel free.'

'You've given us a lot of scope and a plenty of food for thought,' Diana remarked, helping herself to the last biscuit.

'You forget to mention Patrick Vaughan's involvement,' Peter said. 'That's why I'm here. The local rag is all very well but I'm confident that I'll be able to interest Patrick in my style. Think big, that's what I say.'

Alexi shot a glance at Jack. They had argued over Patrick's participation, such as it was. He would appear at the final night's party and cast a quick eye over the participants' efforts – the carrot and stick approach. Alexi was pretty sure that he wouldn't be taking on any of her wannabes any time soon, but his name was nonetheless a draw. Jack had argued that he'd only offered his services because it was a way to keep close to Alexi. Whilst that might well be the case, Jack failed to accept that he had nothing to worry about in that regard. She found such a self-assured man's uncertainty about her commitment to their relationship mostly endearing, occasionally frustrating.

She most emphatically did not need his protection.

'Exactly.' Alexi smiled. 'I shall be interested to see what you come up with. But for now, I shall leave you all to settle into your rooms. The annex and its facilities are for your exclusive use this week but, of course, you are free to use the public parts of the main hotel as well. Get to know one another, exchange ideas, work together if you have similar ideas. There are no rules. Lunch will be served in an hour.'

'By your handsome chef?' Emily asked with a mischievous smile. 'Perhaps he'll be dish of the day.'

Everyone laughed.

'Don't encourage Marcel,' Alexi advised, laughing along with them as she and Jack stood up. Marcel, their temperamental chef, was a lady's man through and through but the only abiding love of his life was his creative food, about which he was passionate. 'If you're thinking of interviewing him, I'd advise against it. He received more than his share of publicity when he was briefly suspected of murdering a contestant in the cookery contest staged here,' she added, thinking it better to get that one out in the open too, 'and now only talks to journalists about his food.'

'Shame.' Grace smiled. 'You're not making this easy for us, are you?'

Alexi returned her smile as she headed for the door. 'Where would be the fun in that?' she asked.

'Well done,' Jack said, taking her hand as they strolled across the courtyard towards the main part of the hotel. There was a strong wind gusting and rain threatened. Again. They'd had more than their fair share of it recently.

'I haven't done anything yet,' she replied, 'other than to give in to pressure and host this course. Still can't decide why I did.'

'You know why,' Jack replied, squeezing her hand.

Alexi nodded, because it was true. Jack had been all for exploiting the murder rate in Lambourn by holding murder mystery weekends, but Alexi had vetoed that idea, thinking but not saying that it was tacky. Besides, they had to do something different to restore the reputation of the hotel and fill rooms. They were in agreement on that point, and this seemed like the obvious way to go. Jack had insisted that Alexi's solid reputation as a journalist would have people flocking to join the course and that had proven to be the case. She was flattered; her ego stoked by the response. But she had insisted upon keeping it small: just six participants this time. If it went well, she'd consider expanding the numbers for future courses.

'Hello, you,' she said, bending to scratch Cosmo's flat ears when he appeared out of nowhere with Toby, a terrier half his size, trailing faithfully in his wake. 'I hope you don't intend to terrorise my guests, although I suppose I wouldn't mind if you hiss at Peter and put him in his place.'

'The civil servant?' Jack asked.

'Yeah, he's going to be a problem. Not sure why he felt the need to come, given that he thinks he already knows it all.'

Jack laughed. 'You'll keep him in line.'

Jack opened the door to the hotel's private kitchen, domain of owners Drew and Cheryl Hopgood, Alexi's close friends. She'd run to Lambourn with Cosmo, her tail between her legs, when her position on the *Sentinel* had become untenable. Her lover and political editor, Patrick Vaughan, had known that redundancies were in the offing but hadn't given her the heads-up. He'd tried to persuade her to take a lesser position, but Alexi knew her worth and was having none of it, forcing a generous settlement out of the paper instead.

Patrick had assumed that country life would bore her and that she would return to London. And to his bed. He'd been wrong on both counts and, murders notwithstanding, Alexi had found both contentment and a man she adored in this most unlikely of locations. She had also invested in Hopgood Hall, encouraging her friends to expand, but her efforts had been rewarded with not one but two murders taking place on the premises.

In both cases, she and Jack had unveiled the identity of the killers, neither of whom had any connection to the hotel. Even so, once the initial influx of guests curious to see the scene for themselves had waned, Alexi was surprised when bookings didn't immediately tail off.

Naturally, Marcel claimed it was his food that held people's interest. Since the restaurant was booked for weeks in advance, that was likely true. Even so, the profits from the restaurant alone weren't sufficient to keep the old house maintained and the business ticking over. Something had to be done to fill the rooms year round and keep the place in people's mind for reasons other than violent death.

'How's it going?' Cheryl asked, looking up from playing on a rug with Verity, her daughter who was just a year old.

'It's going,' Alexi replied, grimacing.

'Relax!' Drew walked into the room. 'The only thing that will be murdered this time is the English language and I dare say it'll recover from the odd misplaced semicolon.'

'Easy for you to say,' Alexi replied, smiling as she took Verity from her mother, barely conscious of sticky fingers digging into her hair.

'I appreciate that you're doing this for our sake,' Cheryl said, taking Verity back when her head lolled on Alexi's shoulder. 'I know you have a lot going on and I want you to know that I appreciate the sacrifice you're making.'

Alexi felt bad for complaining when she still felt responsible for the damage that had been caused in Lambourn only since her arrival in the village. Her head told her that she had nothing to feel guilty about, but her conscience was having none of it. She had overheard more than one person muttering comments about her being a Jonah. About there being no place in the country for townies like her, who didn't understand local customs and traditions. Polly Pearson, the middle-aged owner of a long-established B&B, was Alexi's main detractor and Jack insisted, the source of the gossip. Alexi barely knew the woman and had not, as far as she was aware, done anything to offend her. It wasn't as if Hopgood Hall was likely to take her business. The two establishments were at opposite ends of the market.

'Don't worry.' Alexi smiled her reassurance. 'I'm a woman. Multi-tasking goes with the territory.'

'Well, even if this course is the unmitigated success that I expect it to be,' Drew said, 'don't feel that you have to do it again if the participants drive you bonkers.'

'I can out-bonkers the lot of them,' Alexi quipped.

'How's the outline for the book coming on?' Drew asked.

'Good question.' And one that Alexi didn't really have an answer for.

After the first murder that she and Jack had solved shortly after Alexi's arrival in Lambourn, she had accepted a large advance from a publisher to write a full-length book on the case. It had shot to the top of the non-fiction charts. Everyone wanted to read about murder, it seemed, especially when a well-known public figure proved to be the guilty party. The proceeds, along with her settlement from the *Sentinel*, the sale of her London flat and an inheritance from her late mother, had left her awash with funds. Funds that she'd utilised to help her friends extend their business, resulting in two more murders.

Perhaps Polly Pearson was right to brand her a Jonah.

She had declined the opportunity to write a book on the latest catastrophe, preferring not to draw more speculation in Hopgood Hall's direction. Instead, she'd accepted an advance to write a collection of in-depth exposés about cases of abuse, corruption and violent crime where the perpetrators had evaded justice. Stories that she had written for the *Sentinel* but which had not seen the light of publication because the paper's legal team weren't willing to risk being sued. An opportunity to lay out the facts and highlight the loopholes in the legal system pounced upon by expensive defence barristers was too good to resist.

'Still in the early stages,' she replied, in answer to Drew's question, 'but I have to say that I'm quite excited about the project.'

'The pen is mightier than the sword and all that,' Jack remarked.

'It's a balancing act. Social media is a very powerful weapon but can be misused. I really don't approve of the way that reputations, lives in some cases, can be destroyed on the back of rumour and inuendo. At the same time, I *know* the people I'm intending to write about got away, literally with murder in some instances, thanks to the vagaries of our legal system. The police know it too and are beyond frustrated at the hoops they have to jump through to prove their guilt.' Alexi shrugged. 'We're talking ruthless individuals who think they are above the law. I simply want to set the record straight.'

'I've seen a few mentions online. Your publishers are already getting their PR in gear,' Drew said. 'You will have half the criminal fraternity wetting themselves.'

Alexi laughed and shook her head. 'Sticks and stones. Nothing I say can hurt them, at least insofar as they can't be banged up because they've already been tried and acquitted. Their reputations are another matter though and I won't lose any sleep over exposing them for the scumbags that they are.'

'Quite right,' Jack agreed. 'The public hate injustice. Alexi's name carries some weight. She's known as a serious journalist who checks her facts, not someone out for a cheap thrill, so perhaps the authorities will sit up and take notice. It's high time some of these scrotes who think they're untouchable are named and shamed.'

'True.' Drew nodded. 'Anyway, we'll wait for Cheryl to put Verity down, then we'll have lunch. I take it you have to go back and hold your delegates hands shortly, Alexi.'

'Yep. Once they've had lunch, I'm gonna set them loose.' She grinned. 'Don't say you haven't been warned.'

Drew laughed. 'How much harm can a bunch of wannabe writers do in a small village?' he asked.

2

The participants set about their assignment with enthusiasm over the next two days. Jack was glad to see Alexi gradually relax, despite Peter Foreman's obvious determination to monopolise her attention. The man was an irritating know-it-all who fancied himself as a ladies' man and had Alexi in his sights. But as she herself had told him when they'd talked about it the night before, she'd had more than her fair share of staving off unwanted attentions during the course of her career.

Jack had sensed Alexi's abiding doubts about the wisdom of running the course, even though she stopped short of actually saying that something was bound to go wrong. She was starting to believe the local gossip – the poison spread by Polly Pearson in particular. Ordinarily level-headed, she was halfway to convincing herself that she was a Jonah, but her guilt was misplaced. Nothing that had happened in Lambourn since her arrival in the village had been her fault, but he couldn't deny either that tongues were wagging, or that fingers were being pointed in her direction.

Jack would do just about anything to prevent her from returning to London and that smarmy bastard, Patrick Vaughan.

Despite the fact that she now felt at home in Lambourn, that would be the most obvious course for her to take if anything else untoward were to occur. There was anonymity in big cities and the world's wrongs couldn't be placed at her door if she hid away in the suburbs.

All her attendees were in fine form, if one overlooked Peter's determination to dominate. Jack went out of his way to schmooze with them all, putting them at their ease by sharing amusing anecdotes about his years in the Met. Bill Naylor, the editor of the local paper, played his part too and Jack could sense that the love of his life was beginning to have faith in herself.

'It's going well,' Jack said as they prepared to leave her cottage on the penultimate day.

'If one ignores Peter. Why he thinks he's God's gift is beyond me.' She rolled her eyes. 'He obviously doesn't see what the rest of us do when he looks in the mirror.'

'Do you know what projects they have taken on, as a matter of interest?'

'Let's see. Emily is doing a piece on a single mum who's been threatened with eviction because the father of her kids has stopped paying maintenance and so she can't afford her rent. Archie Walton is looking into how grooms et al exist without any sort of nightlife which, given his career as a bouncer, is an obvious area of interest. He writes surprisingly well. He's interviewed a few grooms and reports their responses without getting all flowery, or over-wordy, which is a common mistake with amateurs. Ranya and Diana have joined forces to report on integration here in a small village.'

'Is there anything to report on?'

'You'd be surprised. Grace has chosen Halloween.'

'And Peter? I assume he didn't get anywhere with Cosmo.'

Aware that he was being talked about, Cosmo looked up at

Jack through wide, unblinking eyes and mewed, making him and Alexi smile.

'Not a chance! I wish he had in some respects because he's chosen to delve into the supposed sighting of the wanted gangster in the Franklin case.'

'Paul Franklin? Ha, good luck with that one.'

'He says he wants to talk to me about something important that happened in London.'

'To do with Franklin?' Jack permitted his surprise to show. 'Why?'

She shrugged. 'Absolutely no idea.'

'You think that's what attracted him to the course? The local supposed sighting, I mean.'

'I really couldn't say. The man makes me uneasy.' Alexi picked up her bag and searched it for her car keys. 'Why he thinks I need to know is baffling. Something about a mutual acquaintance apparently but he won't tell me who.'

'He wants to get you alone so he can wow you with his charm, darling.' Jack frowned. 'Should I be worried?'

'We're eloping next week.' She grinned at Jack when his frown deepened. 'If I even suspected that I'd read Peter all wrong, Cosmo's reaction to his attempts to befriend him would have reassured me. The man's a plonker out to make trouble. Not sure why I feel that way about him. I mean, what can he do, other than attempt to monopolise my attention, which I won't stand for?' Alexi's expression remained resolute. 'I absolutely need this course to be a success and I won't permit him to ruin it.'

'If he gives you any more trouble, I'll get Cassie to do some digging into his background. Everyone has an agenda nowadays so it's better to be safe than sorry, especially after what you just told me about a mutual friend in London.'

'Thanks. Let's hope it doesn't come to that.'

Jack wasn't about to tell her that he'd already had a brief look at all the participants' backgrounds. Or more to the point, his business partner had. He absolutely did not want anything else to go wrong for Alexi or she really would be driven out of Lambourn by local hostility.

And there was only one place and one person she would run to.

Not happening!

Having located her car keys, Alexi kissed Jack and left the cottage with Cosmo at her heels. She was headed for the hotel and her morning briefing. Jack needed to be at the office in Newbury that he shared with Cassie Fenton.

Cassie, a friend of Jack's ex-wife, had attempted to take her place once the divorce was final, but Jack didn't share her feelings. They worked well as a team on investigations though, since Cassie could make computers sing for her and nothing online stayed hidden from her for long.

Cassie had thrown a wobbly when Jack got together with Alexi, and he thought at first that he and Cassie would have to go their separate ways professionally. But she'd gotten over her jealousy and their partnership had endured. Not that Jack and Alexi were likely to socialise with Cassie any time soon, but Jack was fine with the status quo.

He reached the office and was surprised not to find Cassie in her usual place in front of her computers, head down, intent upon whatever flashed up on any of her three screens. He shrugged, thinking it was high time she gave her personal life some priority, but he absolutely wasn't going there so busied himself with his outstanding paperwork. The phones were quiet, and he managed to get a lot done.

He glanced at the clock when his mobile rang, surprised to see that it was almost lunchtime. Cassie's name flashed up on his screen.

'Hey, Cas, what's up?' he asked, resisting the urge to ask her why she wasn't in the office.

'There's a lead on your case. I assume you're in Lambourn.'

'Nope, I'm in the office. Why?'

'Meet me at the Swan in Shefford. I have a potential lead on Amy.'

'Okay. I'm on my way.'

He hung up without asking any questions, locked the office and headed for his car. Cassie did spend most of her time in the office nursing her precious computers, but it wasn't unheard of for her to venture into the field. They were attempting to locate Amy Dawson, the wife of a close friend of Cassie's who'd gone missing, so she had a personal interest in the case.

The Swan was less than five miles from Lambourn, a popular gastro pub/hotel with a terrace backing onto the river. Jack hadn't been able to uncover any connection to Amy in the area; she was from Winchester. Presumably, Cassie's online sleuthing had come up with something important enough to drag her out of the office.

Jack's short journey was made longer by an accident on a narrow country road and it was fifteen minutes before he could get past it. He finally pulled into the Swan's car park. It was half-full of high-end vehicles. A couple of bikes were chained up in a stand by the door. One, a yellow mountain bike, caught Jack's attention. Cassie, leaning against the bonnet of her car, waved when she saw him and walked over.

'What kept you?' she asked.

'Accident. Have I missed something important?'

'You just missed your girlfriend,' she said, looking edgy.

'Alexi?'

'You have more than one?'

Jack shrugged, recalling that Alexi had planned to meet Peter there. Bill Naylor had talked about a case of mistaken identity that his paper had covered in Shefford recently: the case that Peter had taken it upon himself to delve into. The person in question had been wrongly identified as Paul Franklin, a criminal on the run who was wanted in connection with a bullion robbery at Southampton docks that had left a man in hospital, fighting for his life. Just the sort of case that a more enterprising wannabe of Peter's ilk might be tempted to investigate in his pursuit of journalistic fame, which had probably been Bill's intention when mentioning it.

'What brings you here?' Jack asked.

'Amy was seen in the area less than a week ago. Well, not seen precisely but she was definitely here.'

'How do you know?'

'Her credit card was used.'

'That's interesting. She's been missing for a week and not used it once, which made us think that she must be staying with someone. Either that or she's been using cash. What's she hiding from, Cas?' Jack's mind whirled with possibilities as he fixed his partner with a probing look. 'Her husband is your friend. You must have some idea.'

'Neil isn't the problem if that's what you're implying.' Cassie spoke emphatically, almost as though she was attempting to convince herself.

Jack shook a warning finger at her. 'You know better than to make assumptions.'

'I've known Neil for twenty years,' she protested. 'He was a vegan long before it became fashionable. He believes in the sanctity of life, all life, and literally wouldn't harm a fly.'

'We none of us know what we're capable of when boxed into a corner. Besides, there are more ways to intimidate than physical violence. Amy wouldn't have disappeared without a word if she wasn't afraid of him.'

Cassie folded her arms across her chest. A strong wind blew fallen leaves into the air and sent them whirling about in eddies. Yet more rain threatened. Her gesture was defensive rather than an attempt to keep warm and he knew that she wouldn't be receptive to his suggestions of marital disharmony. 'We were working on the assumption that she'd been abducted.'

'But hadn't uncovered any proof to back that theory up. They aren't a wealthy couple but if she had been snatched for some reason other than money then Neil would have been contacted by now.'

'He does deal in sensitive government information.'

Jack nodded. 'So you say, but if he thought she'd been taken in order to extract information from him then why call us in? And why tell the police for that matter?'

Cassie let out a long sigh. 'Yeah, point taken. You're still veering towards her having an affair and leaving Neil for the other man. In which case, why didn't she just tell him she was scarpering?'

'Perhaps because I'm right and he's controlling or mentally abusive. Men of that ilk are very good at hiding their proclivities. Anyway, let's talk to them inside and see if we can get a handle on who used Amy's credit card.' Jack started walking towards the entrance. 'Let's hope it was Amy herself.'

Jack led the way across the car park, scattered with a rainbow of falling leaves still being tossed about by a sharp northerly wind. He entered a pleasant foyer, decorated in orange and black and an array of spiders' webs in anticipation of Halloween, and was greeted by a smiling hostess.

'A table for two?' she asked.

Jack offered her a smile that usually got him what he wanted, at least where women were concerned. He heard Cassie, at his side, inhale sharply.

'We're investigators,' he said, flashing his identification beneath her nose, 'and were hoping you could help us.'

'Not the Franklin case again,' she responded with a theatrical sigh. 'How many more people do I have to tell?'

'The bullion robbery?'

'Like you didn't already know.' The professional smile had disappeared. Without it, Jack could see that she was older than she appeared; hardened and not easily manipulated 'That sort of publicity is bad for business.'

Bill Naylor was still a relatively young man, keen to make a name for himself as a journalist. Jack wondered if he'd dangled that particular case beneath the noses of Alexi's delegates because he thought there was still something fishy about the supposed mistaken identity. Amateurs asking innocent questions often got better results than their professional counterparts, Jack knew. It was a long shot but breaking the story and taking the credit for bringing a vicious thug to justice would be Bill's ticket out of local journalism.

'Actually, we're looking for a missing person whose credit card was used here last week. Can you help us out?'

The woman whose name badge identified her as Sally looked dubious. 'I'm not sure. Isn't that sort of stuff supposed to be confidential?'

'Do you have CCTV?' Cassie asked, speaking for the first time.

The woman shook her head. 'What date are we talking?'

Cassie told her. She and Jack waited as she rummaged through her computer.

'No one of that name booked a room here. If her card was used in the bar, I can't tell you anything about that.'

Jack glanced at Cassie when she opened her mouth and shook

his head. 'Were you on duty on the thirteenth?' he asked, showing Sally a picture of Amy. 'Do you recognise her?'

'Possibly. Not sure. Faces all look the same after a while. I don't take much notice. Too busy.'

'Is there anyone who would know?' Cassie asked, an impatient edge to her voice.

'Even if there is, I doubt they'd tell you anything.' Sally had clearly taken exception to Cassie's abrupt manner. He wished she'd keep her mouth shut and leave things to him. Cassie's decision to remain mostly in the office wasn't solely attributable to her computer skills. By her own admission, she was most emphatically not a people person, especially when she was lied to – a frequent occurrence in their line of work. 'Confidentiality and all that. We were told, after the supposed sighting of that robber guy, to remain professional. I told that bloke who came this morning the same thing.'

'Someone was asking about this lady?' Cassie asked.

'No, about the criminal. I had to get quite shirty with him.' She huffed. 'Honestly, some people.'

'Okay,' Jack said, 'thanks for your time.'

'What the hell!' Cassie demanded as they walked away. 'She knew more than she was saying.'

'Even if that's true, we could have got her to tell us how?'

'I don't know.' Cassie threw up her hands. 'Somehow.'

'Even if Amy *was* here, she's long gone and chances are she didn't leave a forwarding address.'

'Even so.'

'Know when to back off, Cassie. If you're certain that there's something here, tell the police. They *can* demand answers.'

'Yeah, okay.' She still seemed on edge, reluctant to let it go. Amy was her friend's wife, so she was probably permitting emotion to cloud her professional judgement. 'Even so,' she added, glancing at two members of staff taking a smoking break on the back terrace, collars turned up against the wind. 'Since we're here, we might as well...'

Her voice abruptly broke off when a piercing scream echoed from upstairs in the pub. Cassie gasped. Jack's training kicked in and he instinctively ran in its direction. He took the stairs three at a time and discovered a vacuum cleaner abandoned in the hallway leading to the toilets. A woman, presumably the one who'd screamed, sat on the floor, looking as white as a sheet.

Several people had emerged to see what the fuss was all about, one of them clearly the manager, but at a word from Jack, he hung back. Jack entered the gents and felt a dull sense of inevitability when he discovered Peter Foreman, Alexi's troublesome civil servant, slumped against the urinal.

He felt for a pulse but knew he wouldn't find one.

3

'You look tired,' Cheryl remarked, smiling across the kitchen table at Alexi. 'But really, you should be feeling exhilarated. Your course is an unmitigated success. Everyone I meet seems to be singing your praises. You've managed to be both professional and approachable.' Cheryl giggled. 'I think your delegates are a little star struck.'

Alexi laughed and waved the suggestion aside. 'Rubbish! Cosmo is the only star in this set-up.'

Alexi's cat looked up from Toby's basket, rested his chin on the dog's back and mewled in agreement, making the ladies laugh.

'Well anyway, whatever your secret, you're well on the way to putting the past behind us and re-establishing the hotel's standing. Not that it needs re-establishing precisely, despite what you seem to think. Bookings are steady and Marcel's reputation ensures that the restaurant is always full.'

'Even so—'

'Even so nothing. Stop beating yourself up over events that were none of your doing. Drew and I were on the verge of bankruptcy when you came to Lambourn and shook us by the scruff of our necks. Without your foresight, we *would* have gone under. Now we're even contemplating taking a holiday. I know, astonishing or what?' Cheryl added, grinning. 'And we can even afford to pay for it.'

'Then I'm glad. You could certainly do with a break away from this place. You and Drew never stop working.' Alexi stretched her arms above her head and yawned. 'As to the course, it is going well, I suppose, and I do like the attendees.' She chuckled. 'Well, most of them.'

Cheryl's expression turned sympathetic. 'Peter still thinks he's God's gift to journalism in general and women in particular, does he?'

'I don't know what thoughts go through his head, but I do know that he's driving me demented with his neediness.' Alexi let out a protracted sigh. 'I tell you, if he touches my arm, my shoulder, any part of me one more time, he'll get an elbow in places where the sun don't shine.'

'Oh dear. That bad, is it?'

'The sad part of it all is that he's quite intelligent and isn't a bad writer. But then again, he's not nearly as good as he thinks he is.'

'I suppose that rather depends upon what he wants to get out of the course. Does he see it as an escape from being a dreary civil servant by turning himself into... I don't know, the latest John Grisham? Or does he see himself as a whistle blower, writing an explosive exposé of the government of the day's dirty secrets?'

'Perhaps one of those. We all have to dream. Not sure what part of the civil service he works for, though. Could be nothing to do with anything sensitive.'

'How does he get along with the others?'

'He's argumentative, a real know it all. It's... I don't know, it's always as though he wants to create friction within the group.

Archie ignores him but he imposes himself on the ladies and they're all too nice to tell him to take a hike. Well, all bar Diana. She doesn't put up with his bullshit.'

'You realise that single, heterosexual men are in short supply, women of a certain age are supposedly desperate, Peter is good looking and so thinks they should be grateful for the attention.'

'Ha! Dream on.' Alexi threw her head back and closed her eyes. 'Is Patrick still here?'

'Yes, I think so. Well, he hasn't checked out yet, but I haven't seen him around anywhere today.'

'Hmm.'

Alexi shouldn't have been surprised that Patrick had used the course as an excuse to descend upon Lambourn. It bothered her that he was still being so tenacious, to say nothing of the fact that his early arrival – he wasn't due to put in an appearance until the final night – had caused friction between her and Jack. He hadn't actually said anything, but he clearly suspected that Alexi had known he'd intended to stick his nose in before his presence was required.

She wondered how Patrick had managed to get away from the paper. In her day, his workload had been manic, his physical presence necessary to iron out the glitches that arose all the time, but when she'd pointed that out to him, he'd simply shrugged evasively.

'I don't suppose he'll go back now, only to return again tomorrow,' Alexi said. 'Even Peter's irritating presence didn't seem to faze him.' She sighed. 'I wish I knew what his agenda is – Patrick's, that is.'

'He hasn't given up on you, Alexi, that much is obvious. *And* he hates seeing you with Jack.'

'Yeah, I know.' Alexi tapped her fingers restlessly against the tabletop. 'And I can assure you that Jack isn't too happy to have him hanging around. Honestly!' Alexi let out a deep sigh. 'For a tough guy, Jack can be surprisingly sensitive and insecure. I've told him endless times that Patrick and I are history.'

'But you do have a common interest that Jack can't compete with.'

'Journalism? Yeah, that's true or would be but for the fact that I prefer the sort of writing I do nowadays. I can set my own agenda and don't have to freeze my backside off chasing down stories and attempting to scoop the opposition. That's a young person's game.' She yawned again behind her hand. 'Anyway, quite what Patrick hopes to achieve by hanging around is beyond me.'

Alexi's phone rang. She checked the display, sighed again and took the call.

'My agent,' she explained, concluding a terse conversation and picking up her coffee cup. 'The publishers are putting on the pressure regarding the book I've agreed to write. It's getting talked about and they want me to exploit the interest by going on the chat show circuit while the subject's still hot, which I've said all along that I'm not willing to do. I've told all and sundry that I can't give the project much attention this week either but it's clear that particular email's being ignored. They seem to think that my days will be my own whilst my delegates are off pursuing their stories. I've told them that I run round to their various locations, checking on them all, making sure that they don't frighten the horses.' She grinned. 'In this village, I'm speaking literally.'

'You've just done the rounds. Any problems?'

'None, as long as you disregard a professional difference of opinion with Peter but that's old news. He's got one day left to turn something in but so far, he's got nothing. I suggested that he change tack but he won't be told. Still thinks he knows best, seems obsessed with the Franklin case and is convinced that the wanted man is hanging out around here somewhere.'

'In fairness, if he could somehow prove that he was seen in the district, it *would* give him the edge. You did tell them all to think laterally.'

Alexi rolled her eyes. 'How do you prove a rumour?'

Cheryl shrugged. 'By talking to the source of that rumour, I guess.'

'Yep, if someone knew who *had* started it. But no one does and everyone he's spoken to doesn't know where they heard it. He's knocking his head against a brick wall but is too stubborn to admit defeat.'

'He could do a piece about rumours, I guess, and how they gain momentum, using the supposed sighting as an example.'

'Now *that*,' Alexi replied, sitting a little straighter, 'is an excellent idea. Why didn't I think of it?'

'He wanted to talk to you about a mutual London acquaintance, I think you said.'

Alexi flapped a hand. 'Something and nothing, just as I thought. He was only name dropping in an attempt to impress me.' Alexi didn't bother to add that they'd had a difference of opinion – that is to say, a blazing row. Cheryl didn't need to shoulder Alexi's problems.

'Your skills are in demand, darling, and so they should be. But don't let those publishers, Peter, or anyone else bully you out of your comfort zone.'

'Oh, believe me, I won't! If there's one thing I've learned since becoming my own boss, it's that I can make my own schedule. No more chasing deadlines or persuading editors to run with my stories, threats of legal action notwithstanding.'

'Despite your attention being on the course this week, I'm

betting you're still putting in the hours on the outline for your book.'

Alexi flashed a self-deprecating smile. 'How well you know me,' she said.

A wail echoed through the baby monitor. Cheryl sighed and pushed herself to her feet. 'I have a different sort of deadline,' she said, smiling and leaving the room.

Tired, feeling the strain, Alexi was seriously tempted to take a nap. She hadn't slept well during the course, always expecting something to go wrong.

* * *

Jack, for all his experience of violent crime, couldn't quite believe what he was seeing with his own eyes. One of Alexi's delegates, dead. Murdered. Another violent crime with a connection to her. It not only defied belief but would also destroy Alexi, who would be convinced she was to blame.

Personal considerations notwithstanding, Jack's professional instincts kicked in as he cleared the scene and checked for a pulse. He didn't expect to find one given the ligature marks around Peter's neck and his wide-open, staring eyes.

Peter had been strangled, here in the men's room, but how that was even possible and why no one had heard the struggle was another matter entirely. Who would want to kill the man for that matter? As far as Jack was aware, Peter was a stranger in Lambourn. He might be irritating and tenacious but that was hardly grounds for murder.

With a weary sigh, he extracted his phone from his pocket and put a call through to the direct line of his old colleague and friend, DI Mark Vickery, who had investigated the last two murders in Lambourn. But a third, he thought with a sinking heart as he waited for Vickery to pick up, another victim with links to Alexi. What were the chances?

'I'll send the troops and be there as soon as I can.'

Vickery's voice was terse, as though he was having a hard time getting his mind round the situation.

Join the club, mate.

Jack ensured that there was no one lurking in the rooms on the first floor and then stood sentry duty at the top of the stairs to keep people away until Vickery's uniforms took over. A short, stocky man bustled up to Jack, wheezing with the effort that it took him to climb the stairs.

'I'm Alton, the manager. What the hell's going on? I've got a hysterical cleaner down there and the entire place is in uproar.' He tutted. 'It's most irregular.'

'So, I imagine, is having a dead man in the gents. The police are on their way.'

'Dead?' Alton's eyes bulged. 'Dead! But that's impossible.'

Jack fixed him with a look and said nothing.

'What happened?' Alton asked. 'Did he slip and bang his head, or pass out, or something like that?'

Not unless he strangled himself.

'Is he on drugs?' Alton persisted, desperate for an explanation. 'Can't have drugs in my hotel.'

'It isn't natural causes, which is all I can tell you right now. I would suggest that you go back downstairs and keep everyone calm until the police arrive.'

'Just a minute.' Alton puffed out his chest and straightened his shoulders, a bit like an outraged bullfrog protecting his territory. 'I'm in charge here. I make the decisions. Who are you, anyway?'

'Jack Maddox, former detective inspector.'

'Oh, I see.' Alton deflated. 'Are you sure the man's actually dead? This is most inconvenient.'

'Especially for the victim.'

'Yes, yes, of course.' Alton paused to lick his thin lips. 'Was the man – I assume it's a man – a guest?'

'No, he wasn't a guest, that much I can tell you.' Jack gave the man's shoulder a gentle push. 'Now please, if you wouldn't mind.'

Alton took the hint and lumbered back down the stairs, shaking his head and muttering about irregularities.

Jack wasn't left with much time to think about who could possibly have topped Peter, and more to the point why, before Cassie joined him.

'What the hell, Jack?'

'It's Peter Foreman,' he said, grimacing. 'He's been strangled.'

'I know that name.' She looked pale and distraught as she tapped her index finger against her teeth. 'You asked me to look into his background.'

'Not just him. All the people on Alexi's journalism course.' Jack sighed, feeling weary before the investigation had even gotten under way. Alexi, he knew, would feel responsible and it would be the final straw that drove her away from Lambourn. The very thought of it caused his spirits to sink. 'Did you come up with anything interesting on Foreman?'

'Can't say that I did off the top of my head. I'll check when I get back to the office but if there were any red flags then I'd have told you.'

Jack fixed her with a speculative look, wondering if that was true. He wouldn't put it past her to let a disruptive influence like Foreman do his worst on Alexi's course. He wondered now why he'd asked her to look into the backgrounds of the participants, aware that her feelings for Alexi were far from sisterly. He chased that disloyal thought away. Cassie might resent Alexi, but she wouldn't deliberately sabotage her efforts to rebuild her reputation, aware that she was already living under a cloud of suspicion in Lambourn.

Would she?

Not that it really mattered. Cassie hadn't strangled Peter, but she wouldn't cry too many tears if this latest disaster pushed Alexi back to London.

'The cavalry's here,' Jack said as he heard the sound of approaching sirens.

A uniformed sergeant whom Jack recognised led the procession up the stairs.

'In there,' Jack said, pointing towards the men's room.

'Okay, leave it to us.'

Jack and Cassie had barely reached the foyer before Vickery and Constable Hogan, an attractive female DC, arrived. Vickery wasn't smiling.

'The victim's name is Peter Foreman,' Jack said as he shook Vickery's hand. 'A cleaner found him in the gents and screamed the place down. I went to investigate. He's been strangled.'

Vickery didn't insult Jack by asking if he was sure. 'How do you know his name?' he asked instead.

'He's on a journalism course that Alexi's running at the hotel.'

Vickery paused and if anything, his expression turned even more severe. 'I see. Any idea what he was doing here?'

'Trying to get a lead on the sighting of Paul Franklin, apparently.'

Vickery rolled his eyes. 'Him and half the county. Still, there might be something to the rumours if he stuck his nose in and got himself killed because of it, I suppose.'

'That's what I thought,' Cassie said, speaking for the first time.

'And you are?'

'Sorry,' Jack said, 'I'd forgotten that you two haven't met. Mark, this is my business partner, Cassie Fenton. Cassie, DI Mark Vickery and Constable Hogan.'

'Anna,' Hogan said, offering Cassie her hand. 'Pleased to meet you.'

'What brought the pair of you here?' Vickery asked. 'You have a happy knack for being in the wrong place at the wrong time, Jack. Careful, or I might be inclined to feel your collar.'

'I'll come quietly, guv.'

Jack's quip barely raised a smile.

'We're working a missing person's case. Cassie discovered that the girl's credit card was used here last week. We came to check it out and walked into... this.' He waved a hand towards the upstairs bathroom for emphasis.

'Your case have anything to do with the victim?' Vickery asked.

'Not as far as I'm aware,' Jack replied. 'Her disappearance has been reported to your lot. Amy Dawson.'

Hogan made a note. 'We'll look into it,' she promised.

'Any idea why the victim got caught up looking for a man who doesn't want to be found and was probably not here in the first place?' Vickery asked.

'That's what Alexi told him, but he insisted. She has them all writing local interest pieces, except for Foreman, who was going for the sensational.'

'Well, he has his notoriety now, but not for the reasons he imagined,' Vickery replied with a droll smile.

Jack inclined his head. 'My thoughts exactly.'

'Okay, if there's nothing more you can tell me, I'd best take a look for myself.' Vickery and Hogan accepted plastic covers from a constable at the foot of the stairs and slipped them over their shoes. 'Get along if you like and give Alexi the glad tidings. I'll be over to see her later.'

Jack gave his ex-colleague a mock salute and turned towards the car park.

'I'm so sorry, Jack,' Cassie said, trotting to keep up with him. 'I may not be Alexi's biggest fan, but she doesn't deserve more bad luck.'

'No,' Jack replied tersely, 'she sure as hell doesn't.'

'You want me to come back to Hopgood Hall with you and help break the news?'

'Thanks, but it's best coming from me.'

'Okay, if you're sure.'

'If you want to help, go back to the office and send me the notes you took on Foreman and all the other contestants. I've only seen the headlines so far.'

'Consider it done.' Her pause was protracted, causing Jack's head to swivel in her direction. 'One thing I didn't tell you. I'm sure it's nothing. But when I got here, there were raised voices coming from upstairs. A man and a woman. Jack, I'm pretty sure the woman's voice was Alexi's... I'll have to tell the police.'

'Of course you will. I wouldn't want you to perjure yourself.'

'This is awful, Jack.' She touched his arm. 'Call if you need me, professionally or for a shoulder to cry on. Any time day or night. I'm here for you.'

Jack acknowledged her words with a raised hand but didn't turn round as he made his way towards his car, wondering if Cassie was trying to be helpful or spiteful by implying that the tragedy would adversely affect Alexi. A little of both, he reckoned as he started his engine and left a car park now crowded with police cars and emergency vehicles.

Why had Alexi been at the hotel that morning? Cassie had seen her there, and he wished now that he'd asked his partner if the two of them had spoken. Not that it mattered; Alexi would tell him. Besides, if he'd asked Cassie, it would imply that he suspected Alexi of involvement in Foreman's death, which he didn't. Not for a moment. Foreman had come on to Alexi and made a bit of a nuisance of himself, but Alexi was an attractive woman, and if she murdered every man who gave her hassle, there would be a string of corpses in her wake.

Apart from anything else, strangulation wasn't a woman's preferred method of killing. It took physical strength and didn't happen as quickly as the movies made out. Foreman had been taller, heavier and stronger than Alexi and would have fought back.

'Hell, why am I even contemplating the possibility of her involvement?' he asked aloud.

He knew the answer to his own question. The moment Vickery and his team discovered that Foreman had plagued Alexi with his attentions and also learned from Cassie that she'd been at the hotel, perhaps at the actual time of the murder, then they themselves would start to wonder, too. Jack knew that the previous murders had played on Alexi's conscience and damaged the hotel's reputation, despite Drew's insistence that it had enhanced it. Looked upon objectively from the outside, it could be argued that the publicity had enhanced Alexi's profile too and made her richer due to the fact that she'd written about two of the murders and profited from the experience.

'There's motive and opportunity for you,' Jack told his windscreen. 'Means are missing though,' he added, feeling slightly less anxious about the situation. How could Alexi have entered the men's room unnoticed and even if she had, how the hell could she have overpowered Foreman? More to the point, why did he permit himself to be strangled without putting up a fight? It occurred to Jack that his hands had been undamaged – as a trained detective, Jack noticed that sort of thing as a matter of course. If Foreman had tried to fight his killer off, there would have been signs to point to this fact, surely?

Perhaps Franklin, the fugitive, had been to the Swan and was still in the area, hiding in plain sight. If Foreman was even half as tenacious in pursuit of that story as he was in pursuit of Alexi, then Franklin would have heard about it and made it his business to shut him up. It was a strand worth investigating. So too was digging into Foreman's past. Hopefully, that would throw up more clues.

Jack's hands were unsteady on the wheel as he turned into the car park at Hopgood Hall. Everything looked so calm, so normal, but all that was about to change. What he would give to be able to turn the clock back six hours and start the day over. But daydreams were for children. This was real life and Jack would have to deal with the situation, doing everything he could to ease Alexi's burden.

Taking a deep breath, he left his car and walked into the hotel at a brisk pace, still trying to think how best to break the devastating news to Alexi. She looked up and smiled at him when he walked into the kitchen, but her smile quickly faded when she caught his expression.

'What is it?' she asked. 'What's happened?'

Cosmo looked up from the basket that he was sharing with Toby and mewled, clearly sensing the onset of another tragedy.

Jack sat beside Alexi, took her hand in his and kissed the back of it. 'Bad news, darling,' he said softly. 'There's no easy way to say this.' Jack swallowed and increased the pressure on her hand. 'Peter Foreman's dead.'

4

Jack's voice sounded as though it was echoing down a tunnel, his words barely making any sense, perhaps because Alexi's brain had instinctively tuned them out. She felt her body sway and was aware of Jack's arm shooting out to support her as she dredged up the strength from somewhere to face the unthinkable.

'Dead? How? Where?' She shook her head, still feeling bemused. As out of body experiences went, this one was in a class of its own. 'There must be some mistake. This can't be happening.' She looked at Jack with wide-eyed incomprehension. 'I saw him less than an hour ago and he was fine.'

'At the Swan. I know. Cassie told me.'

'Oh, was she there? Why? I didn't see her.'

'She had a lead on our missing woman.'

'Ha! Perhaps your misper was there with Paul Foreman.'

'Glad to see that you haven't lost your sense of humour, darling.' Jack gently pushed the hair away from her eyes, looking worried, as well he might. This was unbelievable. Another tragedy and this time, Hopgood Hall wouldn't survive the fallout. 'Cassie said you and Foreman were arguing. What about?'

'What do you think?' she replied, throwing back her head and closing her eyes, feeling the full weight of this disaster weighing heavily on her shoulders. 'It isn't the first time he's been to that hotel, hassling the staff, convinced that it's a conspiracy. According to him, they're all in on it in order to protect Franklin.' Alexi rolled her eyes. 'The manager, a fussy little man with attitude called Alton, asked me to call him off. He was upsetting the clientele apparently, approaching them in the bar and plying them with questions, refusing to back off when they said they couldn't help him.' Alexi flashed a mirthless smile. 'He probably thinks... thought, that the guests and regulars were all in on the conspiracy too.'

'Did he take on board what you told him and agree to back off? I'm guessing not because it isn't like you to lose your temper.'

'Cassie told you that too, did she?' Alexi shivered. 'Eavesdropping, was she? She'll be loving this.'

'Never mind Cassie. Tell me about your confrontation with Foreman.'

'I told him that making a nuisance of himself would draw adverse publicity to this establishment, but he didn't want to know. He had the temerity to tell me that good journalists develop thick skins and don't take no for an answer. He implied it was where I'd gone wrong and reason why I was let go.' She puffed out her chest. 'I'll admit that I saw red and let rip. He's been getting on my nerves all week with his know-it-all attitude, and this was the final straw. I most emphatically didn't whack him with anything sharper than my own wit, though, tempting though the prospect was at the time.' She glanced up at him. 'How did he die, anyway?' she asked.

'He was strangled.'

'Oh.' Alexi swayed on her chair, devastated for Peter. And for herself and the reputation of the hotel. 'Well, I'm sorry. Really, I am. Strangling isn't quick, or painless.'

'I know you're sorry.' Jack kissed the top of her head. 'I am too but we have to put personal feelings aside and try to figure out what happened. And why.'

'It must have taken some strength to strangle a man of his stature,' Alexi said pensively. 'I mean, he was well built and I doubt whether he just stood there and let someone sling a ligature around his neck. He must have put up quite a fight. Didn't anyone hear a struggle?'

'It was upstairs in the men's room.'

She blinked at Jack. 'What the hell's going on? Why on earth would anyone want to kill Peter?'

She felt tears trickling down her face as she turned towards Jack. He folded her in his arms, and she sobbed on his shoulder, feeling sorrier for herself than she did for Peter Foreman, which probably made her a terrible person. Be that as it may, her mind had recovered from the shock, after a fashion, and it belatedly occurred to her that someone must have borne the man a massive grudge that had absolutely nothing to do with her course. The course had taken Foreman out of his routine and into a part of the world where he wasn't known. It was an opportunity for the murderer to take him unawares. She said as much to Jack.

'If he had pissed someone off to the degree that they wanted to kill him then he must have known about it and been careful in his usual environment.'

'Perhaps, but if he felt his life was in danger then surely he'd have gone to the police.'

Alexi shook her head. 'You know better than that. We don't know what he'd done to make himself a target. Probably something he wouldn't want authority figures to know anything about.'

'You're right. Perhaps he came on the course to get away from his aggressors. Give tempers time to cool and all that.'

Alexi let out a deep sigh and a deeper sob. Jack soothed her back with expansive sweeps of one capable hand, holding her until she felt more in control. Having a meltdown, feeling sorry for herself, would achieve nothing.

'I won't survive this latest scandal,' she said, sitting upright and fishing in her bag for a tissue. 'I might as well accept that I don't belong here and take myself off before anything else happens.'

'And how guilty will that make you look?' Jack asked briskly.

'Yeah, point taken. At least he wasn't killed here at Hopgood Hall.' She bit at her lower lip as she considered her options, which were precious few. Jack was right. She needed to stay here and get to the bottom of things.

Again.

'Is Vickery assigned to the case?' she asked.

'He is. Which is a good thing. He won't cut corners to get a result.'

Alexi nodded. 'Well, that's something.'

'Cassie will have to tell him that she saw you at the hotel,' Jack said softly.

'Fine. I have nothing to hide and no earthly reason to kill one of my course's participants. Quite the reverse.'

'Where did you conduct your conversation with Foreman?'

'On the rear terrace.'

'Did anyone see you?'

She shrugged. 'No idea. Why? Surely you don't think that I—'

'Of course not, but Vickery can't play favourites and will have to treat you with suspicion, same as anyone else who had issues with the man. Especially as you were likely the last person to see him alive.'

'Except for the killer.'

'Yep. Except for him.'

'Interesting that you say him.'

'We both know strangulation takes physical strength, and it didn't look to me as though Foreman had tried to fight back.'

'How would you know? I don't suppose there's anything that could have been knocked over in a men's bathroom.'

'True, but if he was pushed...'

'Heads don't bounce off porcelain,' Alexi finished for him.

'Right.' Jack frowned, presumably with the effort of recollection. 'The scene was... I don't know, undisturbed, I suppose. Like he knew the person who attacked him and didn't feel threatened.'

'Or a stranger walked in to use the facilities and Foreman took no notice of him.'

'He still would have fought back if that was the case.'

Alexi nodded. 'I guess.'

'Anyway, as I was saying, I didn't notice any head wounds, or defensive wounds on Foreman's hands. No broken nails or scraped knuckles and his clothing was undisturbed. There was no blood but then again, that doesn't mean anything. Besides, I didn't look that closely. I was blindsided when I recognised the victim.'

Alexi shrugged, feeling oddly detached from the horror of Foreman's untimely demise and the devastating consequences it would have for her personally. 'Well, that helps me, doesn't it?' she suggested, willing Jack to agree with her. 'I would never have been able to overcome a man of his stature if he was fully alert.'

'I think you could be right about Foreman being on someone's hit list.' Alexi was conscious of the fact that Jack had avoided answering her question. 'There's definitely more to the man than met the eye.'

'We need to delve deeper into his background in that case.'

'Cassie is doing that as we speak.'

Alexi hesitated, unsure how to put her feelings into words. 'Can we trust her?' she eventually settled for asking. This situation was too serious, for herself and the future of the hotel, for her to worry about hurt feelings. 'She isn't my biggest fan and won't shed too many tears if this latest murder sends me scurrying back to London.'

'Not happening!'

Alexi was encouraged by the force of Jack's response.

'I've only just found you,' he added, sliding an arm protectively around her waist. 'You don't get away that easily. Besides, this isn't just about you. There's Drew and Cheryl's feelings to consider.' He allowed a significant pause. 'To say nothing of my own.'

Alexi bowed her head and rested her forehead against Jack's shoulder. 'I hear you,' she replied. 'Besides, running away is not in my nature.'

Jack tightened his arm around her. 'Cassie will deliver, no matter what her personal feelings might happen to be. If I even suspect otherwise, rest assured I will instigate my own enquiries.'

'I'd kinda assumed that we'd do that anyway.'

'I meant without Cassie's input.'

'Thanks. I don't mean to cause trouble between you and her. Well, not any more than I already have.'

'Cassie has her issues, but she'll get past them.' He sat up a little straighter. 'Right. Let's do what we do best and go into damage limitation mode. We can start by thinking of alternative suspects, other than your lovely self, obviously.'

'And Cassie. She was there. Only joking,' Alexi added hastily when Jack frowned. 'The same rules apply to her in that she wouldn't have the physical strength to strangle a fully conscious man even if he did stand passively whilst she gave it her best shot.'

'Patrick,' Jack countered. 'Makes you wonder why he's wasting precious time here in Lambourn when he has a Sunday paper to put to bed.'

'Why would he kill Peter?'

'To make you return to London. I'm guessing you've told him that the locals have branded you as a Jonah.'

'Well yes, but...'

'And he will have seen that Peter was wrecking your course *and* coming on to you.'

Alexi laughed. 'At the risk of sounding as though I'm defending him, I'm pretty sure he's incapable of killing anything other than a good story.'

'Yeah well, a guy can dream.'

Alexi listened to Jack's theory about the missing fugitive whom Peter had been so stubbornly determined to track down.

'You really think the guy *was* here?' Alexi could hear the scepticism in her own voice.

Jack lifted one shoulder. 'It's possible.'

'But you can't prove it.'

'Nor can Vickery disprove it. Casting doubt and all that.'

'If Franklin really is still around then he wouldn't have wanted Peter getting too close.' Alexi frowned. 'Except he wasn't. He had nothing new.'

'That he told you about.'

She conceded the point with a reluctant nod. 'I suppose he might have unearthed something tangible. It would be just like him to keep it to himself and do a big reveal to Patrick, hoping to make an impression. Even so, it's a stretch to assume that Franklin would resort to murder just to keep him quiet. He could have found out easily enough that the course ends on Saturday and that Peter would be scurrying back to London.'

'But what would he do with the fictional information he'd unearthed? A fugitive wouldn't take the chance. Bear in mind that the proceeds from that robbery were enormous and haven't been traced.'

'Then why would a wanted man hang out around these parts, where strangers are easy to spot?'

Jack sent her a meltingly gentle smile. 'We'll ask him when we find him.'

'Ha! Good luck with that one.'

'Darling, if he exists then I'll find him, especially if it removes all traces of suspicion from you.'

Alexi wrapped her arms around his neck and kissed him. 'I don't deserve you,' she said softly.

'You're stuck with me. Get used to it.'

Alexi sighed. 'I'm scared,' she admitted. 'But it's worth pointing out that I'm not in the habit of visiting men's bathrooms, with or without murderous intentions. How could I have known that Peter would be in there alone?'

'It could be argued that you wanted to gloss over the argument you'd just had.' Jack held up his hands in a defensive gesture. 'I know, I know. I'm thinking like a prosecution barrister. Anyway, don't be scared. We've already thought of three plausible alternative suspects.'

'Your own partner, a respected newspaper editor and a fictional fugitive.' She gave a sad little shake of her head. 'In Vickery's position, I'd still look upon me as the most likely suspect. Besides, it's not as if we can make unfounded accusations against Cassie, or Patrick either.'

'We'll think of...'

Jack broke off when Cheryl and Drew dashed into the room.

'Police have just pulled up outside,' Drew said. 'What's going on?'

'I'm so sorry,' Alexi replied, swiping at her eyes with the back of her hand as she broke the bad news to her friends.

'Christ!' Drew let out a protracted breath as he fell into a chair and ran a hand through his hair. 'Not again. What are the chances of it happening to us? It's almost as though someone wants this business to fail.'

'I know.' Alexi dropped her head.

'Alexi Ellis, don't you dare say this is your fault!' Cheryl puffed out her chest and shook a finger at Alexi. 'You are not to blame. It's nothing more than bad luck.'

'Especially for Peter,' Drew added. 'The man might have been a jerk but that's not a crime. If it was, half the village would be under lock and key.'

Drew's attempt at levity did little to lighten the mood.

'Vickery will want to talk to me.' Alexi sighed. 'I was with Peter and was heard arguing with him what could only have been minutes before he was killed.'

'Damn!' Drew said. 'But still, you have absolutely no reason to have killed him.'

'Of course she didn't!' Cheryl cried hotly. 'I was here when she got back from doing her rounds this morning and there wasn't anything unusual about her behaviour. I know my friend. If she'd just throttled the guy, she would have been a mess. Besides, she doesn't have the capacity to kill anyone.'

'Thanks for the vote of confidence,' Alexi replied, sitting a litter straighter, determined not to appear guilty when Vickery entered the room. She knew very well just what an impact first impressions had in such circumstances. She should. She'd been here before.

Twice.

A tap at the door preceded Vickery putting his head round it. 'We meet again,' he said, strolling into the room with DC Hogan in his wake. He did not, Alexi noticed with a quailing heart, look particularly pleased to be back at Hopgood Hall. For her part,

Alexi wasn't exactly delighted to see him either. Predictably, Cosmo got up and hissed at him, before settling back in the basket with Toby. 'You appear to have lost one of your delegates, Alexi,' he added.

'So Jack just told me.' She shook her head. 'I'm still trying to take it in.'

'Do you want us to leave?' Drew asked, indicating both himself and Cheryl with one swipe of his hand.

'No need. These are just preliminary questions.'

'How can I help?' Alexi asked, striving to prevent her voice from wavering.

'You were at the Swan this morning, heard arguing with the victim.'

Alexi glanced at Jack, unsurprised that Cassie had lost no time dropping her in it. Or, as Jack would probably put it, getting things out in the open. All well and good, but unlike Jack, Alexi wasn't convinced of Cassie's impartiality. No holds barred when it came to affairs of the heart, and all that. Jack had never shown a romantic interest in Cassie but if this crime could be pinned on Alexi then she must hope that he'd turn to her for solace.

In short, Alexi neither liked nor trusted the woman and suspected that Peter's death had provided her with all the ammunition she required to create doubts about Alexi in Jack's mind.

'I was,' Alexi replied without hesitation. 'I was also at all the other places where my delegates were chasing stories, checking to see if they needed any help or guidance.'

'Then why the argument with Foreman?' Vickery asked.

'Because he was making a nuisance of himself, bothering guests, drinkers and staff alike by insisting that someone must have seen the elusive Paul Franklin. The manager complained about his behaviour and asked me to call him off. The idea, you see, was to get my delegates patronising local businesses in an effort to... well, to rebuild bridges following recent unfortunate events, not make their lives more difficult.'

She didn't need to explain further. Vickery understood.

'Foreman was like a dog with a bone. He simply refused to let it go. I was at my wit's end. I mean, it wasn't as though I could force him to give it up. Only the manager could bar him from the premises, and he seemed too weak-willed to do anything other than to complain to me and expect me to do something about it.'

'Do you know if he had any specific interest in the case?' Vickery asked.

'No, but I did wonder. London's a big place but Peter was from there and I gather that the criminals responsible for the raid on the bullion shipment at Southampton docks were too.' She shrugged. 'Then again, perhaps Peter decided that if he could get a lead on Franklin, it would be his path to fame and fortune, beating the press and police at their own game and seeing an end to his dreary career in the civil service. He didn't suffer from a lack of self-confidence so I wouldn't put it past him.'

'Is the civil service dreary?' Vickery asked.

Alexi shrugged. 'No idea but probably. It sounds like it ought to be.'

Vickery grunted. Hogan wrote something in her notebook.

'It seems like too much of a coincidence that you got called to the same venue as a murder, Jack,' Vickery remarked. 'Are you absolutely sure that the victim had nothing to do with your missing persons case?'

'I'm not sure of anything right now, Mark,' Jack replied, his expression open and honest. 'Needless to say, I'll look into it.'

'What the hell!' The door flew open and Patrick barged through it. Cosmo stood up, arched his back and hissed like a snake on steroids. He had never liked Patrick and his feelings clearly hadn't mellowed with the passage of time. 'I've just heard. What in God's name happened this time?'

'How did you hear, sir?' Vickery asked. He was already acquainted with Patrick, so Alexi didn't feel the need to introduce the two men.

'I'm a journalist,' he replied, as though that explained everything. 'Are you okay, Alexi?' he added, his face wreathed with concern.

'Never better,' she replied flippantly.

'May I ask what you're doing here, sir?' Vickery fixed Patrick with a look of polite enquiry. 'It's my understanding that you have a Sunday paper to edit.'

'Ever heard of working online, Inspector?' Patrick looked disconcerted to have his activities questioned. 'But since you ask, I'm here to support Alexi's course.'

'Have you met any of the participants before?'

'Nope. Alexi ran the shortlist past me for that very reason and I can assure you that none of them are known to me.'

Vickery's gaze flicked between Patrick and Alexi. For her part, Alexi looked straight back at him. Patrick on the other hand found something to interest him on the phone he'd extracted from his pocket.

'Very well.' Vickery's voice broke the stalemate. 'I'll need to do some digging, ask more questions elsewhere. No doubt you'll do the same, Jack, but tread carefully,' he added with a significant glance in Alexi's direction.

'I hear you,' Jack replied, shaking Vickery's hand and opening the door for him and Hogan.

'I will arrange for the victim's room to be searched,' Vickery added. 'In the meantime, make sure no one goes in there.'

'Will do,' Jack replied, turning to wink at Alexi.

'Was I just accused of committing murder?' Patrick asked, looking animated.

Before Jack could tell him not to be such an insensitive jerk, Alexi placed a restraining hand on his arm. 'Come on,' she said. 'The others will be back soon. Let's go to the annex and break the news to them before they hear it elsewhere.'

5

'Thanks for stopping me from killing the insensitive arse,' Jack said, taking Alexi's hand as they crossed the courtyard.

'My pleasure. One of us being suspected of murder is quite enough to be going on with.'

'Hey, enough of that talk.'

Jack gave her hand a warning squeeze. He needed her at the top of her game if they were to stand any chance of finding out what this was all about before the authorities shut them out. Vickery was giving them a little leeway, but Jack knew that situation couldn't last for long. Vickery might know in his gut that Alexi wasn't the killer, but he still had to play this by the book.

As for Jack... well, he was attempting to disguise his anxiety from Alexi. He didn't believe in coincidence. There had to be a reason why yet another murder had been committed that had connections to Alexi but as things stood, he had absolutely no idea what those connections might be.

But he sure as hell intended to find out.

She laughed. 'It just feels that way.'

'You realise Vickery just gave us an opportunity to search Foreman's room before his troops arrive?'

'He did?' She blinked up at Jack. 'My brain must have seized up because I thought he said to keep people away from it.'

'He's gone out on a limb for you, darling. Giving us a bit of time before his troops arrive. Let's make the most of it.'

'Okay.'

'Do you know what branch of the civil service Foreman was in?'

'No. Does it matter?'

'Not sure. I just want to know more about the man. His entire annoying persona could have been a smokescreen.'

'I suppose anything's possible,' Alexi replied, 'but it seems unlikely. If he *was* hiding an alternative agenda though, the best way to cover it up would be to behave so brashly that everyone avoided him, branding him a harmless and annoying eccentric, I suppose.'

'Getting strangled is pretty unlikely too.'

'Yeah, I take your point. We do need to delve into his background independently of Cassie though.'

'Let's see what she comes up with first. She has superpowers when it comes to online sleuthing that the police can only dream about, and I think it's unlikely that we'd unearth anything she hasn't already found.'

'Because she hacks into stuff?'

'I have absolutely no idea.'

Alexi rolled her eyes. 'Of course you don't. But don't forget that I have contacts independent of the internet. Real people who know people if you get my drift. I'm sure it was the same for you when you were in the force.'

'Yeah, I hear you, but one step at a time.' Jack opened the door to the annex and let her pass through it ahead of him. 'Come on.'

The communal lounge was thankfully devoid of human presence, Alexi's delegates still out chasing down their stories. It gave Jack the opportunity he'd hope for to search Foreman's room without anyone knowing about it.

'Ready?' he asked, pausing at the doorway when Alexi pointed out the right room to him. 'Remember not to touch anything,' he added, pulling latex gloves from his pocket and snapping them onto his hands. 'I only have one pair of these.'

'I'm surprised you just happen to have any about your person. Although, then again, perhaps I shouldn't be.'

The room already felt unlived in. It was excessively neat. The hotel's staff would have been in to make the bed and clean the bathroom, but they had a policy of never moving anything the resident had left lying about. Peter had made their job easier by being so tidy.

'It's not natural,' Alexi said, echoing Jack's own thoughts.

'I tend to agree.'

Jack opened the wardrobe, unsurprised to find Peter's clothes hanging in a neat row, fastidiously organised.

'The man must have had OCD,' he muttered.

'Where are his papers? His course notes?' Alexi asked. 'He was constantly scribbling with pad and paper.' She twirled in a circle. 'Even so, you'd expect there to be a laptop, or something. I suppose he had his phone and wallet with him.'

'Here.' Jack opened a drawer and found Peter's notebooks. He flipped through them with gloved fingers, but nothing jumped out at him. 'There might be something there, but we can't take them until the police have seen them. It's unlikely, though. If he had ruffled feathers to the extent that his life was in danger, I doubt whether he'd have left notes lying about.'

'He might,' Alexi countered, peering round Jack's shoulder at Peter's neat handwriting. 'He fancied himself as an investigative journalist and it looks as though these books contain notes on his various projects. He isn't exactly subtle and might have trodden on toes without even realising it.'

Jack grunted. 'It's possible, I suppose, but unlikely. A good beating would ordinarily suffice if a person sticks their nose in where it isn't wanted.'

'I wish I could read through those notes,' Alexi said, sighing with frustration. 'Perhaps if I go back to the kitchen and find some gloves...'

'Does the name Gates mean anything to you?'

'Yes.' Alexi frowned. 'It's one of the investigations I intend to include in my book. A guy who sold a piece of land in Portugal four times over to trusting individuals. Four that we know about. There could well have been more who were too embarrassed to admit that they'd been taken in. I interviewed several of his victims, but the police couldn't, or wouldn't, do anything about it.'

'If the transactions were done by legal contract, then the police's hands are tied. It's up to the buyer's solicitors to check out the legalities in question. Fraud investigations are complex, time consuming and expensive. This guy was clever; he didn't get greedy enough to make an investigation worthwhile, didn't target people who couldn't afford to take the hit, and he didn't scam them for too much. Certainly not enough to force his victims to endure the embarrassment of admitting they'd been idiots. That's what people like your man Gates depended on.'

'Yeah, that's pretty much what I thought. Gates had gone to ground, scarpered with the proceeds of his latest scam when I tried to track him down. I was convinced that he'd pulled similar cons over the years but the few people who agreed to speak with me wouldn't go on record, probably for the reasons that you've suggested.'

'Even less reason for the police to get involved,' Jack

confirmed. 'Anyway, Foreman has lots of notes on the case. He seemed obsessed by it.'

'Perhaps he was a victim himself.'

'There's a phone number.'

'Let me see.' Jack held the page up and Alexi gave it a protracted look, probably speed-reading Foreman's notes rather than checking to see if the number was familiar to her. Besides, everyone used mobiles nowadays and the need to memorise numbers was outdated. 'He really was tenacious,' she said, shaking her head, 'albeit rather like a bull in a china shop.'

'Time's up,' Jack said, when the sound of approaching voices warned them that Vickery's uniforms were on their way to conduct an official search. Alexi pulled out her phone and snapped a picture of the phone number. Jack realised too late that he should have done so earlier, contenting himself with turning the pages and letting her snap as many as possible. 'Come on.' He put the notebook back and grabbed her hand. 'We don't need to be caught in here,' he added. 'It will make matters worse for us.'

'Let's go out the back way,' Alexi suggested, sending a covetous glance towards the drawer in which Jack had replaced the notebooks.

They let themselves out and sauntered back towards the main body of the hotel by a different route. Cosmo appeared from nowhere and wound himself round Alexi's legs, mewing indignantly.

'How does he do that?' Jack demanded to know. 'We left him in Cheryl's kitchen.'

'Well, he did want to come with us,' Alexi reminded him, bending to stroke her cat. 'He's aware that a crisis has arisen and assumes that his services as security will be required.'

'Let's hope it doesn't come to that.'

Cosmo lifted his head and sent Jack an accusatory look that made them both smile. 'You've hurt his feelings.'

'He'll get over it, won't you, big guy?'

'What are you thinking?' Alexi asked when they'd walked a little further and Jack had fallen unnaturally quiet.

'I'm ruminating upon Foreman's true reason for coming here.'

'Other than to enjoy the benefit of my expertise.'

Jack smiled and touched her arm. 'That goes without saying. He'd be a fool not to learn as much as he could from you and despite Foreman's best efforts to convince everyone otherwise, I'm feeling increasingly convinced that he was no fool. Quite the reverse.'

'From what little I just saw of his notes, I'm inclined to believe you.' Alexi paused, taking her turn to mull the situation over. 'I am now very curious to know what precisely his line of work actually was. The civil service is a bit of a catch-all, isn't it?'

'Yep. People have preconceptions about the civil service involving nothing more taxing than paper shuffling and seldom ask more questions if a person claims to be in that line of work.'

Jack opened the kitchen door for Alexi, but Cosmo squeezed through it ahead of her. Toby greeted his feline friend with wagging enthusiasm, giving the impression that they'd been separated for months rather than minutes. Cosmo withstood the dog's adoration with the aloof brand of indifference common to felines the world over as he settled into their shared basket to resume his snooze with his back to the dog. Toby struggled to squeeze himself into the remaining space.

'You're thinking that Foreman's obsession with the elusive fugitive had something to do with Gates?' Alexi suggested, sitting at the table, resting her elbows on it and supporting her chin on her clenched fists.

'It seems improbable but not a possibility that we can afford to ignore. Foreman was a complex and clever character.'

'Not that clever, considering what happened to him.'

'Apart from that.' Jack waved the suggestion aside. 'Con men like Gates start small. Grifters if you like, pulling small-time cons in crowded places. Most don't get any further, either going straight or reverting to the type of crime that requires brawn rather than brain. The natural con artists rise to the top, get ambitious and spread their wings. I reckon Gates used the land in Portugal as a dry run for something a lot bigger, which is why he went to ground, waiting for the dust to settle.'

'Okay, but what does that have to do with the bullion robbery? Thieves and con men are different animals.' Alexi lifted her head and waved a hand in the air to emphasise her point. 'Well, they're both thieves, but different categories of the same profession. Not natural bedfellows.'

Jack grinned and nodded towards the cat and dog, curled up together in Toby's basket.

'Okay, point taken but I still don't buy it.'

'Perhaps Gates is multi-talented and is the fugitive.'

'The wanted man is called Franklin. Oh, okay, I get it,' Alexi added when Jack simply looked at her. 'Names are fluid.'

'We're clutching at straws, I agree with you there,' Jack said, 'but at the end of the day, it's another avenue for Vickery to explore.'

'One that takes the heat off me.' Alexi nodded. 'I'll go for that.'

'Vickery doesn't suspect you of strangling a fully conscious man, darling,' Jack assured her. 'Or any one at all for that matter. He wouldn't have let us search the victim's things if he had any doubts on that score.'

'Perhaps not but that won't prevent Polly Pearson and her

coven from talking up my guilt. They won't let the facts get in the way of a good conspiracy.'

'Forget the locals,' Jack said briskly, determined not to let her wallow in self-pity. 'Sticks and stones and all that. We'll find out who did this, never doubt it. I know you worry about the hotel but whatever the outcome, it won't go under.'

'I know.' She sighed. 'It's a sad reflection on the morbid curiosity of Joe Public but there's no denying the fact that murder seems to be good for business.'

'Anyway, Vickery probably thinks that you can tell him more about Foreman than you actually know. We'll try not to disappoint him so let's take a moment to think this through,' Jack said. 'What do we actually know for a fact?'

'That Peter Foreman worked a number on me and everyone he met here and made us all avoid him for fear of being subjected to one of his know-it-all lectures. We are unsure what he actually did for a living, but he was probably not an ordinary civil servant. He came to Lambourn with the specific intention of tracking down a criminal wanted in connection with a bullion robbery but we're unsure if he wanted to do so in order to achieve journalistic fame or for more sinister reasons.'

'Exactly. It will be interesting to see what Cassie comes up with regarding his background, if anything.'

Alexi blinked. 'You're always telling me she can find out just about anything.'

'If it's there to be found. People are getting wise to the powers of the internet and know better than to put anything out there if they don't want it found.'

'But National Insurance numbers, stuff like that?'

Jack merely shrugged. If, as he suspected might be the case, Foreman was employed by one of the national security agencies, then they would have created a whole new online background for him. Everything including birth certificate and employment history: stuff they wanted to be found. Anything else would be beyond even Cassie's ability to uncover.

He scowled, worried about what precisely they had stumbled upon.

'We also have to consider the possibility that someone who badly wants me out of Lambourn killed Peter with the intention of driving me out. Cassie would be number one on my list in that respect but for the fact that she'd be no more capable of strangling a grown man than I am. Sorry Jack.' She looked up. 'Any idea what was used to do the deed?'

'No, I didn't notice anything but if I had to guess, I'd say that it was some sort of strong cord. It was pulled very tight and cut into his neck.'

'Why would the killer take it away with him?' Alexi nibbled at her index finger. 'I wonder if there was anything significant about it.'

'Perhaps he didn't take it. It could have been beneath the body. Vickery will tell us, I dare say.'

'It will be interesting to know the results of the post-mortem. I'm wondering if Peter was drugged somehow, which would explain why he didn't put up a fight.'

'Did he seem like he'd been drugged when you spoke with him?'

Alexi sighed. 'No, he seemed perfectly lucid. And I hope he was. If they do find any sort of debilitating drugs in his system then it would make me a more likely suspect. Anyway, I don't see how he could have been drugged and even if he was, would it have worked so quickly? I'm not sure of the timeline but his death can't have occurred more than a short time after I left him alive and alert.'

'Leaving aside Cassie, there's one other person who's been

hanging around for no particular reason and who has a very compelling reason to want you away from here.'

'Patrick.' Alexi bit her lip as she slowly nodded. 'Yeah, I know. That fact hadn't escaped my notice.'

'Foreman seemed a bit star-struck by him *and* he wouldn't have felt threatened if Vaughan followed him into the men's room.' Jack shrugged. 'Or it could have been the other way around. Foreman saw his hero and followed *him*.'

'And Patrick would have the strength to strangle a man.' Alexi shook her head. 'Even so, much as I've lost all respect for him, I can't see him going that far just to get me back. That said, I expect you feel the same way about Cassie's unlikely culpability.'

'We're just trying to make sense of a senseless situation, darling. Giving Vickery different lines of enquiry.'

Alexi's mouth fell open. 'Surely you're not going to suggest that Cassie or Patrick might have...'

'Not unless we unearth compelling evidence to back up our theory. But should suspicion seriously be directed toward you then I might well reconsider.' He stood, pulled Alexi into his arms and held her tight, feeling a fierce protectiveness, a determination to remove all suspicion from her name by finding the real culprit. He had finally found a woman who stirred his passions and challenged his intellect, and he was damned if he would allow anything or anyone to come between them. 'There's no fight I wouldn't take on to keep you safe so get used to it.'

'Thank you,' she said softly, resting the side of her face against his shoulder. 'Right now, when I'm feeling distressed and vulnerable, that's just the sort of reassurance I need to hear.' She lifted her head and met his gaze. 'But once the pity party's over, I'll be ready to fight back. Never doubt it.'

Jack chuckled. 'I don't, not for a minute. Which is why I'm enjoying my momentary domination.'

Alexi laughed as she pulled away from him and punched his arm. 'What now?' she asked, resuming her seat.

'Now we go back to the annex and wait for the others.' Jack peered out the window. 'The uniforms are leaving and taking some of Foreman's stuff with them by the looks of things. Talking of which, that phone number. Any thoughts?'

'Ah, I'd forgotten about that.'

Jack watched Alexi as she pulled her phone from her pocket, scrolled through the pictures she'd taken and brought up the number in question.

'Here goes nothing,' she said, tapping the number into her keypad and putting the phone on speaker.

They both listened to it ringing and then a voice – a familiar voice – asking the caller to leave a message. The voice didn't give a name but then he didn't need to.

Alexi turned to Jack, her face chalk-white, her mouth gaping in astonishment. 'That's Patrick's voice,' she said, stating the obvious.

6

Alexi felt shell-shocked. 'Why the hell would he have Patrick's number? And, for the record,' she added, scrolling through the contacts in her phone, 'it's not one of Patrick's personal numbers, nor one of the paper's lines, at least not as far as I'm aware. Things might have moved on since I left.'

'A burner, most likely. Vickery will check it out.'

'Why have it written down? Most people just add numbers to their contacts nowadays.'

'That's something we shall ask your ex at the earliest opportunity.'

'What does it mean, Jack?' Alexi probably looked as distressed as she felt. 'It makes absolutely no sense. Peter was a civil servant. Perhaps he was a potential whistleblower. That would explain why the two men were in private communication but not why Patrick used a different phone to communicate with him.'

'I can think of a dozen reasons for using a secret number off the top of my head,' Jack replied with a scowl that implied he didn't much like any of them. 'But now isn't the time to speculate,' he added when he heard footsteps approaching. 'We need to tell the others on the course and get their views on Peter.'

Alexi straightened her shoulders. 'Yeah, we do,' she agreed, thinking it best to leave the matter of Patrick's involvement with Peter on the back burner for the time being. Vickery's minions wouldn't recognise Patrick's voice when they checked Peter's phone, always assuming they *had* his phone. If it was a burner though, they wouldn't be able to trace it back to Patrick, which left Alexi in a quandary.

What the hell have you involved yourself with, Patrick?

She would give him an opportunity to explain before she enlightened Vickery. She owed Patrick that much. Much as Jack was reluctant to believe that Cassie had anything to do with the murder, Alexi felt the same way about Patrick. Even so, facts had to be faced. They both had compelling reasons for wanting Alexi to leave Lambourn but just how far would either of them go in order to make it happen?

Cosmo appeared ahead of the approaching delegates and leapt onto Alexi's lap, almost as though he was aware of her need for a little uncomplicated feline affection. Well, as uncomplicated as things ever got with an unpredictable cat of Cosmo's ilk. She smoothed his sleek back as he settled down, still alert and ready to hiss, or worse, at anyone he took a dislike to.

'Hi.' Ranya and Diana walked through the door, chatting animatedly. They abruptly stopped when they saw Jack and Alexi, probably guessing from their serious expressions that something bad had happened. Cosmo gave a mild growl but didn't bother to get up. 'Are we late?' Ranya added, checking her watch. 'I didn't think that the day's debrief was for another couple of hours.'

'It's not,' Alexi replied, 'but something's happened and we wanted you all to hear about it from us.'

'What is it?' Diana dumped a heavy bag on a vacant chair and sat down with an equally heavy thump. There was nothing delicate about Diana's deportment or in the forthright way she addressed others. No nonsense appeared to be her mantra and she most certainly didn't lack self-confidence. The miniscule Ranya, on the other hand, was delicate and self-deprecating. Despite their different characters, the two ladies were living proof that opposites attracted.

'It's Peter,' Jack told them.

'Who's he upset now?' Diana asked, rolling her eyes.

'I'm afraid it's a bit more serious than a few ruffled feathers,' Alexi said. 'He's been killed. Murdered.'

'Murdered?' Ranya's mouth fell open. 'How? Why?' She shook her head. 'I don't understand.'

Diana paled and didn't say a word, which was unusual. Her hands shook and she looked close to tears.

'No more do we,' Jack replied, 'but the police will hopefully get to the bottom of things. They will want to talk to you all.'

'Not much I can tell them,' Diana said, pulling herself together with commendable speed. She may not have had a high opinion of Peter but anyone unused to murder, which was the vast majority of the population, were always affected when it struck close to home. 'The man was a know-it-all and a misogynist. I didn't have any time for him.'

'He wasn't *that* bad,' Ranya said. 'Besides, he's dead, Diana. We should show some respect.'

'I have respect and I'm sorry he's dead,' Diana responded, not maintaining eye contact with any of them, instead fiddling with the cuff of her sweater. 'Even so, I'm no hypocrite and I won't pretend that I liked the man.' She paused to reflect. 'Who would want to murder him, though?'

'Well, that's the question the police will be hoping to find answers to,' Jack said. 'Did he mention anything about his personal life to either of you two ladies?'

'Not to me.' Alexi wasn't surprised when Diana responded first. 'I kept my distance and didn't encourage him to speak to me about anything, otherwise I would have been compelled to upset the balance of the course by putting the irritating man firmly in his place.'

'He told me that he'd almost married several times but didn't want to deprive the rest of the female population of his company by settling for just one woman,' Ranya said.

Diana snorted. 'Sounds like the sort of arrogant statement he'd come out with.'

'Well, he was quite good looking, I suppose,' Ranya said, waggling a delicate hand from side to side. 'And a lot of women are swayed by appearances.'

'I wonder why he felt the need to mention his marital status to you, Ranya, unless he hoped you'd be interested in him.' Alexi smiled. 'He was a bit of a flirt, full of himself. I think we can all agree upon that much.'

'More likely the women he fancied had better sense than to get involved,' Diana said dismissively, 'and told him to take a hike. He thought a lot of himself and was just the sort to punch above his weight.'

'Did he say anything about his line of work to either of you?' Jack asked.

'He told me he was something important in the civil service,' Diana replied. 'Made it sound as though the wheels of governmental departments would grind to a halt without him. I walked away. I wasn't interested in his boasting and couldn't raise sufficient energy to care.'

'He told me that he couldn't talk about his work,' Ranya added, 'which seemed odd, now that I think about it, since I hadn't asked him what he did.'

'He was probably trying to impress you with his importance,' Diana remarked with a dismissive snort. 'I do wonder now why he was on the course, though,' she added pensively. 'For all his pretentiousness, he was quite intelligent. The news was on one morning when we were having breakfast and he actually spoke quite intelligently about the economic migrant situation.' Diana frowned. 'I suppose what I'm attempting to establish is what he hoped to achieve from this course. The rest of us all have our reasons but if Peter's career took up all his time and was as vital to the country's interests as he implied, how could he capitalise on what he got from your leadership, Alexi?'

'Perhaps he was a spy,' Ranya said, giggling but abruptly cutting her amusement short, presumably because she recalled that someone had died.

'He was fastidiously neat,' Diana said. 'Annoyingly so. He tidied up empty plates the moment one of us stopped eating, sometimes even before. I told him that the hotel employed people to do that sort of thing, but he was having none of it. He couldn't seem to help himself.'

'Is there anything about him that in retrospect seemed off kilter?' Jack asked. 'A chance remark? Out of character behaviour? Anything that will help the police get to the bottom of things.'

The two ladies shared a protracted look and simultaneously shook their heads.

'No, sorry,' Diana replied for them both. 'I can't think of any reason for anyone wanting to bump him off, discarding the fact that he was annoying. And if that was a murderous offence then half of us would be potential victims.' She paused. 'It was probably a random attack. Oh, I know that sort of thing is more likely in the city but still, the world's changing...'

'Actually, I overheard him on his mobile the evening before last. He was in the courtyard and he didn't see me. He was arguing with someone but speaking in an undertone, like he was afraid to be overheard,' Ranya said, frowning. 'I'd forgotten about that.'

'Did you hear the name of the person he was talking to?' Alexi asked.

Ranya shook her head. 'No. I heard him say that he'd done all he could and that the rest was up to the person he was speaking with, but I have absolutely no idea what that meant. The other person obviously disagreed, hence the argument.'

'Tell the police about the overheard conversation,' Jack replied, 'and tell them as close as possible the time and date. That way, they'll be able to trace who he called from his mobile phone records.'

Alexi, who had an uncomfortable feeling that Peter might have been talking to Patrick about her, given the fact that Patrick was desperate to get her back, and wished that she could have had access to his phone first.

'If that's all,' Diana said, standing and hoisting her bag over her shoulder, 'I'd like to get showered and write up my notes from today. I don't mean to sound heartless, but life goes on and I fully intend to get our efforts published.'

Ranya flashed an embarrassed smile and followed Diana from the room.

'I wonder if she realises that she just gave herself a motive,' Jack remarked. 'Well, kinda.'

'By implying that Peter's demise eliminates a strong competitor.' Alexi shrugged. 'Not sure she meant it that way. Diana is too self-assured to look upon anyone else as a serious threat to her journalistic capabilities and even if she did view Peter in that respect, she was with Ranya all day.'

'Is she a capable wannabe?'

Alexi waggled a hand from side to side. 'She does good research but it's Ranya who turns their interviews into an account that won't send readers to sleep. Left to her own devices, Diana would simply reproduce the facts in a dull-as-ditchwater manner, rather like the way she speaks and acts.'

'Ranya is her polar opposite. She's quiet and self-effacing.'

'Which is why they work well as a team. Ranya doesn't have the strength of character to, metaphorically speaking, thrust a microphone beneath a reluctant person's nose but Diana is as thick-skinned as they come in that regard. By the sheer force of her tenacity, she could extract an opinion from a stone. But when it comes to turning the results of her bullying... sorry, I mean robust interviewing, into meaningful prose then Ranya gets the chance to shine.'

'Diana was shocked by the news of Peter's death. Did you notice her reaction?'

Alexi nodded. 'I did but I didn't make much of it. We're all shocked.'

Before Jack could ask more questions, the door opened and Archie Walton sauntered through it. Alexi thought it would be easy to look upon him as all brawn and no brain, but stereotyping would be inappropriate in his case. She liked Archie. He had a quick wit but didn't take life too seriously. He'd told her that being a bouncer was a young man's game and he was looking to expand his horizons. He'd had the most basic of educations in a failing comprehensive in the East End but it was clear to Alexi that he was intelligent. He'd told her that he wanted to write a crime novel, using the experience he'd gained on a club's door and the things he'd learned from it as his base.

Cosmo looked up at him, blinked and didn't even bother to hiss. As far as Alexi was concerned, her cat's reaction established Archie as one of the good guys. She glanced at Jack, clearly attempting to suppress a smile. He hadn't missed Cosmo's behaviour and would know what Alexi was thinking. Jack would never admit it in a million years, not even to her, but Alexi suspected that he'd fallen into the habit of trusting Cosmo's judgement too.

'Hey guys, what's up?' Archie asked.

'Not good news,' Alexi replied. 'I'm afraid Peter's dead.'

'Dead?' Archie scratched at his bald head. 'Blimey. What happened?'

'He's been murdered,' Jack told him, clearly not feeling the need to mince his words.

'Murdered? Someone bumped him off, you mean.' Archie looked flabbergasted. 'Here? In sleepy Lambourn. What the hell's going on?'

'That's what we're trying to establish,' Jack said. 'When did you see him last?'

'This morning at breakfast. He was making a prat of himself as usual, banging on about illegal immigration when something came on the news about the small boats and that not enough was being done to stop them. He told us all how the situation should be handled. Easy to spout off when you don't know the facts. I told him to button it, for all the good it did me.'

'Did you get into a fight?' Jack asked.

Archie laughed. 'Nah. I don't pick fights, especially not with bullies who're physically incapable of defending themselves.' He glowered at Jack. 'Here, hang on a minute. I hope you ain't trying to pin this on me. Just because I've been inside, I guess that makes me an easy target.'

'You have?' Jack glanced at Alexi, who gave a brief nod. Archie had told her in confidence that he'd done six months for GBH, but she hadn't seen any reason to enlighten Jack. 'News to me. Why, if you don't mind me asking?'

'I do mind as it happens but still, if the old bill are looking for a suspect, I suppose it will come out anyway.' Archie aggressively rubbed his stubbily chin. 'I got a bit over-enthusiastic ejecting a coked-up idiot from the club when he was harassing a woman, gave him a bit of a hiding. Me temper got the better of me, I'll admit that much but it gets my goat when a man beats on a woman. Anyway, it turned out that the geezer was connected to someone important, his pride was hurt, he got his mates to lie about what happened and I got me collar felt.'

'Archie is going to use his stint inside as a unique selling point when he submits the outline of his gangland novel to agents,' Alexi said, smiling at a man who had become both a friend and a protégé.

'Yeah well, Alexi says everyone has to have an angle to get ahead in the publishing game.' Archie grinned. 'Well, just about any game nowadays, and if my record gets me noticed then who am I to complain.'

'You clearly didn't have a high opinion of Foreman,' Jack said, 'but you're not alone there. What we're struggling to establish is why anyone would dislike him enough to top him, especially here in the country, where he doesn't know anyone.'

'Yeah, I can see the problem, mate. And I sympathise with you, Alexi. Coming after all the other trouble you've had, you really don't need this. So, if I can help at all, crack a few heads together to get answers, I'm your man.'

'Nice offer,' Jack said smiling, 'but it doesn't work that way.'

'Shame,' Archie said, shrugging his massive shoulders.

'At least he wasn't killed here at the hotel,' Alexi said, 'which is something, but the connection to me won't go unnoticed.'

'What happened?'

'He was strangled,' Jack replied.

Archie sniffed. 'A man's crime then.'

'That's the assumption we're working on,' Jack said. 'Can't tell you much else because I don't know anything. The police will be here to talk to you all soon.'

'I look forward to it.' There was a sarcastic edge to Archie's voice. 'He must have been killed sometime after we all left here this morning and I can account for my whereabouts, with witnesses to prove it.'

'I'm sure you can,' Alexi replied. 'We don't suspect you. What we wanted to ask you, to ask everyone, is if you had any private conversations with him and if he gave you any insight into his private life? For all his opinionated rants, he never said much about himself, which is unusual enough to make me suspicious. Given what's happened to him, there was obviously something in his background that he didn't want anyone to know about.'

'Now that you mention it, you're right.' Archie again rubbed his chin, a habit of his that Alexi had noticed when he was deep in thought. 'I asked him once what branch of the civil service he was in, given that he thinks he knows how to run the country. I thought perhaps he worked in the private office of some important minister who couldn't do his job without the questionable benefit of Peter's advice.' He chuckled. 'That would have explained a lot about the state the country's in nowadays. But he didn't run with my question and instead changed the subject. The man liked to boast so his reticence seems out of character, now that I think about it.'

'Yes.' Alexi nodded emphatically. 'It does. And obviously, given what's happened, there was a great deal more to him than met the eye.'

'He severely pissed off someone important.' Archie threw back his head and growled. 'The idiot! I don't think any of us had much time for him, but he didn't deserve to have the life choked out of him.'

'I tend to agree.'

'Emily had more to do with him than the rest of us. I heard her defend him once or twice when others thought he was out of order. She might be able to tell you more about him than anyone else.'

'Thanks, Archie.' Alexi gave the bouncer a warm smile. 'I'll catch her as soon as she gets back.'

'Right. Well, if you've finished grilling me, I'll get out of your hair.'

'Don't look at me like that!' Alexi said indignantly in response to Jack's hurt expression, after Archie had gone. 'I had absolutely no reason to tell you that Archie had been inside, *and* his conviction has nothing to do with Peter's death. The two situations aren't connected. Anyway, Archie told me in confidence. It came up when he mentioned his plans to write a novel based on his experiences. Besides, I know where Archie was this morning and also know he told the truth when he said his whereabouts could be corroborated.'

'Hey, don't shoot the messenger.' Jack held up his hands in a defensive gesture. 'I don't suspect Archie. In fact, I like him. It was just a bit of a surprise, that's all. It will raise red flags with Vickery when he finds out but if Archie's whereabouts can be verified and no previous connections to Foreman come to light, then he has nothing to worry about.'

'Interesting about Emily,' Alexi mused. 'Peter didn't have any good things to say about modern society and what he described as a work-shy generation expecting to live off other people's taxes and yet he was sympathetic about Emily's circumstances.'

'Which are?'

'She's a single mum of two. Her ex left her high and dry, disappeared off the face of the earth and hasn't paid a penny in maintenance. She works two jobs to make ends meet and her mother minds the kids. She's standing for election to her local council, keen to make her voice heard on behalf of others in her situation who are stigmatised as scroungers.' Alexi smiled. 'She's a feisty individual too and I think she'll make a great ambassador for her cause. She wants my help in finding the most diplomatic way to get her views across.'

'Good for her,' Jack replied. 'You have certainly attracted an eclectic mix.'

'Is now a good time to tell you that Patrick vetted the shortlist?' she asked, cringing as she awaited Jack's explosion. To her surprise, he simply sighed.

'Actually, that could be how Patrick and Foreman linked up. I assume he approved Foreman's name.'

'I put it on the list, and he didn't dispute his inclusion.' Alexi paused. 'It will look bad for Patrick if a former link between them comes to light and I know that you will look for one, even if Vickery doesn't. I did ask Patrick to let me know if any of the names were familiar to him. You know how badly I want... wanted this course to be a success and Patrick's offer to look over the entrants' efforts and possibly publish extracts was a big cachet. I didn't want disappointed delegates claiming favouritism.'

'We'll have to assume for now that Patrick approached Foreman for some reason and had him reporting back to him. That would have been the argument that Ranya overheard.'

'Yeah, it looks that way.'

'Goodness, I had no idea that Halloween was taken so seriously as a pagan festival.' Grace breezed through the door with a natural elegance that made her name seem so appropriate. 'I hadn't... oh, is something wrong?' she asked, stopping dead when she observed Alexi and Jack's dour expressions.

'I'm afraid so,' Alexi replied, indicating to Grace that she should occupy a vacant chair. 'Unfortunately, Peter's been killed.'

Grace blinked several times and then swallowed. 'An accident, presumably. I got the impression that he was terrified of race-horses; he let that much slip once, despite the fact that he tried to project a tough image. Peter saw any sort of fear as a weakness to be overcome. I wouldn't put it past him to have befriended an unpredictable thoroughbred, just to prove a point to himself, and got kicked in the head for his trouble.'

'Unfortunately not.' Alexi spoke gently, wishing for her own sake that *had* been the case. 'He was murdered.'

'Good heavens. Why on earth would anyone want to murder Peter?' She scowled as she examined her beautifully manicured fingers. 'He could be incredibly opinionated and overbearing but that's no reason to murder a person.'

'Did you talk to him privately about his life?' Jack asked. 'We're trying to establish a motive but know next to nothing about him, other than that he was a civil servant, although in what branch, we have yet to establish. We do know that he'd never been married and, presumably, had no children.'

'Then you know as much as I do.' Grace lifted her shoulders in a gesture of apology. 'Sorry. I'd really like to help. Murder is just awful.' She paused. 'I'm sorry if this sounds insensitive but will the course continue?'

'Yes,' Alexi replied. 'It's due to end tomorrow anyway. The police will want to talk to you all and so you won't be free to leave for a while. So, if everyone wants to press on, that's what we will do.'

'Well, heartless as it sounds, I'm glad.' Grace collected up her possessions and stood. 'But now, if you will excuse me, I think I need a little time alone to get my mind round what's happened.' She glanced back over her shoulder. 'Do we know who his next of kin was and if they've been informed?'

'I'm sure the police will be on that,' Alexi said, glancing at Jack for approbation.

'That's good, I suppose.'

Even at times of distress, Alexi noticed, Grace still instinctively moved with… well, grace, but she was obviously very upset and had shown a sensitivity that didn't surprise Alexi.

'And then there was one,' Jack remarked, as Grace disappeared from view. 'Hopefully, Emily will be able to give us something, anything, to go on.'

Emily dashed through the doors a few minutes later, as though summoned by the power of Jack's thoughts, a bag flapping open on her shoulder.

'Hey,' she said. 'Just had a call from my mum. Why does a two-year-old find earth worms so endlessly fascinating?'

Alexi smiled. 'Presumably the two-year-old in question is a boy.'

'Of course. Ben takes "going down the garden to eat worms" as a personal challenge.'

'Boys will be boys,' Jack replied, laughing. 'That won't change any time soon.'

'I tend to agree.' She threw herself into a chair. 'Not sure if I'm cut out for all the doorstepping that goes hand in hand with getting elected to local councils. No one wants to talk about anything other than their own pet peeves. It's selfish, to say nothing of exhausting.'

'Sorry to be the bearer of bad tidings,' Alexi said, her expression sobering, 'but I'm afraid that Peter's been killed.' She paused, watching as the colour drained from Emily's face. 'Murdered.'

'No!' She clapped her hands against her cheeks. 'How can that even be possible in such a tranquil place? And why? Who would want to kill Peter?'

'That's what we're trying to establish. As are the police, obviously,' Jack replied. 'You seem to be the only person who had much time for him.'

Emily nodded. 'He was annoying, and opinionated, there's no denying that. Very right wing. I hesitated to tell him about my circumstances because I assumed he wouldn't approve but I was wrong about that. He grew up in care apparently and didn't have a good time of it. He didn't actually say as much but I got the impression that he'd been both abused and neglected.'

'You've already told us more about him than we knew,' Alexi said. 'And it would explain why he was so sympathetic to your situation.'

'Did he tell you why he decided to come on Alexi's course?' Jack asked. 'Everyone else had specific reasons for doing so but Peter wasn't planning to write a book, get elected to a local council or take up writing for a hobby.'

'He spoke about it in cryptic terms.' Emily bit her lip as she paused to consider. 'He said something about doing a favour for an acquaintance.'

'What sort of favour?' Jack asked, sharing a look with Alexi.

'I don't really know.' She shook her head. 'But I think it concerned you, Alexi.'

'Me?' Alexi pointed to her own chest for emphasis.

'He just said that some people were wasted outside of their natural environment and needed to realise the error of their ways.'

'What on earth...' Alexi felt dizzy, incapable of completing her sentence.

'He said that sometimes, people needed to be shocked out of their complacency.'

Alexi tuned Emily out, her mind dwelling upon Patrick's burner phone, the number of which had been in Peter's possession. She glanced at Jack, whose expression was set in stone, and knew his mind was similarly engaged.

7

Jack waited for a tearful Emily to leave the room before turning to Alexi with a concerned expression.

'You okay?' he asked, gently touching her shoulder.

'Not really,' she replied. 'Patrick setting Peter to spy on me and perhaps even sabotage the course I can just about believe.' She flashed a wan smile. 'Even so, I honestly don't think he's capable of strangling anyone. Besides, why would he?'

'Unless Ranya didn't hear the entire argument and Peter had threatened to tell you why he was really here.'

'Patrick has a way with words. If Peter had issued that threat then Patrick would have used his linguistic abilities to turn the tables on Peter and paint himself as the wronged party. I have seen him think on his feet and turn situations like that to his advantage tons of times.' Alexi shook her head. 'We both know that he wants me to go back to London. He expected me to capitulate long before now.'

'Until I distracted you.'

Alexi's smile was more genuine this time. 'Right. So if he was going to kill anyone, you would be the obvious target.'

'Ouch!' Jack shook his head. 'Yeah, I can see that.'

'I can believe that he might use underhand tactics to achieve his aim but the only type of murder that Patrick is capable of committing is through the written word. He was even too squeamish to remove a spider from my bathroom once.'

'What a man!' Jack's expression sobered. 'I know you believe what you say but we none of us know what we're capable of when jealousy supersedes common sense. The man has an ego the size of Wales. You rejecting him was hard enough for him to swallow but the fact that you then took up with me, a humble policeman who doesn't know a dangling modifier from a split infinitive, would have severely pissed him off.'

Alexi smiled. 'You overestimate my charm.'

Jack returned her smile with a meltingly gentle one of his own. 'No, darling, I don't. Patrick is a man who always gets what he wants. He was confident that you'd die of boredom in the country and that you'd return to London after a month or two of licking your wounds. He was absolutely sure of your affections, which is why he didn't warn you beforehand that your job was being axed. He was confident that you'd take the lower position offered because you couldn't bear to be parted from him.' Jack snorted his contempt. 'Prat! But even when you didn't, he still thought you just needed time to come to your senses.'

'Then you came along.'

'Then I came along, inciting a jealousy that has been simmering away ever since. A series of murders in Lambourn, all tenaciously linked to you and this hotel, must have seemed like manna from heaven for Vaughan. They were bound to make you reassess your options and you would finally come to your senses. But instead, you suggested the journalism course, went to him for help and he saw an opportunity.'

Alexi let out a weary sigh. 'It all sounds so plausible when you put it like that. Even so, I still don't see what he can have expected Peter to do to scupper things, short of getting himself murdered.' She threw up her hands. 'I know, I know! In your position, I would suspect Patrick too and I'm not saying he isn't involved. I just can't see him taking such an almighty risk, even putting aside his disinclination for violence.'

'He could have had someone else do the deed.'

Alexi waggled a hand from side to side. 'Perhaps, but wouldn't that lay him open to the possibility of blackmail? Even supposing he knew where to find a killer for hire.'

'Such people aren't *that* hard to find, especially not for a person with his resources. Believe it or not, a woman was recently found guilty of conspiracy to murder her husband. She found someone to do the deed by Googling "Hitman for Hire".'

Alexi gaped at him. 'You're joking.'

Jack grinned. 'I kid you not. And she didn't even have enough sense to delete her search history. There's no cure for stupid.'

'Patrick is many things, but no one's ever accused him of being thick.'

'Well, darling, he's hung around for no obvious reason and no one's seen him today. It does make me suspicious, but then I have a suspicious mind, especially when someone thinks they can mess with your life and reputation.'

Alexi tipped a protesting Cosmo off her lap and wrapped her arms around Jack's neck. 'I appreciate your caveman values, but I don't need protecting and you are not going to talk to Patrick alone.' She removed her arms so that she could hold up a hand to prevent him from interrupting her. 'With all that testosterone floating about, it's bound to get physical, and I don't want to have to bail you both out.'

'Leave him to rot,' Jack quipped.

'This is serious!' She stood up and tugged at Jack's hand.

'Come on, let's see if we can track Patrick down and give him a chance to explain.'

Cosmo, tail erect and twitching, led the way to the door.

Jack and Alexi returned to Cheryl's kitchen. Both she and Drew were there, with Verity in her carrycot. They both looked up, wearing identical worried frowns. For all their attempts to remain stoic, Jack could see that this latest tragedy had pushed them close to breaking point. Alexi clearly could too. She let out a gentle cry and ran to Cheryl, wrapping her arms around her neck.

'It will be okay,' she promised.

Jack nodded dutifully in support but was unsure if it ever could be.

'What's happened?' Drew asked. 'Are you getting anywhere?'

'Early days,' Jack said, sitting down and leaning back so that Cosmo could occupy his lap. Toby yapped indignantly and scraped his paws against the leg of Jack's chair.

'You're in demand,' Cheryl said.

Jack grinned. 'So it would seem.'

'We think there was more to Peter Foreman, civil servant and general know-it-all, than we imagined,' Alexi told her friends.

'A reasonable assumption, given that someone killed him,' Drew replied, nodding. 'No one goes into a bathroom on spec and strangles whoever happens to be in there for the hell of it.'

'But why, here in Lambourn?' Cheryl asked, frowning. 'Surely, there's more chance of getting away with murder in a big city like London.'

'Not necessarily,' Jack told her. 'Most people in busy cities mind their own business but there are cameras absolutely everywhere. Even so, it was a risky thing to do in this part of the world, which implies desperation on someone's part. But at least there are no cameras in pub bathrooms, or anywhere else on the premises for that matter. I know because I checked. And there weren't many people around at that time of day either. If the killer arrived on foot, or on a bike or electric scooter say, then no one would remember a vehicle.' A recollection of that yellow mountain bike flashed through Jack's mind.

'Yeah, I hear what you say,' Drew replied. 'Even so, the killer took a hell of a chance, which does imply desperation.'

'Perhaps he wasn't supposed to die and was attacked as a warning,' Cheryl said hopefully.

Jack shook his head. 'Afraid not.'

Cheryl sighed as she fussed over the sleeping baby.

'We did discover something disturbing,' Alexi said into the ensuing silence.

'What?' Drew and Cheryl asked together.

'A connection between Peter and Patrick.'

Jack subjected Alexi to a close scrutiny as she spoke, wishing he could read her thoughts, worried about her stout defence of her former nearest-and-dearest. Did she still feel a connection to the weasel? They were joined by a long history of a shared career and Jack couldn't compete with that.

Cassie had her own reasons for wanting Alexi out of Lambourn. Jack was well aware that she hadn't given up on winning his affections, albeit by default. How would he feel if Alexi accused her of committing the crime? Ten to one, he'd spring to her defence, simply because he *knew* she was incapable of killing anyone. But wasn't Alexi making the same claim about Patrick?

Damn, this business would drive a wedge between him and Alexi if he didn't handle it with kid gloves.

Kid gloves it would have to be then since he was more than ready to fight for what he wanted. And what he wanted was Alexi's full and complete commitment to their relationship, no half measures.

'What sort of a connection?' Cheryl asked.

Alexi explained about the mystery phone number and how they had established that it belonged to Patrick.

'Blimey.' Drew scratched his head. 'I know he wants you back, Alexi, but that's a bit extreme even by his ruthless standards.'

'Yeah, I know.' Alexi stared at her feet. 'It does make you wonder why he hung around all week rather than going back to London where he's needed; I'm with Jack on that one.'

'Perhaps ask him before condemning,' Cheryl suggested.

'That's what we intend to do,' Jack said. 'Is he here?'

'Actually, no,' Cheryl said, sharing a worried look with Drew. 'He went out this morning, came back earlier and then went out again.'

'But he's not checked out?' Alexi asked. 'Well, he wouldn't,' she added, answering her own question. 'He has to be here for the end of course party tomorrow.'

'His things are still in his room,' Cheryl confirmed.

'Look,' Drew said, 'let's not get ahead of ourselves. I don't like the guy any more than you do, Jack. The way he treated Alexi was well out of order but even so, if you really thought his name was in the frame, you'd have already told Vickery.'

'Patrick's up to something, Drew,' Alexi said, looking weary and very concerned. 'I just hope that whatever reason he had for being in touch with Peter was journalistic rather than murderous.' She turned to face Jack and summoned up a smile. 'We should talk to him, see what he has to say for himself and then encourage him to speak with Vickery. If he dithers then we'll do it for him.'

Jack felt relief sweep through him as he reached out to touch her hand. 'Deal,' he agreed.

'At least we don't have the press camped outside again,' Cheryl said. 'Either news of the murder hasn't broken yet or the pack have descended upon the Swan.'

Jack knew that as soon as Alexi's connection to the victim became public knowledge, they would be besieged and there was sod all he could do to protect her from the avalanche of speculation, other than to identify the real killer. That was what he did best, he reminded himself. He was a detective, a damned good one, and would never get a better opportunity to use his skills to ensure that Alexi emerged with her reputation intact.

'How about a bite to eat?' Drew asked, as always thinking of food in a time of crisis. 'Can't catch criminals on empty stomachs.'

Cosmo jumped from Jack's lap, wound himself round Drew's legs and cried pathetically, making everyone laugh.

'Okay, big guy.' Alexi stood and went to the cupboard where his food was kept. 'I get the message.'

'It's only five o'clock,' Jack said, in response to Drew's suggestion, 'but sure, why not?'

'Not sure I can eat anything.' Alexi shuddered as she watched Cosmo tucking into his food.

'You know better than that,' Jack chided. 'You won't be any good to anyone if you pass out through lack of sustenance.'

'I'll arrange it then,' Drew said, heading for the hotel's kitchen.

The food when it arrived was delicious, but no one seemed to have much of an appetite, not even Jack. Possibilities tumbled through his mind like a washing machine stuck on the spin cycle but nothing about the reasons for the murder of a seemingly ordinary man made much sense to his detective's brain. Really, until they could establish more about Foreman's circumstances, they never would.

Jack's phone rang just as they finished their meal.

'Cassie,' he told Alexi as he checked the screen and took the call. 'Hey, Cas,' he said. 'What you got for me?'

'Frustratingly little,' she replied, sighing. 'Are you aware that Peter Foreman didn't exist before 2000?'

'What?' He'd put the call on speaker and watched as Alexi's mouth fell open. 'A false identity?'

'Looks that way. Sorry, Jack. I've looked everywhere and can't find anything with his birth date and name before 2000. He was born a full-grown man with the dawn of the millennium.'

'He told someone here that he was brought up in care,' Jack told her. 'Does that help?'

'Not unless I know *where*. Sorry.'

'Don't be. Just a minute,' he said, when a thought occurred to him. 'Alexi, did Foreman give you a contact number?'

'Sure.' She reached for her phone, pulled up her records for the course and reeled the number off.

'See if you can get into these phone records,' he said, repeating the number. 'It might give us something. We don't know if the police have his phone or if the killer took it.'

'The police will access his records either way.'

'You're better. And faster.'

'Flattery will get you everywhere.' She gave a brief little laugh. 'I'm on it. Anything else?'

Jack looked at Alexi, who shook her head.

'That's it for now. Soon as you can, Cas.'

Verity, who had slept peacefully through the entire drama, woke at that moment and started to grizzle.

'Someone else needs feeding,' Cheryl said, picking up the carry cot and heading for the door.

'And I'm needed in the bar,' Drew added, standing also and opening the door for his wife. 'I dare say that you'll want to speak to Patrick alone when he gets back anyway.'

'Don't let us drive you out of your own kitchen,' Jack said.

Drew waved the apology aside. 'Busy, busy, mate,' he said as he disappeared through the door. His head reappeared almost immediately. 'Patrick's car just pulled up outside,' he said. 'How's that for timing?'

'Game on,' Alexi muttered, straightening her shoulders.

Jack knew that his first port of call would be this kitchen, where he'd hope to catch Alexi alone. *Not happening!*

'Ready for this?' Jack asked, squeezing Alexi's hand.

'Nope,' she replied tersely.

* * *

Cosmo stood up from Toby's basket and made a sound that could have been anything from a mewl to a growl, even before the door opened. Jack knew that the feline hated Patrick, confirming Jack's suspicion that Cosmo was an excellent judge of character. There was something of the night about Patrick Vaughan and Jack didn't believe a word that came out of his self-serving mouth.

'It's your show, darling, but I'll back you every step of the way.'

Alexi smiled as she straightened her shoulders, looking battle-ready. 'I'm tougher than I look. I need answers, Jack, and I need them now. Today. Patrick at the very least sent someone to spy on me and at worse, could have done something a damned sight worse than that.'

Jack squeezed her hand and nodded, glad that she hadn't totally dismissed the possibility of Vaughan having committed murder.

'Drew said I'd find you here.' The man of the moment burst into the room and smiled at Alexi, but his smile quickly faded when he noticed her hand clasped in Jack's. 'Hi guys,' he said, recovering quickly and flashing a wider smile that Jack thought contrived. 'Any updates yet?'

'Sit down,' Jack said, releasing Alexi's hand, his tone silk on steel.

'Just a minute...' Patrick glowered at Jack but something in the set to Jack's features made the editor comply. 'What's on your mind?'

'Peter Foreman,' Alexi said, glowering at Patrick.

Jack thought he noticed a modicum of unease pass through Patrick's expression, but it was gone again before he could be sure. 'The murder victim.' Patrick shook his head. 'How can I help?'

'Cut the crap.' Jack spoke quietly but with sufficient venom to ensure Patrick's complete attention.

'I'm not sure I like your tone.'

'We need to know what your connection to Foreman is,' Jack told him.

'I don't have... Look, I don't have time for this. I'm sorry he's dead, but I barely shared a dozen words with him and I'm sure he's no great loss. What's with the inquisition? I didn't do anything to frighten the man off, except perhaps to tell him, tell them all, a few home truths about the "glamour" of our profession.' He smiled at Alexi, intentionally excluding Jack from that comment. 'I thought I was doing you a favour by lending my support to your course but if this is all the thanks I get for it then—'

'Cut the act, Patrick,' Alexi said quietly. 'This is devastating for me. We need you to step up for once and tell us the truth.'

Vaughan barely reacted to Alexi's harangue, but only, Jack sensed, because he was there. The man knew more about Foreman than he'd so far let on but understood the importance of body language and was too slick to make elementary mistakes. He was a player, a newspaper man who wasn't above bending the rules and getting down and dirty. If he'd had anything to do with the murder, he'd had more than enough time to control his response.

'What happened precisely?' he asked, shifting his bulk to sit sideways on his chair, ignoring Cosmo's angry hissing. He looked worried now, perhaps wondering what he and Alexi had found out.

'What we need to know is how you were connected to him,' Alexi said, her tone firm, controlled. Yet Jack sensed she was anything other than in control. In fact, she was perilously close to breaking point.

'Me?' Vaughan's eyes widened. 'I wasn't, other than on this course.'

With a sigh, Jack grabbed his phone and dialled the number they'd taken from Foreman's notes. A phone in Vaughan's pocket started ringing. Vaughan instinctively reached for it, then glanced up at Jack and swore softly beneath his breath.

'Shall we start again?' Jack invited.

'We thought we'd give you an opportunity to explain before we tell the police that you own that phone,' Alexi added.

'Thank you for that.' Vaughan smiled briefly at Alexi and bowed his head in acknowledgement of the courtesy. 'He was doing some research for me on a story we're hoping to run.'

'Then why the burner phone if it was legitimate newspaper business?' Jack asked.

'It was... off the books.' He sent Alexi a prolonged look. 'You know how it is sometimes. The situation was delicate. Until we had all the facts, we couldn't decide if the story was worth running *and* we didn't want the opposition getting wind of it.'

'Who *was* Peter?' Alexi asked. 'We know his identity is comparatively new.'

'He worked for a government agency. That's all I can tell you because that's all I know. They let him go recently but he never said why and I didn't bother to ask because I knew I wouldn't get an honest answer. He said it was a young man's game and that he'd had enough.'

'But?' Jack prompted.

'One of my best journalists came across him when chasing down a story.'

'The gold robbery,' Alexi said.

Vaughan sent her a sharp look. 'Right.'

'If he worked for the security services, that investigation wouldn't have been their remit, so what was his interest?' Jack asked.

'That I couldn't say.' Vaughan spread his hands. 'That's the honest to God's truth.'

Jack snorted, convinced that he wouldn't recognise the truth if it jumped up and bit him on the arse.

'But you did meet with him, told him about my course and encouraged him to apply,' Alexi said through clenched teeth. 'You knew he'd be accepted because I asked you to vet the list of applicants.' Alexi tapped her fingers on the surface of the table. 'You knew one of the robbers was supposedly hiding out in this area and the course would be a good way for Peter to get close and ask questions.'

'*And* you wanted him to report back to you on Alexi,' Jack added harshly. 'You probably hoped to hear that her relationship with me was on the rocks. Perhaps you even asked him to try and make it so.'

'It wouldn't have broken my heart,' Vaughan replied, meeting Jack's gaze and holding it in a challenging fashion. 'Alexi's talents are wasted in this backwater.'

'And another murder linked to Alexi would make it easier for you to entice her back to London,' Jack pointed out.

'Good God! Do you really think so little of me, Alexi, that you could even entertain such a thought?'

'I know you, Patrick.' Alexi shook her head. 'I wouldn't put anything past you. You stop at nothing to get what you want and can be utterly ruthless.'

'In pursuit of a story. That's the way it works. You know that. This is different. It's personal.'

'Glad you're able to differentiate,' she replied, a sarcastic edge of her voice.

'Did Foreman get definitive proof that Paul Franklin is hiding out hereabouts?' Jack asked.

'I have absolutely no idea. He said he'd tell me when there was something to tell.'

'He went about his investigation in much the same way as he fooled all of us on this course into thinking he was a waste of space,' Alexi said. 'If he was intelligent enough to be employed by one of the security services then his persona had to have been a bluff.'

'To make you avoid him and stop asking questions he'd prefer not to answer, is my bet,' Vaughan said.

'That approach might work on a residential course if he wanted to keep the other delegates at bay,' Alexi said musingly, 'but why draw attention to himself by asking aggressive questions about Franklin at the Swan?'

'To draw Franklin out?' Vaughan suggested. 'Sounds as though he succeeded too.'

'Possibly,' Jack said grudgingly. 'We need to know more about him, and you need to tell Vickery everything you've just told us.'

Vaughan nodded. 'Yeah. I've got nothing to hide.'

'Other than a controlling nature and desire to manipulate me,' Alexi added hotly.

'No, darling, never that.'

'Save it!' Alexi said sharply. 'I don't want to hear it.'

'You have got things to hide though,' Jack pointed out. 'Like how Foreman came to your attention in the first place.'

'My journalist came across him asking questions about the bullion robbery. I looked into his history and found what you did insofar as he didn't exist before 2000. So I made contact with him.'

'Just like that?' Jack asked sceptically.

'Sure. Why not? Alexi will tell you, in our world, that's what you do. You also have to take stuff at face value, at least until the time comes to establish your facts.' He spread his hands. 'Look, all I can tell you is that Foreman was a loose cannon, not good at following orders. He told me that much, which is probably why his career tanked.'

'He had a personal interest in the bullion robbery,' Alexi added.

Vaughan shrugged. 'Seemingly so, but I have absolutely no idea what that interest was.'

'Okay,' Jack said, turning to face the newspaper man. 'Let's assume that we believe you and put Foreman's murder to one side for a moment. Instead, why don't you tell us why you've been hanging around and, more to the point, where you've been today.'

'To visit my mother,' he said without hesitation.

'Try again.' Alexi's voice was brittle. 'Your mother's in a care home in Surrey.'

'Not any more. I wasn't satisfied with the treatment she received there so I moved her to Winchester six months ago.' He held up his hands. 'You can check.' He reeled off the name of the care home and Jack made a note of it.

'We will,' Jack said. 'So too will the police.'

'I don't doubt it.' Vaughan seemed more relaxed. 'So, what now?'

'Now you talk to Vickery and tell him what you've told us,' Jack repeated.

'No, I mean how can I help with your enquiry? I feel kinda responsible.'

'Nothing you can do,' Jack replied shortly, 'other than to keep this out of print. It will make matters worse for Alexi if her connection to the victim becomes common knowledge. If you care about her, you'll put her interests ahead of your career.'

Vaughan inclined his head. 'Consider it done. Or not done. But if the others pick up on it...'

'A local murder won't interest the big boys,' Alexi said with authority, 'unless they latch on to Peter's connection to whichever department he once worked for. And you can bet your life that if that happens, they'll be shut down.'

'Alexi went to the Swan to meet with Foreman because he wanted to discuss a mutual acquaintance with her,' Jack said.

'Really?' Vaughan elevated his brows.

'It could only have been you,' Jack continued. 'He was over-heard arguing on the phone, protesting that he'd done all he could and mentioning Alexi by name.'

'Could have been talking to anyone. Did he mention my name?'

'So much for wanting to help,' Alexi said, allowing her disgust to show.

'You're not prepared to 'fess up.' Jack shook his head, aware that Vaughan was fishing, wanting to know how much they knew before dropping himself in it. 'Not that it matters. We know the time of the call and once the police have looked through his phone records, we'll know who he was talking to. They'll draw their own conclusions from the fact that you aren't willing to admit it.'

'I might have had a heated discussion with him,' Vaughan admitted, 'but it may or may not have been the one that was over-heard. I take a lot of calls.' When met with a stony silence, Vaughan sighed. 'Look, I did ask him to give me the lowdown on this place and his opinion on how well you fit in, Alexi. I care about you and hate to see you wasting your talents.'

Jack wasn't convinced that was all there was to it but only two people knew the truth. One was dead and the other would never condemn himself, so he'd let it go.

For now.

'Is the course going ahead?' Vaughan asked into the ensuing silence.

'Yeah, big finale tomorrow as planned, although it will all seem a bit flat now,' Alexi replied.

'Okay, well I'll be here for that.' He stood up, ignoring Cosmo's increased growling. 'But now, if you'll excuse me, I'll get in touch with Vickery. Call me if I can help in any way,' he added, addressing the comment to Alexi before he left the room.

8

———

'The plot thickens,' Alexi said as they watched Patrick leave. 'Did you believe him?'

'I hate to say this but yeah, I did, at least insofar as he didn't kill the guy, or arrange for him to be killed. I think there's stuff he didn't tell us, though.'

'About where he'd been this afternoon? I thought you'd ask.'

'He wouldn't have told me. Besides, it's where he was during the time of the murder that's germane and he's already told us that. It will be easy enough to check.'

'Right.' Alexi nodded. 'You think he knows more about Peter's background than he let on?'

'Yeah, I'd put money on it and that is relevant. Say for the sake of argument that he does work for a government agency that flies below the radar.'

'The security services?'

'If someone from that life decided for some reason that he was a loose cannon with too much sensitive information rattling around inside his head, it would explain why he was bumped off.

It happens and your old mate would know that. He probably smells a story and so wants to keep the details to himself.'

Alexi nodded. 'I wouldn't bet against it. But surely, if whatever Peter knew was sensitive enough to get him killed then Patrick would be skating on thin ice if he pursued the issue too?'

'He won't do it himself,' Jack said with authority. 'I might not know much about journalism, but I recognise a man who sits back and lets others take the risks while he takes all the accolades.' Jack paused. 'Is it normal to recruit outsiders to chase down stories?'

'Occasionally. It's plausible but I'm still not sure why he selected Peter. He was a bit hazy on that point. Unless, of course, the elusive bullion robber really *is* in the area. Peter was tenacious, and not discreet in his pursuit of him, so Franklin shut him up permanently before more attention was drawn to him. If that's the case then Peter's death was nothing to do with mysterious government agencies and everything to do with a desperate individual who has no intention of having his collar felt.'

'Yeah, possibly.' Jack yawned and stretched his arms above his head. 'Vaughan wasn't truthful when he said he didn't recall the overheard phone conversation. We've let on that we know about it and given him time to come up with a plausible explanation when Vickery raises the subject, which he will. I'll make sure of that.'

'Spying on me is vile and something that I believe Patrick to be perfectly capable of, but I can't see how it would have anything to do with the murder.'

'Just another example of a controlling individual who doesn't take rejection well.'

Alexi sighed as she smothered a yawn with the back of her hand. 'So, what now? Where do we go with this?'

'I think we need to dig out more information on that bullion robbery. It's obviously relevant. I'll get Cassie on it.'

'I remember the previous bullion robbery. It was audacious but security has gone up several levels since then and it was supposed to be impossible to replicate.'

'Maybe our friend Franklin, who's accredited with being the mastermind, couldn't resist showing off.'

'Unless Peter thought that Gates, the con man he had all the notes on, was the driving force.'

Jack conceded the point with the tilt of his head. 'It's possible.'

'I'll speak to a few old contacts. They might have heard stuff; unsubstantiated rumours that can't be put out there.'

'Good idea. Half the country is fascinated by the robbery and want to know what happened to the bullion.'

'It can't be put in suitcases and flown out the country.' Alexi gave the situation more thought than it had thus far merited on her part. 'A boat perhaps but we're a long way from the sea here in Lambourn so why would one of the suspects hang out in the area?'

'All sorts of reasons. Laying low while the dust settles in all probability. Patience is a virtue in such situations. The thing is, the majority of villains can't resist spending above their means straight away. My ex-colleagues caught the majority of the culprits for that very reason, but Franklin got away and none of the guys who've been collared are claiming to know where he or the bullion are.'

'Perhaps they don't actually know.'

'Hm, possibly.'

'I wonder if Franklin has connections in this area?'

Jack shook his head. 'If he has, the police will be all over it. It wouldn't be safe. Even so, if he's a patient man then this wouldn't be a bad area to hide out, keeping a very low profile. There are hundreds of houses of all shapes and sizes scattered about and very little police presence. Without any leads to go on other than that alleged sighting at the Swan... well, they can't waste resources by patrolling such a wide area with absolutely no idea which part to home in on.'

'I'm going to dig deep into Franklin's background,' Alexi said, feeling fresh energy coursing through her system. It was the sort of area where she'd excelled in her previous career. She loved solving puzzles, the more obscure the better. She had the patience of Job and was willing to put in the legwork, especially when the cause was one so vital to her own survival in Lambourn. 'From what I've read, he's highly intelligent and was once an investment banker.'

'A different kind of criminal activity,' Jack quipped.

'Yeah, perhaps. Not sure why he left that line of work or if he has any family.' She rubbed her hands together. 'That would be a good place to start.'

'Whilst I intend to take a closer look at the rest of your fledglings.'

'The course?' Alexi blinked. 'Why? None of them had any reason to kill Peter. Besides, we know where they all were.'

'Sure.' Jack paused. 'Probably. But they were the closest to Foreman here in Lambourn and you know as well as I do that there's more to people than meets the eye. I'm just being thorough is all. Besides, I'm not convinced about this fugitive from justice angle, especially since it was Vaughan who brought it up. He definitely knows more than he let on. He's aware that Foreman was obsessed with finding Franklin, so he's put that idea of Franklin being involved in the murder out there, perhaps in the hope of distracting us.'

'From what?'

'Well, there's the question.'

'Knock, knock.' Vickery put his head round the door. 'Anyone at home?'

Cosmo answered with an indifferent hiss.

'He's warming to you,' Alexi said, smiling.

'Come in,' Jack said. 'No DC Hogan?'

'She's with the uniforms over in the annex, talking to your delegates.'

Vickery sat at the table and accepted Alexi's offer of coffee. She got up to pour him a mug from the pot kept permanently on the go on the hob. He thanked her when she placed it in front of him and resumed her seat.

'What news?' Jack asked.

'Just had an interesting conversation with your editor, Alexi,' he replied, stirring his coffee.

'Ex editor,' Alexi said. 'Yeah, we did too and suggested that he speak with you. I take it he told you about the burner phone.'

'He did, and about his connection to Foreman, which has got me worried. If he was once with one of the agencies then I'm surprised that no one in a suit has been down here, warning me off.'

'I thought that only happened in the films,' Alexi said.

Vickery took a sip of his coffee. 'Really couldn't say. Never been in this position before.'

'Do we know yet how Foreman came to be strangled without putting up a fight?' Jack asked.

'Nope. Post-mortem in the morning. We'll know more after that but if I had to guess, I'd say he was either taken completely by surprise and had no time to fight, perhaps because he knew and trusted his assailant, or else he was somehow drugged. Obviously, his system will be tested for traces of anything nasty.'

'Any sign of the murder weapon?' Jack asked.

'No dice on that one either. Bloody criminals have no consideration nowadays.'

Alexi smiled. 'I blame all the police procedural shows on TV.'

Vickery nodded. 'They don't help. Everyone's an expert nowa-days.' He drained his coffee in a single gulp. 'He was strangled with a cord of some type, that much is beyond doubt.'

'It would have taken a lot of strength to choke a man of his size, even if he was incapacitated,' Jack said. 'I doubt whether a woman could have done it.'

'A strong woman could have if he'd been drugged, but we're getting ahead of ourselves with all this speculation.'

'I've spoken to everyone on my course and they can all account for their whereabouts. In fact, I saw all of them at various stages of the morning,' Alexi said.

'Even so, they were the only people down here who knew the victim so their alibis will have to be verified.'

'On the assumption that none of them did it, and bear in mind all but one of them are female, then someone else down in Lambourn presumably did know him,' Jack pointed out.

'You think the fugitive *is* hiding out around these parts?' Vickery glanced at Alexi. 'You buy Vaughan's story in that he had Foreman poking into it?'

Alexi shrugged. 'I guess.'

'You don't sound too sure.'

'That's because I'm not, but it *is* plausible. Patrick's a news-paper man through and through. If I say he'd kill for a scoop, it's not far from the truth. And I have known him to use outsiders with an interest in a particular story to do the digging.'

'He wasn't especially subtle about it though, if that's the case,' Jack pointed out. 'He bothered so many people at the Swan that the manager asked Alexi to call him off.'

'Perhaps he was trying to get a message across to Franklin,' Vickery replied. 'We're going through his notes now and we'll see what we come across. Hopefully, something to point me in the right direction because I'll be honest with you, right now I have sod all to go on.' Vickery scratched his head. 'This is a weird one, that's for sure.'

'It's hard to know if it was something more personal, given that we don't know anything about his former life.'

'We've sent someone to check out his flat in London,' Vickery said. 'Apparently, it's like a monk's cell: small, neat and unlived in. Uniforms are talking to the neighbours but so far, no one's admitting to seeing or knowing anything about the occupant of that flat. Some even thought it was unoccupied.'

'Did he own it?' Alexi asked.

'No. We're checking with the letting agents but I don't suppose that will get us far.'

'He had a laptop,' Alexi said, 'but it wasn't in his room. Presumably, he had it in his car with him.'

'He had a Ford Focus, right?'

'Yes, dark blue,' Alexi replied.

'Well, there was no sign of it or his laptop at the Swan and no car keys were found on the body. His mobile wasn't on him either. We'll get onto his provider for a record of his calls.'

'The murderer took off with the car and his stuff,' Jack said, thumping his fist against the tabletop. 'Damn!'

'We're looking for the car but don't hold out much hope of it helping us if we do get our hands on it,' Vickery replied. 'It's either tucked up in a garage somewhere or will turn up abandoned. Either way, it will give us sod-all clues, that much's for sure. This killer has been very careful to cover his tracks which *does* make me wonder if it was a professional hit.'

Jack nodded. 'Me too,' he said.

'If Peter's pad in London was relatively unlived in,' Alexi said pensively, 'and if he was previously involved in dark deeds for one of the country's security agencies, presumably it was a cover and he actually lived elsewhere.'

'Yeah.' Vickery gave a glum nod. 'We're looking but don't hold your breath.'

'Have you considered approaching MI5 or MI whatever and asking if they've lost touch with a former agent?' Jack asked.

'Above my paygrade.' Vickery shuddered. 'I'll tell my guv'nor and that will be his call.' Vickery pushed himself to his feet. 'Best be getting on. I'm sure I don't need to tell you that we've got this and there's nothing you can do to help.'

Jack grinned as he took Vickery's outstretched hand in a firm grasp. 'I'll let you know what we dig up,' he said.

'I didn't hear that.' Vickery smiled at Alexi, avoided Cosmo, who gave a desultory hiss, and left the kitchen.

'If he needs our help, it wouldn't kill him to ask for it,' Alexi said.

'He's on thin ice. He can't officially allow civilians to do his investigating for him, you know that. But he's not too proud to admit that he's stumped and knows we can stick our noses in without having to jump through all the hoops that restrict the possibility of his achieving a conviction. If, on the other hand, we track the killer down...'

'And he knows that we'd do our own sleuthing anyway.' Alexi grinned. 'We can't help ourselves, especially because technically, I'm a suspect.'

'Remind me never to get on your wrong side,' Jack said, shuddering.

'Seriously though,' Alexi said, her expression sobering. 'If the post-mortem shows that he was drugged somehow then my name will have to be in the frame. I was there. It could be argued that I knew Patrick had put Foreman on my course in order to try and scupper my relationship with you. Peter was a good-looking guy and did come on to me big time. When I confronted Peter with my suspicions and he admitted it, I got angry and—'

'And just happened to have some sort of drug about your person that he willingly ingested. You then followed him into the men's room and strangled him with your belt.' Jack shook his head. 'No one seriously suspects you, darling. Besides, once Foreman confirmed his true purpose, it would more likely have been Vaughan that you chased with a carving knife.'

'True enough, but local opinion is still stacked against me.'

'The locals are a superstitious lot who enjoy a good gossip. Nothing this exciting has happened in Lambourn for... well, forever and Polly stokes the rumours because it's good for her business. Everyone has an angle. You know that. Anyway, they aren't the ones investigating the crime.'

'Just as well, or trial by public opinion would see me banged up for life.' Alexi sighed. 'Anyway, where do we start?'

'Like I suggested before Vickery joined us, we could do worse than to delve into the backgrounds of the others on your course. If for some obscure reason one of them had a reason to kill Fore-man, something might pop if we dig deep enough.'

'Need I remind you that they all have alibis?'

'Not necessarily. They were all doing their research locally. Any one of them could have legged it to the Swan, done the deed and then scarpered in Foreman's car.'

'If one of the ladies did it, she would have had to drug him first and wait for the... Of course!' Alexi snapped her fingers. 'Your suspicious mind is thinking that she planned ahead and dropped something in his morning tea. Something like Rohypnol would take a short while to become effective, too short probably.' Alexi drummed her fingers impatiently. 'But Diazepam has a slower release time *and* tends to make some users manic.' She stared at Jack. 'Peter was heard shouting and acting wildly, even by his stan-dards. That annoying little man at the Swan said he was ranting and slurring his words. Damn!' She looked up at Jack. 'I really don't want the culprit to have anything to do with me. It's bad enough that the victim was on my course.'

'It's just one line of enquiry, darling. Something for us to do while we wait for the results of the post-mortem.'

'Okay, let's do it.'

'At home, I think. You're not entertaining your attendees tonight, are you?'

'No. It's the only night when they'll be left to their own devices. A chance to tidy up their submissions and exchange views.' Alexi frowned. 'I'd really like to be there, to hear what they have to say about Peter's murder.'

'Best not,' Jack replied. 'They're grown-ups and can deal with it in their own way. Let's give Cheryl and Drew their kitchen back and take this beast back to his own domain.' Jack nodded towards Cosmo, who looked up from Toby's basket and treated Jack to an imperious stare. 'If that suits your highness,' he added to the cat.

Cosmo made them smile when he got up, stretched and trotted towards the door.

'I'd give a lot to know if the killer took Peter's car as a convenient means of escape or if his laptop was his prime target,' Alexi said as they headed for Jack's car.

'His wallet, full of cash and cards, wasn't taken,' Jack said as he slid behind the wheel. 'But his phone was, so there was something on his electronic devices that the killer didn't want found. Presumably that something wasn't replicated in his written notes, which were still in his room.' He started the engine and backed out of his parking space.

'Or else the laptop being in the car was entirely coincidental. We don't know how the killer actually got to the Swan so perhaps he needed a method of returning to whence he'd come pretty damned quick.'

'I don't like the fact that the murder took place so close to the time that you went to meet with Foreman,' Jack said, as he paused at a junction, indicating left. 'It's almost as though someone wanted to trade on your connections to other recent murders by having you there.'

'True, and I'm not too delighted about it either. You're wondering, I suppose, if any of my lot knew Peter wanted me to meet him there to talk about our "mutual acquaintance", Patrick, and used the opportunity to set me up.' She blinked. 'There were others in the room when he mentioned it, but he spoke very quietly and I don't think there was anyone close enough to overhear.'

'Just something to mull over,' Jack replied as he swung his car onto the drive of Alexi's cottage. 'Come on,' he said, smiling as Cosmo leapt from the car ahead of Alexi and prowled off into the garden, resuming his interrupted rodent watch from earlier that day. 'I'll run you a bath, try to relax.'

'You've got yourself a deal,' Alexi replied, kissing his cheek as she headed for the stairs.

9

Physically and emotionally exhausted, Alexi fell asleep in the bath, soothed by scent of the jasmine oil she'd liberally added to the water and the fragrance of the candles that flickered on the shelf above her head. Jack put his head round the door what seemed like five minutes after she'd closed her eyes. The fact that the water had cooled and her fingertips were in danger of imitating prunes told her it was more like half an hour.

'Come on, sleepyhead,' he said, holding out a towel. 'I've made us a light supper.'

'Hmm. Something does smell nice,' she agreed, flicking water at him as she stepped from the bath. She allowed Jack to wrap her in the waiting towel, rather as though she was a child, incapable of caring for herself. And right at that moment, she needed babying. For just a few minutes, she would cede responsibility for herself to Jack and allow him to take care of her, making her feel cherished.

She needed to feel cherished.

And that worried her a lot. Alexi had always been self-sufficient, even when she'd been dating Patrick. Especially then. She hated showing any signs of vulnerability and wouldn't have lasted for five minutes in the male-dominated newspaper world if she wasn't able to play the boys at their own game. She and Patrick had kept their relationship under wraps. No way was she about to give other journos the opportunity to imply that she'd slept her way into her position. She'd worked too damned hard to be judged upon anything other than her merits.

She had carried that attitude with her into Lambourn. At first. But these murders, especially the latest one, had sapped her energy and made her doubt herself. Perhaps the locals were right. Perhaps there was such a thing as bad karma and she spread its toxic fumes wherever she went.

Way to go, Alexi.

Shaking off her negative vibes, Alexi dressed herself in comfy lounging clothes and headed downstairs. Jack had opened a bottle of wine, which they shared without talking of anything contentious, enjoying the eggs that Jack had scrambled for them. But it was all a pretence. Alexi knew that Jack's quick brain would be assessing Peter's murder and attempting to make sense of it. The subject was uppermost in Alexi's mind too and she was as much in the dark as Jack when it came to finding out who. And why.

'It's still early,' she said, after they'd eaten and cleared away. 'I'm going to hit the internet for a while, see what I can unearth.'

Wallowing in self-pity would achieve nothing. Besides, Alexi was most definitely not the passive type and needed to feel that she was doing something to move the matter forward. She was, after all, an investigative journalist to the core and research, triple-checking facts and not taking anything at face value were areas where she excelled.

Jack rolled his eyes. 'I was hoping to distract you with my

masculine charms,' he said, batting his lashes at her and making her smile.

'Later,' she said. 'I really want to get an angle on this, if only to divert suspicion away from me and the hotel.'

'Understood.' His expression sobered as he dropped a kiss on the top of her head. 'I'll give Cassie a call. See if she has anything for us yet.'

'Yeah, let's hope she's come up with something to point us in the right direction.'

Alexi was disappointed when Jack strolled into the garden to make his call, almost as though he didn't want her to overhear his end of it. She smiled when Cosmo emerged from beneath a bush dripping with moisture and wound himself around Jack's legs. Jack dropped the hand not holding his phone and stroked his head.

The relationship between Jack and his work partner had become difficult since Alexi's arrival on the scene. She was well aware that Cassie was hoping that Alexi's relationship with Jack would run its course so that she could step in and pick up the pieces. She'd tried to do that when his marriage had broken up, but Jack had pushed her back, relegating her to his business life. Cassie probably assumed that if Jack was unlucky in love for a second time then he *would* turn for solace to someone whom he'd learned to trust.

How patient was she prepared to be? That was a question that Alexi had often asked herself when she was feeling insecure. She and Cassie tended to avoid one another but she was always there, in the background, and in the corner of Alexi's mind, a ticking bomb biding its time. She had no doubts whatsoever about Jack's commitment to her but often wondered what Cassie would do if she got tired of waiting for cracks to appear. With her online sleuthing skills, she would have had no trouble digging into the backgrounds of Alexi's delegates *before* Jack asked her to do so.

What had she found out?

How she had latched onto Peter's interest in Franklin and knew where he would be that morning was open to question. She'd told Jack that a lead on his missing woman case had led her to the Swan and that she had no idea that Peter or Alexi would be there. Alexi wasn't sure if she believed it. It seemed like one hell of a coincidence, but she wouldn't risk doing Cassie's job for her and testing Jack's loyalties by voicing her suspicions without water-tight evidence.

Cassie *could* have gone to the Swan with the specific intention of killing Peter and framing Alexi. Not that Jack would accept that possibility and Alexi conceded that it seemed extreme, even for a woman who was as obsessed as Cassie. Stranger things had been known to happen though – a woman scorned and all that. But contemplating murdering a fit man and carrying out the deed were two very different matters. Apart from anything else, if Peter hadn't been drugged, how had Cassie managed it?

With a sigh, Alexi turned her attention to the bullion robbery, reading everything she could find on the subject. It did seem more likely, she conceded, that someone connected to Franklin, or Franklin himself *if* he was hiding out in the area, would have shut Peter up permanently when he refused to back off.

She Googled Paul Franklin's name and was almost over-whelmed by the amount of coverage he'd received online. There was a picture of a middle-aged man with thinning hair and striking blue eyes. He could be overlooked in a crowd, but for eyes that radiated a combination of intelligence and mischief. They were vibrant enough to hold a person's attention and saved him from being ordinary. Of course, he could wear coloured contacts to disguise them now. That or glasses with tinted lenses. He probably did, she reasoned, and would likely have allowed a beard to grow too.

It was autumn and chilly. If he had shown himself in public, he could have worn a hat or even a hoodie without drawing attention to himself. But if he'd well and truly gone to ground, biding his time, why take the chance? Cabin fever, perhaps. Alexi wished she knew more about the supposed sighting. Had he been alone or in company? And if he'd disguised himself, how had he been recognised? Was the sighting a rumour started by the editor of the local rag to talk up a story that would get him recognised by the big boys? Bill Naylor was anxious to get a break and the whereabouts of Franklin was the question on everyone's lips.

Alexi sighed. So many questions. So little to go on.

She turned her attention to Franklin's career with a well-known investment bank. The reasons for his departure were not mentioned. The bank seemed to have cut all ties with him, which made Alexi suspicious. She picked up her phone, scrolled through her contacts and called John Parsons, an old colleague who'd worked on the financial pages of the *Sentinel* for as long as Alexi could remember.

She watched Jack pacing around the garden, still in deep conversation with Cassie, wondering what they'd found to talk about for so long. She hoped he wouldn't tell Cassie everything they'd found out. Not that there was much to tell but Alexi was reluctant to put her trust in her rival for Jack's affections.

Don't let your imagination drive a wedge between you and Jack. You'd be playing into Cassie's hands.

'Alexi Ellis, as I live and breathe.' John's strong voice boomed over the airwaves. 'An unexpected pleasure. The place just isn't the same without you.'

'Kind of you to say so, John. How are you?'

'Fair to middling. What gives? I take it this isn't a social call.'

'If you're trying to make me feel guilty for not keeping in touch then you're doing a bang-up job.'

'Don't worry about it. We're all busy. The pace of life nowadays gets in the way of friendships. Besides, I'm as guilty as you are for not picking up the phone.' His rich chuckle echoed down the line. 'Right, we got that out of the way. Now, what can I do for you?'

'Any idea why Paul Franklin left Hanson's?' she asked, cutting to the chase.

'Good heavens, you're not chasing the bullion story too, are you? Franklin is turning into a modern day Lord Lucan, with sightings all over the place. Spotting him has become a national pastime.' Alexi recalled her earlier musing on that particular subject and nodded in agreement, even though John couldn't see the gesture. 'Anyway, to answer your question, I'm not sure. My contacts are being surprisingly tight-lipped on the subject, but I hear on the grapevine that he was dating a woman who worked with a rival bank and it's alleged that he stole sensitive merger information from her laptop.'

'Ah.'

'Ah about covers it. This was during the pandemic when they were both working from home.'

'Blimey! No wonder it was kept quiet, and he was let go without being prosecuted. Neither bank would want that sort of negative publicity.'

'Precisely. The fact that his girlfriend got the push too indicates that there's some truth to the rumours.'

'Any idea of the lady's name?'

'Melanie Cosgrove.'

'Thanks, John.'

'No problem but a word to the wise. Be careful. I used to wine and dine Franklin in exchange for financial insights back in the day. I've seen him lose his temper over nothing and he can be a vicious bastard when he goes into one. He has oodles of charm though; the ladies gravitate towards him despite the fact that he doesn't have film star looks. There's just something about his brash self-assurance and the aforementioned charm, to say nothing of an extravagant and generous lifestyle, that makes him popular with both sexes. He's clever too. Far too clever to beaver away for someone else for the rest of his days, which is why I have no trouble in believing that he was behind the robbery. He would love pitting his wits against the powers that be and coming out on the winning side.'

'If he's violent and presumably has connections then it would explain why all the guys who have been caught are keeping their mouths firmly shut.'

'It would indeed.' Alexi heard someone calling John's name in the background. 'Have to go. Keep in touch.'

Alexi cut the connection and leaned back in her chair, mulling over what she'd just learned. She Googled Melanie's name and was confronted with a professional shot of a fresh-faced young businesswoman with a confident smile who was exceptionally pretty. She had a waterfall of curly, red hair and freckles decorating the bridge of her nose. They suited her colouring. Alexi had never been able to understand why freckles were considered by many in the beauty industry to be blemishes.

'Where are you now, Melanie?' she asked aloud, hammering away at her keys.

She was unsurprised when there was nothing on record to suggest that she'd moved to another bank. She might have been an innocent victim but if she really had left her laptop open and unattended then she would be considered untrustworthy at best. People in the banking world didn't get second chances if they made those sorts of errors.

'Hey.' Jack strolled back into the room, pocketing his phone. 'I know that look. You're on to something. What have you got?'

Alexi told him what she'd just learned.

'Bloody hell!' He looked stunned as he absently rubbed the back of his neck. 'The banking world sounds like a nursery for would-be criminals. I'm betting Franklin graduated with first-class honours.'

'Yeah. I'm wondering if his girlfriend was in it with him or if she was an innocent victim of a charm offensive. John reckons that women adore Franklin and if he really was honing his dishonest skills then I imagine he'd not hesitate to exploit his popularity. He probably got up close and personal with Melanie for that specific reason. And because of the pandemic, he imagined he'd get away with it.'

'His pride was hurt when he got caught so he needed to show the world how clever he actually is by pulling off a bullion raid that was supposed to be impossible.'

'I'm looking to see if anyone by the name of Cosgrove has a property in this area.'

'Unlikely. It's the first thing the police would have looked for.'

'If they knew of his association with her. It's in the interests of his ex-employers and hers to keep that sort of thing under wraps. The banks will be thinking of their investors who'd likely get cold feet if they even suspected that their hard-earned dosh was at risk.'

'Cynical but true,' Jack said with a smile.

'Well anyway, a brief search hasn't thrown anything up.' Alexi leaned back in her chair and rotated her stiff shoulders. 'I'll take a closer look at Melanie, though. Cosgrove could be her married name. She might have parents living here under a different name. Although, if she did, I'm sure Peter would have been all over it. Unlike your ex-colleagues, he would have got the same information as me from Patrick.' Alexi paused to massage the small of her back with one hand. 'You were talking to Cassie for a long time,' she remarked casually. 'What did she have to say?'

'She got excited when she found Archie's record, but we already knew about that. She suspects him of involvement with Foreman.'

Alexi scowled. 'On what basis? Just because he's been inside?'

'What would you think if you didn't know the man?'

'Yeah, but I do know him. And he was my last port of call here in the village before I drove out to the Swan. There's no way he could have got there before me, killed Peter and legged it back to Lambourn, not least because Peter was alive when I got there, and I was able to argue with him. He was obnoxiously coherent too, banging on about civil liberties and his right to ask whatever questions he wanted to. I've been thinking back and if he had been drugged in advance then he wasn't showing any signs of it. Quite the reverse.'

'Archie rides a motorbike so could have cut across country lanes, got there before you, hid his bike and done the deed *after* your row,' Jack said gently. 'Then gone back for his bike later. We did wonder how the killer got to the Swan.'

Alexi conceded the point with an abrupt nod, her attention still on her screen. 'Perhaps. I'm willing to keep an open mind while we search for a link between him and Peter. What else did Cassie have to say?'

'She's still looking into your others. We were talking about my missing person, her friend Amy Dawson. What with all the excitement, I haven't given the case any priority. Not that there's anything new to give priority to. The lady's disappeared and I still think she's run off with another man but Cassie's having none of it. According to her, Amy's marriage was solid.'

'You mentioned that her husband worked for a government

agency and has access to sensitive information.' Alexi tapped a
pen against her teeth as she thought her fledging idea through.
'Sensitive information is what Franklin steals and he has previous
when it comes to using his charm on females to get what he
wants.'

Jack nodded. 'It's possible but I very much doubt that Neil
discussed his work with his wife if it was *that* sensitive. Besides, he
would have signed the official secrets act, which is a big deal.
Signatories don't break that particular bond without compelling
reason. And often, not even then.'

'Perhaps history repeated itself and she got into his laptop, or
whatever.' Alexi held up a hand in protest. 'Don't look so sceptical.
Franklin is supposed to be clever but he's also a man with an axe
to grind. His reputation is tarnished because his bank caught him
out. He found a good way to restore his pride, got away with it,
loves all the attention and wants to do something even more
outrageous. Serial killers have been known to do what they do
simply to get their names recognised, albeit for despicable
reasons.'

'But if Franklin got away with all that bullion, why would he
need to steal government secrets?'

'Because he can. It's a game to him; he's overconfident and has
upped the stakes. "Look at me, I'm too clever to be caught".'

'You think he and Amy are shacked up together?'

Alexi wobbled a hand from side to side. 'It's one theory and
she *does* have links to this area.'

'To Winchester. And I've checked out every one of them
personally. She hasn't been seen by any of her friends or been in
contact with them. There's been no activity on her social media
accounts and her phone is either dead or switched off. If she's
alive then she doesn't want to be found.'

'Has Cassie checked her phone records?'

'Of course. Nothing suspicious. If she was in contact with Franklin before she disappeared then she had another phone.'

'What's her husband like?'

'Dull, was the impression that I got. A man who likes order and method in his life.'

'Do they have kids?'

'No. Cassie said that Amy doesn't want them.'

'Unusual, but not unheard of,' Alexi said pensively.

'Cassie does admit that Neil is a bit of a workaholic. Amy works in a charity shop three days a week. Her husband made a point of telling me that he earned enough to support them both in style and that she didn't need to work. It seemed like a badge of honour to him.'

'Working isn't just about the money. But I'm guessing that if she felt a pressing need for a career, she could have insisted.'

'Not if Neil is as controlling as I think. Cassie doesn't believe it but what young woman in this day and age doesn't choose to work if she doesn't have anything else to fill her time with? And I can't find out that Amy had any consuming hobbies. Her friendships were tenuous too. I got the impression that Neil didn't encourage her to get too close to her girlfriends. He wanted to be her sole focus.'

'You're thinking that she'd be up for a bit of fun if Franklin approached her?'

'Well, it's possible. I don't believe in coincidences. Franklin was supposedly seen at the Swan and Amy's card was used there.' Jack smiled at her. 'What would you think?'

'Do we know what branch of the civil service that Neil Dawson works in?'

Jack shook his head. 'He said it was classified.'

Alexi rolled her eyes. 'Of course he did.' She'd been flipping a pen between her fingers but placed it back on the table and sighed. 'We know that Franklin used his banker girlfriend and, as far as we know, dumped her when she'd served her purpose. The question is, did he dump Amy, did he fall for her, or did she have a fit of conscience, threatened to tell all and had to be silenced permanently? I gather she's quite a looker so it's possible that they're together. If Franklin is lying low, then stimulating female company would be the diversion he needs.'

'Yeah, she is pretty. And the life and soul, apparently, when she gets the opportunity. But then so too is Neil, according to Cassie. Can't see it myself but you know as well as I do that people have a public persona that isn't a true reflection of their characters. The whole world is a stage...'

'Then the chances are that she did get bored with having nothing to do all day. I find it interesting that she was "allowed" to work in a charity shop. I'm guessing that Neil thought it made him look good, having a wife who gave her time to a good cause. I also think that if she did steal information from his laptop then he might well have reported her missing *and* called us in, just in case the theft comes to light.'

'He's covering his own back?'

'It wouldn't hurt to go and ask him,' Alexi reasoned. 'If he thinks we know then he'll probably 'fess up, if only to prevent us from telling his employers.'

'I wonder what can be so delicate. I suppose it depends upon which section of the service he worked for but if it's anything to do with military intelligence then he would have to put his hand up, surely? National security would be at stake.'

'What would Franklin do with information of that stature?'

'Who can say?' Jack shrugged. 'Threaten to sell it to our enemies. Flog it to your ex-colleagues. He's still a man with a reputation that he wants to exploit, don't forget.'

'It seems more probable to me that he got early warning of...

oh, I don't know. A cabinet reshuffle. A minister's indiscretion. Something like that.' She paused. 'There's a budget coming up, isn't there?'

Jack nodded.

'Well, what if he got hold of its contents?'

'He'd make a killing on the markets if he knew what was being announced beforehand,' Jack said, grimacing. 'Come on, get your coat.' He glanced at his watch. 'Neil Dawson should be home by now. Let's put our theory to the test.'

On cue, Cosmo appeared from the garden and waited at the front door, tail twitching.

'Looks as though our security detail is coming along for the ride,' Jack said, bending to stroke the cat and laughing. 'How the hell does he know?'

'I keep telling you, he's psychic,' Alexi replied, pride in her voice as she slipped her arms into her jacket and picked up her phone and bag. 'Okay, what are we waiting for?'

10

———

Jack drove swiftly towards Winchester with the radio tuned to an oldies station that he hoped would distract Alexi. She loved vintage music and was guaranteed to sing along, albeit out of tune. Even so, he knew it would only be a matter of time before she realised that he'd said very little about his conversation with Cassie and would demand answers, as she had every right to.

Jack had told her the essence of their conversation but nothing about its implications. There was already enough tension between the two women and Jack had no intention of stoking it by dwelling upon Cassie's possessiveness. He had been burying his head, he accepted, hoping that she would eventually accept that he was totally committed to Alexi. But although Cassie hid her feelings better and even went out on the occasional date, Jack was still uncomfortably aware that she hadn't given up on him.

Cassie had dropped acid remarks about Alexi's presence at the crime scene at the vital time into their phone conversation. She wasn't even being especially subtle about it. She also mentioned Vaughan several times, asking why such an important man with such a relentless schedule would lend his weight to the course *and* hang around for so long before his presence was needed.

Sowing the seeds of doubt in Jack's mind, but Jack was ahead of her. He already knew that Vaughan would do just about anything to entice Alexi back to London. His only concern was that this time, he might actually succeed.

Not while there's still breath in my body.

They drove mostly in silence, cocooned in their own thoughts, Alexi's voice occasionally breaking a silence between them that was, for the first time ever, uncomfortable. Jack occasionally touched her thigh, smiling at her when the news came on and the anchor made some inane comment. Alexi winced at the woman's lack of professionalism, just as he'd known that she would. As a tenacious journalist herself, she was allergic to speculation and sloppy research.

'This is it.' It was dark but Jack still recognised the street of upmarket modern houses, spaced well apart, that he had visited once before.

'Pretentious yet dull,' Alexi remarked, peering at the houses as Jack slowed to a crawl, looking for a parking space. 'Status symbols and just the sort of place that I'd expect a pedantic civil servant to favour. I'm betting that he and his neighbours all mow their lawns at the exact same time on a Sunday morning.'

Jack laughed as he found a place to park and cut the engine. 'Now who's being stereotypical?' he asked.

'Only a little.'

They left Cosmo in the car with a window cracked open and headed for number twenty-seven.

'There are lights on,' Alexi said, stating the obvious as Jack led the way up a short gravel drive, 'but no car in sight.'

'Bet he garages it.'

'Who does that nowadays?' Alexi giggled. 'Don't tell me...'

'Pedantic civil servants,' they said together.

Jack laughed too. 'Wouldn't want the motor to get dirty.'

'Does Amy have a car?'

'Yes, a small Fiat and it's here...'

'In the garage,' they chorused.

Jack rang the bell. The porch light came on and the door was opened almost immediately by the man he remembered too well. He wore a suit and his tie was still perfectly knotted, implying that he'd just got home. Surely even a man as uptight as Dawson would lose the tie almost as soon as he walked through his door.

'Mr Maddox.' Dawson raised a brow, looking irritated rather than anxious. 'I wasn't expecting to see you tonight. Did we have an appointment that I've forgotten about, or do you come with news of my wife? I have been going out of my mind,' he added after a significant pause.

He didn't look especially worried to Jack but then again, perhaps he wasn't the sort of person to wear his heart on his sleeve. Jack would give him the benefit of the doubt.

For now.

'No news yet,' Jack replied with a regretful shake of his head, wishing he could warm to the guy. He didn't have to like his clients, but he would feel a whole lot better if he thought they had a common goal. As far as he could tell, the inconvenience of a missing wife whom he supposedly adored had not caused any alterations to Dawson's routine, as evidenced by the suit. 'But we do have a few more questions for you. This is my colleague, Alexi Ellis.'

Dawson subjected Alexi to an exacting scrutiny from behind his horn-rimmed glasses and nodded curtly. He looked highly suspicious, not to say furtive, and didn't offer her his hand. Jack knew that Alexi, already predisposed to dislike the man, would take exception to his prejudice. Jack did too.

'Now isn't a convenient time,' Dawson said. 'You should have called.'

Hardly the reaction of an anxious man, Jack thought, sharing a glance with Alexi.

'You have something more important to do than help us find your wife?' Jack asked curtly. A blast of wind caused Alexi to shiver inside her thin jacket and heavy rain began to fall, adding to Jack's irritation with his client for keeping them standing outside.

'Of course. You must excuse me. My mind is all over the place.'

You could have fooled me.

'You'd better come in.'

Dawson opened the door wide with obvious reluctance. He led them into a spotless and soulless lounge. As had been the case on his previous visit, absolutely nothing was out of place and not a speck of dust dared to make its presence felt. Two oil paintings were hung on opposite walls, probably originals, almost certainly expensive but definitely not to Jack's taste. There were no framed photos, no throw cushions or feminine touches. The two solitary ornaments – large and ostentatious – gave the place the feeling of a museum. A show house but never a home.

No wonder fun-loving Amy had legged it. Jack wondered what had taken her so long.

'Sit down.'

Dawson indicated a leather couch and Alexi and Jack lowered themselves onto its cushions. They didn't give at all, causing Jack to wonder how anyone was supposed to get comfortable on such a hard piece of furniture. It was probably expensive and intended for show rather than snuggling down in front of the TV. Jack glanced around and noticed that there was no TV, at least not in that room. He refrained from shaking his head, instead wondering how the couple had spent their evenings.

Dawson sat across from them in a wingback chair and crossed one leg over the other. Jack noticed that the crease in his trousers was razor sharp. He'd presumably been wearing his suit all day but there wasn't a single crease that wasn't supposed to be there, indicating that a huge amount had been invested in the man's attire. It was most likely bespoke, made to measure. Dawson wasn't bad looking but was cold, aloof, probably controlling – a place for everything and everything in its place, as evidenced by the inside of his house – and definitely vain. Appearances mattered to him a great deal, especially his own and anyone connected with him.

Yep, Jack thought, definitely controlling.

'Now, how can I help you?' he asked, not offering them refreshment and instead getting straight to the point.

'Cassie came across your wife's credit card being used in a hotel called the Swan, which is close to Lambourn.' Jack paused, waiting for a reaction, an interruption. Nothing. Not even a flicker of surprise crossed the man's impenetrable expression. Jack reckoned he'd make a good poker player. 'Do you know it?' he persevered. 'Was it somewhere you went together?'

'When was this?' Dawson asked sharply, evading Jack's question.

'A few days ago. Last week.'

'I don't know the place.' Dawson dismissed the suggestion with a flap of one wrist. 'I don't make a habit out of frequenting pubs and nor does Amy.' Funny, Jack thought. He'd referred to the place as a hotel but Dawson, who supposedly didn't know the place, called it a pub. 'We're not big drinkers and prefer to make our own fun rather than watching idiots getting drunk and making fools of themselves.'

'I imagined that would be the case,' Jack replied, making sure not to catch Alexi's eye. She would be entertaining similar thoughts about Dawson's pomposity and Jack could only remain professional if he didn't look at her.

'If Amy's card was used there, it must have been stolen,' Dawson added. 'I assume you've checked, shown her picture, to see if anyone remembers her.'

'Of course, but with no luck.'

'Well, there you are then.' It was clear from Dawson's lack of concern that the matter was unworthy of further discussion.

'What do you think has happened to your wife?' Alexi asked, speaking for the first time.

'Isn't it obvious?' he snapped, glowering at Alexi with ill-disguised contempt.

'Not to me,' Alexi replied with commendable calm. Jack knew she would be boiling inside, disgusted by the man's lack of emotion, to say nothing of his bad manners. 'I don't ordinarily ask questions that I already know the answer to.'

Dawson briefly bowed his head. Jack got the impression that he didn't like women who stuck up for themselves. He didn't like women much at all come to that. A controlling misogynist who always had to have the last word and wouldn't countenance being contradicted.

'I think someone has taken her and is biding his time before making demands for her return.'

Alexi sent him an incredulous look. 'You actually believe that?'

'If she had met with an accident then it would have come to light by now,' he replied emotionlessly. 'If she had left me, which she has not; we are happily married with never a cross word.' He jutted his chin pugnaciously, as though defying them to refute that somewhat desperate-sounding assertion. 'But if she had, if she'd had some sort of mental aberration then she would have at least left a note and taken clothes and her car with her. No one has any reason to harm her, so it stands to reason that she's being held somewhere against her will.'

Dawson nodded, clearly supposing that his logic couldn't be faulted, and folded his hands neatly in his lap. Everything he did was neat and precise. Jack knew it would be a waste of breath to point out the glaringly obvious insofar as no woman in her right mind would endure life in this gilded cage for long. Especially not one as attractive and vibrant as Amy was purported to be.

'May I ask what branch of the civil service you work in?' Jack asked.

Dawson's entire body jerked, and he blinked repeatedly behind his glasses. Finally, they had got a reaction out of him, but not for the reasons that Jack had imagined would be the case. 'What has that to do with anything?'

'I shan't know until you answer my question,' Jack replied easily.

'I get the impression that you're clutching at straws, Mr Maddox.'

'I get the impression that you're prevaricating, Mr Dawson,' Jack shot back at him. 'And that makes me suspicious.'

'How dare you suggest that I had anything to do with my wife's disappearance!' He puffed out his chest like an indignant peacock defending his territory against all comers. It could have been Jack's imagination, perhaps he was seeing what he wanted to see, but he convinced himself that there was a modicum of fear behind the man's bluster. He glanced at Alexi, who was watching Dawson intently, and wondered if she had seen it too. 'We were devoted. Ask Cassie if you doubt my word.'

'Please answer the question.' Jack's voice was disproportionally quiet in the wake of Dawson's outrage. 'I think we both know that it could have a bearing on the situation.'

'Because of the nature of my work?' Dawson nodded, as

though answering his own question. 'I suppose it's possible, if unlikely. I hold a senior position in a little-known department. That's all I can say on the subject for security reasons.'

Jack and Alexi shared a look. Dawson had just confirmed what had seemed like the most unlikely speculation when they'd come up with it earlier.

'You must work long hours,' Alexi said into the ensuing silence. 'Didn't Amy get bored or feel unfulfilled? After all, she had no proper job and no children to occupy her time.'

'Amy kept herself busy, looking after our home.' He allowed a significant pause. 'And me.'

Blimey, Jack thought, wondering what era the guy thought he was living in. Thankfully, it had been decades since the little woman stayed at home, dutifully waiting hand and foot on her man and never daring to express thoughts or opinions of her own.

'Do you bring your work home with you?' Jack asked.

'What? No, of course not.' Dawson's cheeks now bloomed with colour, but his indignant protest lacked teeth and Jack knew then they were definitely on the right path.

Jack glanced through the open door to the hall stand, upon which sat a perfectly aligned laptop case.

Dawson stood. 'I think you'd better leave. When I asked Cassie for her help, I didn't expect to be subjected to a groundless third-degree myself.'

'Just trying to establish the facts,' Jack replied, standing too and indicating to Alexi that she should follow suit. 'That's what you're paying me for.'

'I think our business arrangement has run its course. Send me your final bill and I'll settle it.'

Dawson moved into the hall and opened the front door wide, mindless of the cold wind that competed with the blast of hot air from his central heating.

'As you wish,' Jack replied easily.

'What I wish... what I hoped for was that you would find my wife. Why I would have engaged your services if I had anything to do with her disappearance is a mystery to me.'

'Perhaps to disguise the fact that you have mislaid government secrets?' Alexi suggested as she walked out into the cold. 'It was a pleasure meeting you,' she added, sarcasm oozing from her words. 'I'm with you, Mr Dawson. I can't begin to imagine why Amy would have chosen to leave you. Good evening.'

They walked rapidly back to the car through pouring rain in silence and were greeted indifferently by Cosmo, who turned his back on them, as was his custom whenever his services weren't in demand and he was obliged to wait in the car.

'What a prat!' Alexi blew air through her lips. 'Not you, darling,' she added, leaning over and scratching Cosmo's ears when he let out an indignant mewl. 'God! No wonder Amy was bowled over by Franklin's charm. That's what must have happened, don't you think?'

'More than likely.' Jack fired up the engine and a welcome waft of warm air filled the inside of the car. 'He gets through life by being overbearing. Not many people dare to challenge him, both at home and, I suspect, at work. He's been in his position for a long time, probably knows where all the political bodies are buried, and so thinks he's invincible.'

'And a woman hater.'

'And that. But he's no actor. He had trouble hiding his reaction when you mentioned the misplacement of sensitive information.'

'Well, I'm glad to see the back of him and at least now we know that his wife and Franklin could well be together. I hope she's having fun.' Alexi rippled her shoulders. 'She sure as hell deserves it. My only surprise is that she endured marriage to that arse for ten years. She deserves a medal.'

'No question. But as to seeing the back of Dawson, I think it unlikely that's the last we've seen of him.' Jack paused at a junction. The road was clear so he turned left and put his foot down. 'He'll think about what we said and accept that we're not intimidated by his bluster. He'll realise we know, or suspect, what happened and will go into damage limitation mode, which will require him to eat humble pie.'

'That I will pay good money to see,' Alexi replied with satisfaction in her tone. 'It will be a new experience for him.' She paused. 'How could Cassie possibly look upon the man as a friend?'

'You'll have to ask her that.' Jack knew better than to go there. 'What I do think though is that Franklin's unlikely to be our killer.'

His attention was focused on his driving, but he still sensed Alexi's confusion. 'Why?' she asked.

'He's a newly fledged criminal who depends upon his brain rather than physical intimidation. He probably doesn't even look upon what he does as criminal activity. If he's clever enough to get away with it... well, it's a victimless crime. A game, if you like.'

'Hmm.' Alexi bobbed her head. 'I see what you mean. He's fine with ripping institutions off but would be horrified by the thought of physical violence. Besides, why would he kill Peter? Like you said earlier, Franklin-spotting has become a national pastime, and no one can actually prove that he was at the Swan any more than they can prove he was at any of the other sightings. He probably gets off on knowing that he's being pursued but still managing to outwit his chasers.'

'My personal feeling is that the editor of the local rag was persuaded by Patrick to encourage Peter's interest in the case by mentioning the sighting.'

'Peter had already been asked by Patrick to delve into it so why would Patrick engage the services of Bill Naylor?'

'Dunno. To reinforce the rumours, perhaps.' Jack indicated to turn into Alexi's lane and waited for a car to pass in the opposite direction. 'All I'm saying is that I can't see Franklin breaking cover to kill Peter just because he was asking questions.'

'No.' Alexi shook her head. 'When you put it like that, nor can I. Do you think that he and Amy were in the Swan and that it was her who used her card?'

'Yeah, on balance, I think I do. Franklin likes to play games, to take chances, because he thinks he's smarter than everyone else and that will prove to be his downfall.'

'He'll get cocky.'

'Yep. Probably.'

'So,' Alexi said, opening her door when Jack brought his car to a halt on her drive. The rain had stopped. Cosmo leapt though the gap and disappeared into the garden. 'If it wasn't me, then that leaves the rest of my delegates, Patrick and...'

'You can say it,' Jack replied, walking round his car and slinging an arm around her shoulders. 'Cassie is also a suspect.'

'Not a viable one any more than I am but yes, she has as much reason as Patrick for wanting me out of Lambourn.'

Jack grimaced, watching Alexi as she extracted her key from her bag and opened the front door. They were greeted by a welcoming waft of warm air. The log fire in the lounge had burned low but Jack added fuel and soon had flames dancing up the chimney again.

He then sat on the sofa, grabbed Alexi's hand and pulled her down beside him.

'We'll get through this, darling. None of it is your fault and nothing and no one is going to come between us.' He squeezed her hand. 'I need to know we're agreed on that much.'

Alexi smiled as she reached up and touched Jack's cheek. 'Thanks for having faith in me,' she said softly.

'Damn it, woman, I'm not daft enough to mess with a female who's capable of strangulation.'

'Ah, I see.' Alexi tilted her head to one side. 'You *do* think I did it, but self-preservation has kicked in and you've gone all subservient on me.'

'You know me too well.' Jack pulled her against him and kissed the top of her head.

'So, what now?'

'Now we wait for the result of the post-mortem. That will tell us if Foreman was drugged, which I suspect he was.'

'Unless a woman enticed him into the men's room. I've been thinking about that. He fancied himself with the ladies and if someone said that they knew something about Franklin but needed to talk somewhere private, he wouldn't have hesitated.'

'Then she rendered him unconscious by bashing the back of his head with... with what? There are no convenient blunt objects in a bathroom.'

'She had something with her?'

Jack probably looked as sceptical as he felt. 'Okay, she took him by surprise, somehow knocked him out and then strangled him.' Jack nodded. 'It could have gone down that way. If he was strangled standing up then he would have bashed his head when he fell, always supposing that he *did* bash his head. We don't know anything for sure yet.'

'If it happened that way then it would put Cassie and me firmly back in the frame.'

'No conviction without a motive, darling, and you don't have one.'

Jack didn't have to point out that Patrick and Cassie both did, even if he thought Cassie incapable of going that far. Vaughan wouldn't get his own hands dirty but in his line of work, he undoubtedly knew people who knew people.

Cassie was as possessive as ever and frequently asked Jack how his relationship with Alexi was going. She could never completely disguise her reaction when he responded in the positive. Perhaps she'd grown tired of waiting for the affair to run its course and had seen an opportunity to take matters into her own hands. But it all came down to the fact that she couldn't possibly have known that Foreman would be at the Swan that morning, or that Alexi had arranged to see him there.

'I think we need to dig very deeply into the backgrounds of your delegates,' Jack said, standing and pulling Alexi to her feet. 'But right now, I have other priorities.' He slipped an arm around her waist and waggled his brows suggestively.

She laughed up at him. 'No change there then.'

'Tomorrow's the last day of the course. How involved are you?'

'Fortunately, not very. I meet and greet in the morning, then Bill Naylor is giving them a tour of the local rag production facility. They're spending the afternoon tidying up their submissions and handing them in before dinner. Patrick's already seen their outlined pieces but will make his final judgement on the basis of the submissions themselves. You and I will have to be at the dinner.'

'Wouldn't miss it,' Jack replied.

'They are staying for lunch on Sunday and leaving after that. Although, since the murder, they might have changed their minds.'

'We have tomorrow then to see what we can turn up. Not much time but we'll put it to good use.'

The cat flap rattled. As intuitive as ever, Cosmo knew it was bedtime and preceded Alexi and Jack up the stairs, tail aloft.

11

Alexi slept surprisingly well despite the fact that she was acutely aware of time running away from her. If they were to stand any chance of solving the crime before her delegates went back to their ordinary lives, they would need to make significant headway today. If one of them *was* the guilty party, then that person must have had a compelling motive: jealousy, revenge, a massive grudge – all of the above?

Not that she seriously thought any of her wannabes capable but she knew that Jack would examine their whereabouts at the vital time for himself, despite Alexi having visited them all. He never took anything at face value and expected people to lie to him as a matter of course, not always because they were guilty of anything but because there were aspects of their lives that they would prefer not to have subjected to public scrutiny.

'What time is the post-mortem likely to take place?' Alexi asked Jack as he drove her and Cosmo to Hopgood Hall.

'Probably already underway,' Jack replied. 'It was first on the list today. Murder victims tend to get priority.'

'Will Vickery let us know what was found?' she asked.

'I'm sure he will, darling.' He pulled up in the hotel's car park but didn't cut the engine.

'You going somewhere?' she asked.

'To the office. Cassie's got into Peter's phone records. I want to see for myself what she's come up with.'

'If I didn't know any better, I might think that you don't trust her to tell you the truth.' Alexi spoke lightly, making a joke out of a deadly serious suspicion.

'You know me, I like to be hands on, especially with something this important. I'll be back in a couple of hours.' He kissed the side of her face. 'Stay strong.'

'Ring me if you come up with anything.'

Jack winked at her. 'Count on it. Same goes for you.'

Alexi was about to leave the car when she noticed a gaggle of locals standing outside the front door, gossiping. She groaned when she noticed Polly Pearson in their midst, her mouth working overtime as she waved her arms about.

'That's all I need,' she said, with a heavy sigh. 'What that woman has against me is a mystery. I've barely ever spoken to her.'

'Sticks and stones, darling. Ignore her. Or better yet, set Cosmo on her.'

Jack's flippancy made Alexi smile. 'That ought to do it.' She leaned over to kiss his cheek, aware of Polly and her coven watching them intently. 'Later,' she said.

'Isn't it time you left this village?' Polly shouted as Alexi climbed from the car. Cosmo arched his back and hissed at the woman. 'We don't need you hexing the place.'

'Morning, Polly. Ladies.' Alexi smiled at them but didn't break stride as she headed for the hotel. Cosmo hissed again and they all instinctively jumped out of his way. Jack, who hadn't yet driven off and had clearly witnessed the scene, honked his horn. Alexi knew he'd be laughing. 'Hard at work I see.'

Feeling tired and guilt-ridden before the day had even started, Alexi made for Cheryl's kitchen and gratefully accepted a mug of coffee from Drew.

'Is Cheryl with the baby?' Alexi asked, concealing a yawn behind her hand.

'Naturally. I'm sensible enough to know where I come in the pecking order in this family.'

He smiled as he spoke, but Alexi could see the strain around his eyes. This latest murder was a massive blow for him and Cheryl. If not for her own peace of mind, such as it was, the situation that needed to be resolved before the press got wind of it and descended upon them en masse, speculating, drawing conclusions, adding two and two and coming up with seventeen.

'Good to have it confirmed that you know your place,' Alexi quipped.

'What's the latest?' Drew asked.

Alexi gave him a rundown on their visit to Dawson and the conclusions they'd drawn from it.

'Blimey!' Drew scratched vigorously at his scalp. 'No such thing as a quiet life for you and Jack. It would be nice if Franklin was the killer though,' he added pensively.

'Much nicer than it turning out to be anyone connected to us.' Alexi nodded. 'I agree with you there.'

'It would take the spotlight off us and be bound to generate business. Every man and his dog would come trundling down here, determined to unearth Franklin's hideout and we'd make a killing. Whoops! No pun intended. That would be tacky.'

Alexi laughed 'Just a bit but business is business and if you don't cash in, you can be as sure as hell that someone else will. Polly Pearson in particular. Perhaps that's why she spreads so much gossip about me. It's good for her business as well.'

'Probably. She's a queer fish, that one.' Drew paused, kettle in hand. 'If Franklin didn't do it, who do you think did?'

'There's the question. We're awaiting the results of the post-mortem. If he was drugged before being strangled and therefore unable to fight back, it puts my name firmly in the frame.' Alexi paused. 'And Cassie's. Patrick's too.'

'I can see that Patrick has a compelling motive. Cassie as well. But why the hell would you want to kill one of your delegates, even if he was annoying? Apart from anything else, it's bad for repeat business.'

'I was there and overheard arguing with him. Fortunately, Jack thinks that lacking a motive will keep me out of the clink. I on the other hand would much prefer to clear my name rather than giving Polly and her coven more fuel for speculation, which means finding the real killer.'

'The killer made off in Foreman's car and if Cassie saw you leave in your own then you're in the clear.'

'She'd hate to be the one who cleared me,' Alexi said, chuckling. 'But it could be argued that I dumped Peter's car and then came back for my own.'

Drew shook his head. 'Why?'

'Dunno. We think his laptop was in it but I could have helped myself to it and left the car, given that Peter's keys were missing.'

'What was on the laptop that the killer wanted access to?'

'That's another very good question.'

Drew sat across from Alexi with his own coffee in front of him and rubbed his chin pensively. 'You mentioned that Foreman has connections to the security services. If that's the case, Alexi, and he was bumped off by one of his own because he'd... I don't know, become a loose cannon or something, then you'll never get to the truth.'

'I know that and so does Jack. But if all else fails, he's threatening to leak Foreman's previous line of work to my ex-colleagues.'

'They wouldn't publish without confirmation and if confirmation was sought then a D-notice would be slapped on the offending paper long before the presses started rolling.'

'True but then there's trial by social media.'

'Whatever it takes.'

'If a D-notice was forthcoming, at least it would confirm our theory.' Alexi threw up her hands in frustration. 'A fat lot of good that would do us though because we wouldn't have a cat in hell's chance of proving some shadowy figure's culpability. We would know or suspect the truth, but a cloud would continue to hang over this place, so let's hope that Peter was killed by an ordinary citizen with an axe to grind. He did have a tendency to rub people up the wrong way and so perhaps someone followed him down here and saw an opportunity away from home soil to do the deed and avoid being a suspect.'

Drew waggled a hand from side to side. 'A bit tenuous.'

'A girl can dream.' Alexi drained her mug and stood up. 'I'd best get this show on the road. I'll only be half an hour. Once I've sent my fledgling reporters on their way, I'll work upstairs in the lounge, if that's okay. I need to do some serious digging into their backgrounds whilst I wait for Jack to get back and for the results of the post-mortem to come through.' She paused with her hand on the back door. 'I don't suppose I'll find anything that Cassie hasn't but at least I'll feel as though I'm being proactive.'

Drew waved her off. Cosmo had sneaked through the door and seemed determined to tag along with Alexi. She hadn't allowed him anywhere near her delegates for long up until now simply because she couldn't trust him to behave himself. If he took a dislike to a person, he could be unpredictable. Grace especially had pushed for him to join them though and Alexi was happy to provide her clients with a distraction from Peter's untimely death.

'You're the distraction,' she told her cat. 'Bear that in mind and play nice or there will be consequences. No biting ankles or coming over all macho.'

Cosmo sent her an imperious look and stalked on ahead of her, entering the annex with a regal swish of his tail, if tail-swishing could be deemed regal. With Cosmo, nothing was off the table. Her cat appeared to know that Alexi needed his coopera-tion right now. He behaved himself and even permitted Grace to pet him: one small mercy. Ranya seemed wary of him but everyone else displayed genuine interest in a cat who had his own fanbase on Instagram. Pictures were taken and, as Alexi had hoped would be the case, Cosmo's presence eased the heavy atmosphere. By the time Alexi shooed Cosmo out of the annex, everyone seemed more relaxed.

Bill Naylor turned up on time, gagging for information about the murder. Alexi had nothing new that she cared to share with him but promised him full details once anything came to light with the proviso that he didn't publish anything in the meantime other than the basic facts.

She was halfway across the courtyard when Ranya called her name and came panting up to her.

'Is something wrong?' Alexi asked.

'Not exactly.' She screwed her hands together and Alexi noticed that her nails were chewed down to the quick. 'Look, this is probably nothing and I don't want you thinking that I'm speaking out of turn.'

'If it's to do with Peter's death then you have a duty to tell what you know,' Alexi said gently.

The girl nodded and bit her lower lip. 'It's been playing on my conscience.'

'What has? You don't have to tell me if you'd prefer not to, but you must tell Inspector Vickery. It will be withholding information if you don't and that could get you into trouble. Peter's dead, remember, and although he was a bit of a pain, I'm sure none of us wanted that for him.'

'No, of course not.' She swallowed and glanced over her shoulder toward the annex, clearly worried that her conversation with Alexi was being observed.

'Come into the kitchen,' Alexi said, glancing up at a leaden sky and shivering when a cold blast of wind buffeted them. 'It's more private and definitely warmer.'

Alexi was glad that Drew was no longer around. Toby was now the only occupant of the kitchen and he greeted Cosmo with an enthusiasm that made Ranya smile.

'Now, sit down. You have a few minutes before going off with Bill, so tell me what the problem is.' Alexi leaned across the table, a friendly, intimate gesture that reduced the distance separating them; one that she had frequently used in her previous line of work when attempting to put an interviewee at ease.

'It's Diana,' she said, twisting her hands together again. 'She said she didn't know Peter when you asked us but that isn't strictly true.' She swallowed. 'The first night of the course, we'd all gone to bed but I heard Diana in the annex lounge, talking to someone. It sounded... animated between them and I confess that curiosity got the better of me. I opened my door and could see Peter's back. Diana was whisper-shouting at him, if you know what I mean.' Alexi nodded. 'Diana was waving her hands around, getting worked up, but Peter seemed to be placating her as best he could.'

'Did you hear what they were disagreeing about?' Alexi held her breath as she waited for the girl's response.

'Yes. About being in care.' She stared directly at Alexi for the first time through huge eyes that radiated a combination of fear and confusion. 'From what I can gather, they were in the same place at the same time.'

Alexi was gripped by a mix of exhilaration and confusion. This could well be the elusive lead she'd been seeking. It was something anyway. A start. A connection to the victim.

'Are you sure you heard right?' she asked.

'Absolutely.' Ranya nodded emphatically, growing in confidence now she'd started talking about a situation that had clearly been plaguing her conscience. 'Diana seemed to be urging Peter to do something about... well, something. She didn't specify but he clearly understood and told her to back off. He said it was too late, he'd moved on and raking it up again would serve no purpose for anyone involved.'

'Involved in what?'

Ranya shook her head. 'I have absolutely no idea.'

It sounded to Alexi as though Peter could have been abused whilst in care but what that had to do with Diana was less clear. If Diana had been a victim of the supposed abuse, and that was a big *if* since presumably not all kids in care were exploited, then she could have been offering Peter the benefit of her advice. Alexi knew her imagination was in danger of running away with her. Even so, if she was right then she couldn't imagine Diana keeping quiet about any maltreatment now that she was an assertive adult. The woman was far too forthright to let embarrassment stand in the way of righting a wrong and perhaps she'd been urging Peter to follow her example.

'What I don't understand,' Ranya said, frowning, 'is why Diana denied knowing Peter when you asked us about our relationship with him.'

Alexi wondered about that too. 'Thanks for telling me all this Ranya. It might be important.'

'You won't tell Diana that you got this from me.' Anxiety now formed the bedrock of her expression. 'I don't want her to know that I eavesdropped or have her think I've told tales out of school.'

Both ladies stood and Alexi patted Ranya's shoulder. 'Don't worry. She'll never know where I heard it from. Thanks again for letting me know.'

'It seemed like the right thing to do.'

'It was.'

Alexi stood at the window watching Ranya, head bowed against a strong wind and yet more rain as she scampered back to the annex. Alexi mulled over what she'd just learned, wondering what she should do about it. Pass the information to Vickery and let him sort it out or deal with it herself?

There was never any real possibility of her letting Vickery loose, she quickly accepted. She was here, on the spot, and these people were her delegates. She'd speak with Diana, find out what it was all about, and *then* tell Vickery. She'd lost the opportunity to do anything immediately since her group would shortly be leaving for their tour of the local rag's production facility. It would have to wait until they returned at lunchtime. That would give her an opportunity to discuss the situation with Jack, and to find out what, if anything new that Cassie had dug up.

'She isn't the only one with resources,' she told Cosmo as she picked up her laptop and headed for the upstairs lounge, escorted by a haughty cat and tail-wagging dog.

Alexi had barely settled down before her phone rang.

'Hey,' she said, smiling when Jack's name flashed up on the screen. 'Missing me already?'

'Always.' She could hear the responding smile in his voice. 'Anything new?'

'Actually, yes. How long will you be before you get back here?'

'Now who's feeling needy?' He chuckled. 'About an hour.'

'Then it can wait. I'll tell you when you get here. So, why did you call?'

'Vickery called me with the post-mortem results.'

'Ah.' Alexi bit her lip. 'And?'

'We're right, I'm afraid. It seems he was drugged.'

'I see.' Alexi swallowed, aware now why Jack had called her. He wanted to be the one to break the bad news and couldn't be sure that she wouldn't hear it from Vickery first, always supposing he was planning a return visit to Hopgood Hall that morning. 'Well, actually I don't see. How can they know so quickly?'

'There was a speck of dried blood that concealed a puncture wound on the back of his neck. Tests are being carried out but Vickery is working on the assumption that he trusted whoever he entered that bathroom with and—'

'And that person injected him from behind with something to instantly incapacitate, then throttled him. Blimey, that implies a lot of anger, to say nothing of premeditation.'

'Precisely.' Jack's tone was sombre.

'And also throws our theory that a woman wouldn't have had the strength to do it out the window. Yes, Jack, I got that part.'

'I know, darling, but it would take a massive amount of strength to strangle a man as brutally as Foreman was killed, even if he was unable to fight back. I saw for myself that the cord, or whatever was used, cut deep into his neck.'

'Has Cassie found out anything interesting?' Alexi didn't want to speculate about the strength necessary to cause strangulation. There was absolutely no point.

'She got into Peter's phone records, like I already said. I have a list of numbers he called recently. I'm working my way through them. I'll do that here than head on back. See you soon.'

'Yeah, later.'

Alexi felt weighed down by the strength of her depression and took a moment to wallow in self-pity. It was bad enough that people seemed to make a habit of being killed around her. Being suspected of committing this latest murder though was enough to depress anyone. Why her? Why now?

She gave herself a mental shake, aware that there was no time to feel sorry for herself. If she was to clear her name, the only effective way to do so would be to find the actual killer, and time was running out in that regard. Peter and Diana had a history, but that didn't on the face of it imply that Diana had throttled her childhood friend. Why would she?

Archie had a record but no obvious reason to kill Peter. Ranya was too small to throttle anyone, even if the victim couldn't fight back. Emily and Grace could both probably have managed it but again, it came back to motive. As far as Alexi was aware, none of the attendees had met beforehand, other than Diana and Peter.

So, unless some shady figure from Peter's previous life had done the deed, she was left with Patrick and Cassie, both of whom definitely had their reasons for wanting Alexi out of Lambourn.

All well and good, she thought, leaning back in her chair and sighing, but if one of them had killed Peter, she didn't have a hope in hell of proving it. Patrick had made sure he was miles away at the time, visiting his mother.

As for Cassie... well, Alexi had absolutely no idea where to start. Jack was touchy when it came to the subject of his business partner. Alexi could, she supposed, tell Vickery about her suspicions but she would then also have to tell him why they had arisen. It would make her and Cassie sound like two possessive women brawling over their man. It would also put the kibosh of Jack's business partnership with Cassie, to say nothing of putting strain on her own relationship with him.

A strain that it might not be able to withstand, thereby doing Cassie's work for her.

Alexi accepted that she was stuck between a rock and a hard place. And no nearer to narrowing the field of suspects down. She would shelve all thoughts of Cassie's involvement, trusting Jack to raise the subject if any evidence came to light that pointed the finger of suspicion in Cassie's direction. There was nothing else she could do.

She idly wondered how Cassie had managed to hack into Peter's phone records so quickly and, apparently, effortlessly. Alexi knew she was a whizz with computers, could make them sing for her, but even so. She sat a little straighter as a possibility occurred to her. If hacking was a doddle for her, what's to say that she hadn't hacked into Alexi's phone too? Her blood ran cold at the thought. She had sent an email to her delegates, reminding them that she would be visiting their various research places on the morning of the murder, and listing the places in question, just so that there was no misunderstanding.

'Damn!' she muttered.

It was only a thought, a possibility, and she had absolutely no way of knowing if Cassie, driven by the force of her jealousy, had violated Alexi's privacy to that extent. How to find out? Now that the idea had occurred to her, she would have no peace until she discovered if her phone had been hacked.

She knew that obvious ways of being able to tell were higher than usual data usage, continuous pop-ups, a shorter than usual battery life, amongst other signs. She hadn't noticed any of those things but she wouldn't expect to, she reasoned, not if Cassie had just popped in to have a look around and crash Alexi's schedule. She was too canny to leave a spying device on the phone that would have been found in the event of Alexi being arrested. But if she had taken a quick look-see, she would have known that Alexi had arranged to meet Peter at the Swan that morning. Since the pub was the place where her missing friend's card had been used, it probably seemed like a sign.

And too much of a coincidence.

Had Amy's card actually been used? As far as Alexi was aware, Jack hadn't seen the evidence. He would have taken what Cassie told him at face value because he trusted her.

She glanced out the window. There was still a strong wind blowing but the rain had stopped. Alexi's head felt too full for her to be able to think coherently. She needed fresh air, an opportunity to let her jumbled thoughts untangle themselves. When stuck with thorny questions in the past, a meander with no particular destination in mind usually resulted in inspired decision making.

She made her way down the stairs with her animal escort and almost ran into a lady standing at the reception desk, which wasn't manned.

'Oh, can I help you?' she asked.

'You're Alexi Ellis,' the woman said, smiling. 'I recognise you from your byline photo in the *Sentinel*. I'm Sarah Watt. I have a room booked. I'm *so* excited to be attending your gala dinner tonight.'

'Ah, pleased to meet you.' Alexi extended her hand and Sarah shook it firmly. All of the attendees had invited guests to the final night's dinner, but Alexi had no idea who had issued an invite to Sarah. She examined the lady a little more closely. She had to be in her early twenties and was slightly overweight. There was nothing exceptional about her but her beaming smile and enthusiasm for life were infectious.

'I am so excited,' Sarah gushed, her wide smile illuminating her face. 'What are the chances of both my mother and my father registering for the same course? You could have knocked me down with a feather when Mum rang to tell me.'

'I'm sorry, Sarah. Emily didn't tell me you were coming.'

Sarah blinked. 'Emily? Who's Emily? Is she organising the dinner?'

'No, Emily is the only person on the course, as far as I'm aware, who is a mother. I just assumed...'

'Oh, I see. Mum's ashamed of me again, is she?' Sarah laughed good-naturedly. 'Mum is Diana. Diana Horton and my father, whom I've been trying to trace for a couple of years now, without success I might add, is Peter Foreman.'

12

In a grim frame of mind, Jack drove back to Lambourn without giving the road ahead much of his attention. He'd stumbled upon discoveries that had disturbed him greatly. It would be easy to jump to the most logical conclusion but despite what he now knew, he wasn't ready to burn his bridges quite yet. There were two sides to every story and if he bandied about unsubstantiated allegations then his partnership with Cassie, one based on trust, would never recover.

The problem was, he didn't have time to dither and so must trust his instincts. He would have to tell Alexi, and Vickery, and tell them soon. But he needed the time it would take him to drive to Hopgood Hall to try and make sense of a situation that he didn't want to believe was possible.

Even though it made sense on so many levels.

He arrived in Lambourn and was no closer to deciding what to do about this latest development than he'd been when leaving Newbury. Cosmo greeted him at the top of the steps, a bit like an anxious father demanding to know where he'd been and what time he called this.

'What's happening, big guy?' Jack asked, dropping a hand to stroke the cat's head. 'Where's your mum?'

Cosmo responded by trotting ahead of him and meowing impatiently outside Drew's kitchen door, tail twitching with irritation. Alexi's intuitive cat was trying to tell him that something untoward had occurred and to express his annoyance because he'd been shut out of it.

'What now?' he muttered, assuming that Vaughan had gotten Alexi alone and was launching a toxic charm offensive, using this latest murder to work upon her dwindling resolve and tempt her back to London with an offer of an enhanced position at the *Sentinel*. The fact that the paper probably regretted letting her go, given the dissatisfaction still being voiced by readers, Vaughan would be effectively killing two birds with one stone. He'd have his star reporter back and could pretend to the paper's owners that she'd seen the error of her ways and returned of her own volition. He would arrogantly assume as well that she'd return to his bed.

Not happenin'!

But instead of the newspaper man, he opened the door and found Alexi deep in conversation with another woman. A complete stranger.

'Oh, Jack, there you are.' Alexi looked up at him with a sunny smile that failed to completely conceal her anxiety.

'Hey,' he replied, strolling into the room. 'What did I miss?'

'Jack, this is Sarah Watt, Diana's daughter,' she added with a significant look. 'Diana, my partner, Jack Maddox.'

Jack didn't miss a beat, even though he was as surprised as Alexi appeared to be by the appearance of the prodigal daughter. He and Alexi knew that Diana had never been married and had made erroneous assumptions on that basis.

'Good to meet you, Sarah,' Jack said, extending his hand.

'You too.' She eyed Jack speculatively.

'What brings you to Hopgood Hall?' Jack asked, helping himself to coffee and joining Alexi on her side of the table.

'Sarah has a room booked. She's attending the dinner tonight with Diana. She only just this minute got here. And here's the thing: she just told me that Peter Foreman is her father.'

'Shit!' Jack muttered beneath his breath, sending Alexi a *does-she-know* look. Alexi responded with a miniscule shake of her head.

'I have never met my father,' Sarah told him. 'Mum would never talk about him when I asked questions growing up. She got quite agitated about it and so in the end, I stopped asking. She had me when she was very young, still a child herself, and I figured it was a part of her life that she'd wanted to put behind her.'

'How old was she when you were born, just as a matter of interest?' Jack asked.

'Only just sixteen.' Sarah took a sip of her coffee. 'The thing is, Mum and Dad grew up in the same care home. She never talks about that either, but I got the impression that it wasn't a happy time for her. Well, some terrible stories of abuse are emerging about such places nowadays, aren't they? Anyway, she and Dad turned to one another for comfort with the inevitable results.' She pointed to herself for emphasis. 'But now, against all the odds, Mum and Dad enrolled on the same course and I'll finally get to meet him. I mean, what are the chances?'

That was a question that Jack would like an answer to as well. He didn't believe in coincidences, but they happened, and this had to be one. Didn't it? There were dozens more applicants than there were places on the course so even if Diana was determined that Foreman should meet his daughter, there was no way that she could have inveigled the 'accidental' reunion, much less discover that he'd even applied.

Then again, Vaughan had a big say about who was accepted on the course, given that he was the star turn. He would be more than capable of engineering matters. They knew he'd been in contact with Foreman and got him on the course for a specific reason. But even if he knew that Foreman had fathered a child with Diana, it was less obvious why he'd bother to bring them together. There had to be a reason, though. Vaughan was a master manipulator and Alexi was always centre stage in his thoughts when it came to his machinations.

Sarah was gregarious, bouncing on the edge of her seat like a child on a sugar rush, open and friendly. Jack could see nothing of the dour, no-nonsense Diana in her character, but she was quite pretty and had a look of Foreman about her. He might not have given his child his time but at least she had inherited his looks.

'I'm surprised that you're so keen to meet your father, given that he hasn't wanted to know you,' Alexi said softly.

'Yeah, I hear you, but I dealt with my anger issues in that regard years ago. I saw a therapist who helped me make sense of it. Mum was fifteen when I was conceived but Dad, wait for it, was only thirteen.'

'Blimey!' Alexi said, glancing at Jack.

'Well exactly. Explains a lot, doesn't it? Goodness alone knows what they went through as kids. In their shoes, I probably wouldn't have wanted to accept the responsibilities of parenthood, given their only example of parental care had been at the hands of indifferent abusers. Mum did want a child though and to her credit, she did her best for me. We never had much money, but she made sure I got a good education and also made sure I knew how to stand up for myself. That seemed to matter to her more than anything, perhaps because she'd witnessed so many helpless children being exploited.'

'Your mother told you that she'd met your father again unexpectedly,' Jack remarked.

'She called me last night. She thought I was still in Italy and wouldn't be back in time for tonight but, of course, I made that happen.'

'It seems odd that she did tell you,' Alexi mused. 'Given that she's never wanted to speak about him.'

'It would have been a shock, I expect, meeting him here so unexpectedly and she wasn't thinking straight,' Sarah said. 'I suppose it's natural enough for her to want us to meet but she thought it would never happen because my father didn't want to know, so she discouraged me from asking questions. But coming upon him here, by coincidence, forced her hand. She told me and left me to make my own decision about whether or not I came, thereby assuaging her own guilt, if you like. Anyway, she probably guessed that I would come. I'm a grown woman now. I won't be making any demands on my father. I'm not used to having him in my life, won't fall apart if he shows no interest in me and will at least have met him.'

Jack glanced at Alexi. The likeable lady had waited all her life to meet the man who'd fathered her and was about to be bitterly disappointed. It wasn't fair to keep her in ignorance and he wondered which of them should break the bad news. Alexi nodded, picking up on his unspoken communication and inviting him to go ahead. *Thanks!*

'Sarah, I am so very sorry, but I have devastating news for you.'

'Is it Mum?' She leaned forward anxiously. 'Something's happened to her. I can sense it.' Her gaze darted round the kitchen, as though expecting to find her mother hiding behind one of the appliances. 'Is she okay?'

'It's not Diana. She's fine.' Alexi swallowed and picked up the baton. 'Unfortunately, Peter Foreman was found dead yesterday.'

'Dead?' She blinked. 'No. That's not possible. We hadn't even met yet. How? Was he ill? What happened?'

'Someone killed him, I'm afraid,' Jack told her, reaching across the table to squeeze her trembling hand. 'Your mother obviously didn't ring you to tell you the news.'

'That's because she didn't know I was coming to the dinner tonight,' Sarah replied. 'I have been in Italy for a couple of days, scoping out new hotels that our agency is thinking of promoting. It was a reward for being top salesperson a few months ago. I didn't expect to be back in time so told Mum I couldn't make it but as soon as I knew my father was here, I made it happen. I booked a room here and intended to surprise her.' She looked glum yet her attitude remained stoic. 'Not quite the surprise I had in mind.'

'I'm so very sorry,' Alexi said.

'Yes, well, what you've never had, you don't miss.' She let out the prolonged sigh of a disappointed woman. 'Perhaps Mum was right to say that I should let the subject of my father rest, but I never could. Not really. But now I will have to, I suppose.' She wiped a single tear from her cheek with the back of her hand. 'Is it wrong of me to feel relieved that your bad news wasn't about Mum?'

'Of course not.' Alexi smiled at Sarah. 'You just said it yourself, you never even met your father so it's only natural that you'd feel protective of the only parent you've ever known.'

She nodded. 'True. He didn't want to meet me, but I don't suppose he killed himself, just to avoid the encounter. Anyway, what actually happened to him.'

'He was murdered, I'm afraid,' Jack told her.

'Murdered!' Stunned, her eyes widened and her mouth gaped.

'Good heavens! I'm told he was a civil servant. Who the hell would want to kill a paper-pusher?'

'That's what we're trying to establish,' Alexi told her.

'Well, there's nothing I can tell you to help, I'm afraid. I'd learned never to mention him in Mum's hearing. It upset her. But,' she added, leaning her elbows on the table and resting her chin in her splayed hands, 'I've always believed that he was the love of her life, despite the fact that they met so young.'

'Bonded by bad experiences?' Alexi suggested.

'Precisely.' Sarah fell into momentary reflection. 'I've never known her date and she has never expressed regret about not being married. She doesn't seem to like or trust men very much, but I found a crumpled picture of her and dad in her room once, taken when they were both kids. She doesn't carry baggage, emotional or physical, so why keep that picture?'

'Why indeed,' Alexi replied. 'You told me earlier that you spent a lot of time attempting to track your father down in your earlier years but had no success.'

'I couldn't find any trace of a John Bishop after he left that care home.' She spread her hands. 'It's like he disappeared off the face of the earth.'

Alexi and Jack exchanged a look. They had established Peter's true identity.

'He changed his name for some reason,' Alexi said.

'A new start.' A note of bitterness entered Sarah's tone. 'Either that or he didn't want to face up to his responsibilities.'

'I'm sure that isn't the case,' Alexi replied, although Jack knew she couldn't possibly be sure of any such thing.

'Look, this is all a bit much,' Sarah said. 'I think I'd like to go to my room and mull things over. I'd rather not see Mum for a while. Well, I expect she's busy with the course and wasn't expecting to see me anyway so...'

'Of course.' Alexi stood up. 'Come on. I'll show you the way.'

'It was nice to meet you,' Jack said, standing too and feeling very sorry for the young woman, 'but I wish it could have been under better circumstances.'

'Me too,' Sarah replied with a wan smile, following Alexi from the room.

* * *

Alexi settled Sarah in her room, made sure she had everything she needed and left her to it. This latest development threw up more questions than answers and was a subject that she and Jack urgently needed to discuss. At least now, she thought as she ran down the stairs, they knew Peter's real name. It was a start, but she doubted whether it would get them much further forward.

She returned to the kitchen with that thought predominant in her mind.

'Phew!' she said, flopping back down into her chair and running a hand through her tangled hair. 'I didn't see that one coming.'

'Nor me,' Jack replied. 'The plot thickens.'

'Should we tell Vickery?'

'Given that Foreman was her absent father, I guess he needs to know. Obviously though, the first thing we need to do as soon as she returns is to speak to Diana.'

'I agree with you there. Ranya approached me this morning. She heard Diana and Peter in dispute about something on the first night of the course, so they'd definitely recognised one another. Whether they'd met before the course is another matter. According to Ranya, Diana was urging Peter to do something about... well, they weren't specific on that point. I assumed it was to do with abuse in care, or something like that. Ranya heard him say that it was too late and to let it go.'

'You're supposing now that they were discussing their daughter,' Jack replied, 'which would make sense.'

'What I'd like to know... one of the many things I'd like to know is how they both finished up on this course.'

'Well,' Jack replied, taking a deep breath, 'we know Vaughan got Foreman onto it for his own reasons.' He scowled. 'Whether those reasons are the ones he 'fessed up to is another matter. He got him on the course and was in direct contact with him. But if he found out about Foreman's love child, what did he hope to achieve by bringing the two childhood lovers together again after all these years?'

'Hard to say,' Alexi agreed, drumming her fingers restlessly on the tabletop. 'Perhaps, for some reason, Peter asked him to. Then again, Patrick is a schemer, never leaves things to chance, and you can be sure that he'd have had his reasons.'

'Yeah.' Jack knew that he was stalling, afraid to reveal what he'd discovered back in Newbury. 'Alexi, I need to tell you something.'

She sent Jack an inquisitive look. 'You seem unnaturally serious all of a sudden. Are you about to turn me in to Vickery?' she quipped.

'I'm not sure what to—'

'Hang on, they're back.' She turned at the sound of voices and peered out the window. Her delegates, bundled up against the cold, were crossing the courtyard. 'No time like the present. I'll ask Diana to join us.'

Before Jack could say his piece, she was up and out the door.

'Coward,' he muttered. 'Not you,' he added when Cosmo looked up at him accusingly.

'I'm glad you enjoyed the tour,' Alexi said as she approached the kitchen with Diana. 'All newspapers but especially local ones are struggling to survive in the printed form and so I do what I can to support their efforts. Nothing beats seeing your words reproduced in ink for posterity. The feeling never gets old. Trust me on this.'

'What's this all about?' Diana asked when she entered the kitchen and Jack stood up. 'I have things to do, facts to check before the submission deadline. Can't it wait?'

'Sit down, Diana.'

The calm authority in Jack's voice caused her to comply, albeit with an impatient tut.

'We're attempting to find out who killed Foreman,' Jack told her. 'And why.'

'I think we'd all like to know that.' She brushed the question of Peter's murder aside with a careless flip of one wrist, seemingly unconcerned by the demise of the man she had supposedly carried a candle for all these years. 'What do you need from me?' she asked impatiently, glancing at her watch.

'I gather you and Peter had a heated discussion late on your first night here,' Alexi said.

Diana jerked forward in her chair, the first genuine reaction that Alexi had seen from her. 'Who told you that?' she demanded to know.

'Is it true?' Jack asked.

Diana muttered something unintelligible beneath her breath and folded her arms defensively across her chest. 'It has nothing to do with you,' she said, sounding less than convincing and looking furious at being called on it.

'You're not stupid and know that isn't true,' Jack responded. 'You either tell us or you tell the inspector. Your choice. But be aware, withholding relevant information from a murder enquiry is a serious offence.'

'Tell us about your history with Peter, or should I say John,' Alexi said, her voice soft with sympathy and in direct variance to Jack's harsh tone.

'You know about that.' She shook her head, not waiting for an answer. 'You're good at what you do, I'll give you that.' She allowed a significant pause, her eyes shooting daggers in Jack's direction. 'I knew John when we were both children, growing up in the supposed care system. But we went our separate ways, and I hadn't seen him for more than twenty years, until we ran into each other here.'

'There was no public acknowledgement of your prior acquaintance,' Alexi said. 'None of the shocked exclamations that you'd expect when two people meet accidentally after years of separation.'

'He's changed his name and we've both aged. A lot. I honestly didn't recognise him at first.'

'Did you change your name?' Jack asked.

'No. I never saw the need.'

'Then he must have recognised you.'

Diana harrumphed as she shuffled her bulk into a more comfortable position. 'If he did then he gave no sign. He barely looked at me and was more concerned with cosying up to you, Alexi. I had to remind him who I was when I caught him alone that evening and even then, he seemed to have trouble believing it.'

'That must have stung,' Alexi said, sympathy in her voice.

'The past is the past. And that's what we were arguing about. I've been able to put it behind me and move on without feeling the need to change my identity. John clearly hadn't and I tried to make him understand that it isn't too late to get help. He will always be hampered by his demons if he doesn't.'

Jack nodded. 'You still cared enough about him to try and persuade him.'

'You had to have been there to understand what it was like. We were helpless pawns in the hands of grown-up deviants. The staff and benefactors could do what they liked with us and those who weren't involved went into self-preservation mode and pretended not to know.'

'I'm sorry,' Alexi said. 'I'd like to think that's no longer the case but am not sufficiently naïve to believe all forms of abuse have been wiped out.' She shook her head. 'Innocent kids being violated. The mere thought of it turns my stomach.'

'It was mostly the boys that the perverts entertained themselves with. John was exceptionally pretty and so naturally, he suffered more than most. He never spoke much about it, but I tried to be there for him as a friend. I could sense the anger building up in him though.' She let out a long breath. 'He was just fourteen when our director was found floating face down in the Thames estuary, not far from our home, if you can call the place a home. He was John's main antagonist.'

'And you suspected John of finishing him off?' Alexi asked.

Diana shrugged a meaty shoulder. She wouldn't be bad looking, Alexi thought, if she shed a little weight, wore makeup, did something with her hair – made the best of herself. But Alexi also knew that victims of abuse often felt worthless, as though they deserved their suffering and had brought it upon themselves. She had just said that Peter, or John, had been selected because he was a beautiful child. In making herself as plain as possible, she was displaying classic denial, Alexi thought.

'I never asked John and he never volunteered the information. Anyway, shortly after that, he simply walked out and never came back.' The tough individual who never let emotion affect her looked briefly vulnerable. 'He never even said goodbye,' she added, so quietly that Alexi barely caught the words.

Alexi glanced at Jack, wondering if he agreed with her in that Diana had spoken the truth, insofar as it went. Someone had to raise the question of Sarah, who could walk in on them at any time, and Alexi really didn't want to be the one to do it.

'Did he know you were pregnant at the time?' Jack asked.

Diana's mouth fell open. 'How the hell did you...'

'Sarah's upstairs,' Alexi said softly. 'She wanted to surprise you. And her father.'

'Oh God!' Diana placed her elbows on the table and buried her face in her splayed palms. 'I need to see her. Does she know?'

'Yes,' Alexi replied. 'She took the news stoically.'

'I never should have told her he was here. She's asked about him so often during the years, but she was better off not knowing anything about that hellhole where we were raised. Besides, I had no idea how to contact him, even if I'd wanted to. Not that I did. I had no intention of disappointing Sarah by introducing her to a man who wouldn't even acknowledge her.'

'I'm sure you did what you could to protect her,' Alexi said.

'I did tell John that I was pregnant, but he didn't want to know. He told me to get rid of it. Said that we wouldn't be doing a child any favours if we brought it into this world.'

'That sounds harsh,' Alexi replied, 'but given his own experiences, and bearing in mind that he was still a child himself, you can understand his point of view.'

'I knew it would be a shock, but I thought that when he'd had time to think about it, he'd realise that we could do a much better job of parenting, young as we were, than the people who'd abused their responsibility for our welfare. We were so very close, you see, John and me. I was older than him: his surrogate big sister helping him to forget what they did to him.

'Eventually, hormones took over and we made love. I will never accept that we had a fling, or whatever else you might call it. I was in love, and no one will ever convince me that John didn't return my feelings, at least insofar as he was capable of feeling any emotion. Those bastards who abused him had stripped him of all compassion. He told me once, on one of the rare occasions that he broached the subject, that the only way to get through it was to detach his mind from what was happening to his body.'

'I've heard that said by other abuse victims,' Alexi said.

'You kept track of him over the years,' Jack stated.

'What? No! How could I?' she blustered. 'He changed his name. I had no way of finding him.'

'As a matter of interest,' Jack said. 'What was the name of the man who finished up in the Thames?'

Diana stared at Jack through narrowed eyes. 'Peter Foreman,' she said reluctantly.

13

Alexi and Diana both gaped at Jack.

'You knew that when you asked me?' Diana said accusingly. 'How could you possibly?'

'Educated guess,' Jack replied. 'Foreman wrecked your friend's life and the sort of abuse you described is not something you get over. Not ever. Taking his name would remind him that he was strong, a survivor. I saw a few examples of that when I was in the Met.'

Diana snorted. '*Wrecked* is putting it mildly. Foreman was hugely respected and admired for guiding such a well-adjusted bunch of parentless kids. Ha! His sort of care we could all have done without. Nothing's the way it seems, is it? He ruled behind closed doors with a rod of iron and, from what I can gather, used that rod for a very different purpose when he and his friends "entertained". Do you know, he forced alcohol on John and his other *special* boys to help them to relax.'

'It sounds horrendous,' Alexi said quietly.

'You don't know the half of it.' Diana shook her head. 'What I don't understand, I'll never understand, is why John took Foreman's name. I didn't think much of it when I realised there was a Peter Foreman on this course. It's a fairly common name. It didn't occur to me that it would be my John, not for a moment.'

'It was probably his way of dealing with the trauma,' Alexi replied, expanding upon Jack's earlier remarks. 'Better than counselling. His way of reminding himself that he'd overcome the worst possible start in life and risen above it.'

'I guess,' Diana said, looking anything other than sure.

'Do you think he killed Foreman?' Jack asked.

'I wouldn't blame him if he did,' Diana replied without hesitation. 'But to answer your question, I have absolutely no idea. He wouldn't talk about his death, other than to say that the world was a better place without him in it.'

'Did the original Foreman have any family or especially close friends, do you know?' Jack asked.

Alexi awaited Diana's answer with interest, aware of Jack's reasons for asking it. He wondered if someone from the pervert's past had sought the ultimate form of revenge. It was definitely another angle to consider but Alexi wondered why, if that was the case, the person had waited for so long to procure the revenge in question. Perhaps, she reasoned, because they hadn't been able to find him, which in turn begged the question: how had they come across him in Lambourn? It all seemed highly implausible.

'He was married with two daughters: the epitome of the happy and respectable family unit,' Diana said scathingly. 'Proper little daddy's girls the daughters were but they were safe enough. Foreman preferred pubescent boys.'

Jack nodded and Alexi knew that he'd have Cassie find out what had happened to Foreman's relations.

'What are the chances of you and Foreman ending up on the same course, a course with only six places available on it?' Jack asked, his tone hard and business-like.

'You think I somehow knew he was on this course, so I beat all the competition and got accepted on it as well.' She made a scoffing sound at the back of her throat. 'Then, when he refused to see Sarah, I got the hump and strangled him.'

'Who told you he'd been strangled?' Jack asked.

'Everyone knows,' she replied off-handedly.

Alexi glanced at Jack, wondering if that was true. A lot of people *did* know, including Bill Naylor, and Alexi's delegates had spent the morning with him. They would have asked questions about Peter's death and chances are, Bill would have mouthed off about what he knew.

Diana seemed to be on firmer ground now. She was being deliberately evasive, confrontational... passive aggressive. Even so, Alexi agreed with her assessment of the situation. There was no possible way for her to have gotten herself on the course, just so that she could meet Peter again and compel him to recognise their daughter. If she had kept tabs on him and known he was on the course, she would have been better advised to have come down to Lambourn with Sarah, feigning an interest in a horse-owning syndicate or something equally plausible, and accidentally bumping into him.

It *had* to be a coincidence.

Unless Patrick had forced them together again for reasons of his own. She wouldn't put it past him.

'Look,' Diana said, leaning her forearms on the table and pushing her face towards Jack. 'I didn't kill John; I had absolutely no reason to. Was I upset because he didn't recognise me, and because he didn't want to know me once I'd told him who I was? You bet your life I was! He's the father of my child and, in case it's important, the only man I've ever been with. But he was damaged, badly damaged by what was done to him as a child, and nothing was ever going to change that. I expect it still gave him nightmares. As he himself put it the other night, his form of *normal* wasn't something he'd wish on his worst enemy.

'The argument I had with him that first night was about Sarah. I wanted them to meet, I felt it was important, more for his sake than hers. I wanted him to realise that something good had come out of our toxic past. Sarah is well-balanced, vibrant and... well, normal. No hang-ups or demons. I felt it would be good for him to know that and he actually said he'd think about it.' She breathed a deep sigh. 'Anyway, I don't expect you to take my word for it. I suppose I will have to tell the police about our ancient connection.'

'It would be best,' Jack said.

'Anyway, you know where I was that morning, Alexi, and Ranya will confirm it, so I couldn't have killed John.' She pushed herself to her feet. 'But now, if you'll excuse me, I need to see my daughter.'

'Of course.' Alexi smiled. 'Thanks for being so candid.'

'Can you tell me the name of the home where you grew up?' Jack asked.

'Like I could ever forget it.' She reeled off a name and address and Alexi made a note of it. 'It was shut down ten years ago and turned into flats. I'd be surprised if the occupants of those flats don't have nightmares caused by the bad vibes that haunt the place.'

'What do you think?' Alexi asked, the moment the door closed behind Diana.

'What I think is that she's one resentful woman.'

'If half of what she told us about her upbringing is true then I'd be more surprised if she wasn't.'

'Yeah, I hear you. And I think she did tell the truth about that about most things, but she was holding something back too.' Jack leaned back in his chair and crossed one foot over his opposite thigh. 'I still have trouble believing that the two of them finished up on your course through coincidence.'

'I'm with you on that one. But the only way it could have been done is if Patrick manipulated it, and that I can believe. I gave him a long list of possibles, and he whittled it down to twelve. We agreed on the final six between us.'

'Look up that list. See if Diana's name was on it.'

Alexi raised a brow. 'You think Patrick planted her name on that list and gave her the green light?'

'It's one possibility.'

Alexi reached for her phone and scrolled through her documents until she found the original list of applicants that she'd sent to Patrick. Jack looked over her shoulder and then at her when a thorough check failed to produce Diana's name.

'What the hell...' Alexi spread her hands in a gesture of helplessness, anger bubbling up inside her. 'Patrick's up to his grubby neck in this business, isn't he? He just won't take no for an answer.'

'Looks that way. He's obviously getting tired of waiting for you to come to your senses and is attempting to give you a push in the right direction.'

'Right now, I'd happily push him into the path of a string of galloping racehorses,' Alexi replied savagely. 'He is so arrogant, so conceited, so every damned thing!'

'And is insanely jealous and that jealousy is eating away at him. He can barely hide it whenever we're in the same room. He looks at me in a stupefied way, as though he can't see what the attraction is. He didn't think that a humble ex-copper would be sufficient stimulation for your quick brain and that you'd grow weary of me. I'm not part of your world, not sufficiently sophisticated. He assumed you'd get bored in the country and that our relationship wouldn't last. But it has and his jealousy has pushed him over the edge.'

Alexi harrumphed. 'Off a cliff, if I have any say in the matter.' She paused. 'I thought you would have been happy to be proven right about him.'

Jack smiled and shook his head. 'I'm not that shallow, darling.'

'What is it that you're not telling me?' she asked, canting her head and regarding him quizzically. 'You tried to say something before Diana joined us.'

'Ah. About that.' Jack rubbed his chin, clearly uncomfortable.

'Come on, out with it. It can't be that bad.'

'Actually,' he said, taking Alexi's hand and kissing the back of it in a courtly gesture, 'it's not good.'

Alexi said nothing, quelling her anxiety as she waited for him to get to the point. She had never seen him so unsure of himself before and that worried her more than whatever he was about to tell her possibly could. She loved this man, loved him absolutely, even though he still had his hang-ups about Patrick. She'd thought that she'd loved Patrick but now that she'd experienced the real thing, she knew that she never had.

Not really.

Not in the passionate, all-compassing way in which she loved Jack.

Jack's comment a few moments ago about not fitting into her world had been telling. He hid his insecurities well, far too well for her to have realised that he worried about not being her intellectual equal. That was utter tosh! His thought process was logical, often inspirational. Sometimes downright brilliant. They had different skills that combined to make them a formidable team when it came to problem solving.

'It's Cassie,' he eventually said, breaking the uneasy silence that she had permitted to stretch between them.

'Yes.' Alexi frowned as she tamped down the jealousy she felt at the mention of her nemesis's name. 'What about her?'

'I'm afraid you might have been right about her.'

'In what way?'

'She was in the kitchen when I arrived at the office this morning. She'd left her mobile on her desk. It rang and I noticed the number that flashed up on the screen.'

'No name? It wasn't one of her contacts?'

Jack shrugged. 'All I can tell you is that it's the same number that Foreman had in his notes.'

Alexi gasped. 'Patrick's burner?'

'Yep. You know me, I have a good memory for numbers, and it was definitely the same one.'

'What did you do about it? Did you tackle her?'

'No. I sat at my desk and pretended I hadn't seen it. I needed time to think about the implications.'

Alexi thought the implications were pretty obvious, even though she was as shocked as Jack. One or the other of them wanting to drive her out of Lambourn she could understand. But the two of them teaming up in a combined effort to make it happen? It made total sense.

And no sense whatsoever.

'By the time she came back to the office, the phone had stopped ringing. She checked the missed call log, looked furtive and glanced at me. But she said nothing and nor did I.'

'What the hell does this mean, Jack? Well, it's obvious what it means,' Alexi added, answering her own question.

'They both want you out of Lambourn, but would they go so far as to commit murder and then try to put your name in the frame?' Jack's response implied that they were thinking along the same lines. 'That's what I've been trying to decide.'

'We will have to talk to them,' Alexi said, feeling anger radiating from her core, despite the fact that on some levels, Cassie and Patrick teaming up didn't particularly surprise her. Both of them were tenacious when it came to getting what they wanted.

'Absolutely, but one of the reasons why I didn't speak to Cassie immediately is that I wanted to talk to you about it first. If I had tackled her, you can bet your life that she would have warned Vaughan, giving him time to come up with a plausible explanation. Always supposing they didn't prepare one earlier that is, just in case they were rumbled. Vaughan doesn't leave anything to chance.'

'Perhaps that's why Patrick called her. We'd spoken to him and he wanted to keep her in the loop.' Alexi suppressed a sigh, feeling bone weary, her brain sluggish when she needed to be at the top of her game. 'Did she return his call?'

'Not while I was there, obviously, but presumably, she did so as soon after I left. She asked questions about what progress we'd made but I didn't tell her anything. Apart from Foreman's call log, which presumably she'd already gone through herself and found nothing untoward other than calls from Vaughan's burner—'

'And we have to assume that Patrick's either told her that we know about it, or intended to do so when he rang her this morning.' Alexi took a moment to reflect. 'My money's on her already knowing. Patrick would have wanted to keep her up to speed.'

'Yeah, more than likely.' Jack leaned back in his chair, long legs splayed out in front of him, and momentarily closed his eyes. 'We know Vaughan didn't kill Foreman but there's nothing to say that he didn't pay someone else to do it.' He held up a hand to prevent Alexi from interrupting his train of thought. 'Why he'd do so when he'd sent Foreman down here for a specific reason is less obvious.'

'If he did,' Alexi said scowling. 'Personally, I don't believe a word that comes out of his conniving mouth. We now know that he got Diana on the course so that she could be reunited with her long-lost nearest-and-dearest but have absolutely no idea how he knew about her, or why he felt the need to play Cupid.'

'Vaughan is up to his grubby little neck in this business,' Jack replied. 'If Foreman was known to Vaughan, we'll gloss over how that situation came about for now. But if... say, Foreman did investigative work for him, then there's every chance that he'd tell Vaughan about his earlier life.'

'Why would he do that? Diana says he never talked about it.'

'A good point,' Jack conceded.

'I agree about him doing Patrick's leg work. He uses the most unlikely people to dig up intel for him on various stories. More time efficient than journalists, who get bogged down chasing their tails. And civilians blend in more easily. Reporters might as well have signs on their backs.'

'Not everyone wants their five minutes of fame.'

'True. Peter played his part to perfection on my course. None of us saw beyond the bluster, the know-it-all attitude, to say nothing of his flirting making me want to keep him at arm's length.'

'Thinking about your earlier point, Foreman probably didn't go into detail about his time in care. But if Vaughan already knew where he was brought up, his journalistic nose probably wanted to know why he changed his name. So I'm reckoning he could have found out more about the home, picked up on rumours of abuse that have probably surfaced and found out about the friendships he forged there by... I don't know, talking to others who were there at the time. He might even have found out about Peter's daughter.'

Alexi nodded. 'More than likely. Patrick has people like Cassie who can get into records buried deep in online storage. All highly unethical, but all papers are guilty of doing it.' She allowed a long pause before addressing the elephant in the room. 'And talking of Cassie...'

'Yeah, I know.' Jack picked up a pen and flipped it through his fingers. He did that a lot, Alexi had noticed: a subconscious gesture that he employed either when deep in thought or if he was worried about something. In this case, very likely both. 'Despite what we now know about her, I have trouble believing that she killed a man who outweighed her by fifty pounds simply to get you out of my life.'

'That's where we disagree,' Alexi replied. 'I share your doubts about her ability to murder but I do think there is little she wouldn't do to see the back of me. Do we know what Peter was injected with to make him unable to defend himself?'

'Not yet but Vickery reckons belladonna. Deadly nightshade to you and me.'

'It's used as a recreational drug, isn't it, but I've never heard of it being injected before.'

'Seems that it can be. Drug-users will always find a way to get their next high. Not that you get high on it, apparently. It's more likely to produce hallucinations—'

'Like LSD?'

Jack shrugged. 'You're asking the wrong person. One of the reasons Vickery thinks that's what could have been used is that Foreman's pupils were dilated and that's a classic sign, apparently.'

'Where the hell would the killer have got it from?'

Jack chuckled. 'You know better than to ask that question. Anything is available if you know where to look and can pay the price.'

'Right.' Alexi fixed Jack with a level look. 'Can you see Cassie thrusting a syringe into Peter's neck?'

'No,' he said without hesitation. 'But I do think that she and

Vaughan could have arranged the murder. I also think that her part was to get me there and point out that you'd just left.'

Alexi felt relief sweep through her system when Jack put into words her own suspicions. She had feared that he might jump to Cassie's defence and emphatically deny any involvement on her part. Had he done so then Patrick and Cassie would have got their wish because it *would* have driven a wedge between her and Jack. As it was, she smiled at the man she adored, thinking that she should have known better. This damned murder business was playing havoc with her judgement.

'Another murder and being under suspicion of committing it was supposed to be the straw that broke this particular camel's back,' she remarked, thinking it had come pretty damned close to doing so, and still very well might.

'If we're right then we have to imagine that Diana was brought in as a scapegoat,' Jack continued, 'in the event that suspicion focused on either of them.'

'Then again, Diana herself could have done it,' Alexi reasoned. 'We know that Peter and Diana didn't get on the course together by chance.'

'That did seem farfetched.'

'Such things do happen,' Alexi said. 'There are endless documented accounts of far more remarkable coincidences. For instance, I recall reading about a set of twins in America somewhere who were separated at birth and grew up without any knowledge of each other's existence. They were both named James on their adoptions, they both became police officers, and both of them married women named Linda.'

'Seriously?'

'Yep.' Alexi scrolled through her phone, reminding herself of the details. 'Each of them had a son,' she read aloud, 'one named James Allan and the other one named James Alan, and each also had a dog named Toy. Both brothers later got divorced, and both ended up remarrying women named Betty.' She put her phone aside and sent Jack a challenging look. 'Explain that one if you can.'

He smiled and shook his head. 'Obviously, I can't but I take your point. Something about the power of telepathy, I guess. Even so, I'm glad that wasn't the case here. We never could have sold it to Vickery. Juries like facts. Anyway, Foreman and Diana ended up on the same course by design. She was determined that he would finally accept his daughter, and her, into his life. I mean, she'd waited long enough and has never looked at another man. When he said no, she lost it and...'

'And planned such a complex murder in which I'm a suspect.' Alexi shook her head. 'She couldn't have done so on the spur of the moment but who's to say there hadn't been contact between them before they came on the course? We only have Diana's word for it that there had not been. Perhaps Peter wanted her to be here for some reason and asked Patrick to make it happen.'

'Then why ignore her?'

Alexi threw up her hands. 'How would I know? I'm just thinking out loud. But it's possible, don't you think?' She was aware how desperate she sounded. 'The one fact not in question is that Patrick got Diana onto the course.'

'Diana's name remains on the list of suspects,' Jack said, smiling. 'And we'll tell Vickery what Vaughan did, unbeknown to you. Let him explain that one,' he added, rubbing his hands together in gleeful anticipation.

'There is still an outside possibility that your fugitive did the deed,' Alexi said. 'We shouldn't discount his involvement. Perhaps Peter did somehow find him and discovered that he's hanging out with Amy. He could have threatened to tell Amy's husband where she was unless Franklin made it worth his while to keep schtum.'

She grimaced. 'Unlikely, I know, but so are all our other scenarios. And we know that Peter lacked empathy. It was driven out of him by the abuse he suffered as a child.'

Jack nodded. 'It's a well-known fact that a lot of abuse victim become emotionless, incapable of caring about anything or anyone other than themselves.'

'Yes, and by the sounds of things, Peter was a classic example. He was life and soul of the party in our group, but I bet he was a different animal in private, when his demons would come out to plague him.'

'Abused kids often grow into abusers,' Jack remarked. 'We are all products of our upbringings.'

'Is there any way of discovering if he was employed by the security services?' Alexi asked.

Jack shook his head. 'That's a job I would ordinarily pass to Cassie but I doubt if even she could hack into MI5 or MI6 without being caught. Anyway, I don't want her involved until we've spoken to her.'

'We *are* going to speak to her?' Alexi asked, her voice small, hesitant.

'Of course. But I suggest we get her and Vaughan here at the same time.' He grinned at Alexi. 'No colluding permitted beforehand.'

Alexi nodded. 'Take them by surprise?'

'Precisely.'

Cosmo looked up from the basket he shared with Toby and mewled, making them both smile. 'Don't worry, baby,' Alexi told her cat, 'we're not beaten yet.'

'I want to look into the governor of Foreman's care home too,' Jack said. 'A lot of time has passed and I know it's a long shot but perhaps one of the survivors in his family knows how to bear a grudge.'

'A growing list of possibilities and not an iota of proof to support any of them.' Alexi leaned her elbow on the table and rested the side of her face glumly on her clenched fist. 'It's hopeless.'

'Don't despair, darling. It's early days. Now then, give your friend Vaughan a call. Ask him to meet you in an hour. I'll do the same with Cassie and we'll see what they have to say for themselves when we confront them.'

14

Jack listened to Alexi's end of her call as she got through to Vaughan. God, how he hated the sound of the creep's name. If he was the cause of these latest problems for Alexi then Jack wouldn't be responsible for his actions. One thing he knew for sure was that he would move heaven and earth to find the killer, thereby removing any suggestion of a stain on Alexi's character. And then he would deal with Cassie. Their partnership would not survive her disloyalty and he would have to set up shop alone.

There was nothing else for it. He knew in his heart of hearts that he should have done it long ago.

'He's in Winchester again but he's on his way back,' Alexi said as she cut the connection, threw her phone on the table and sighed.

'Right, good.' Jack smiled at her. 'We'll get answers. Anyway, my turn.'

Before Jack could call Cassie, his phone rang and Cassie's name came up on the display. Jack shared a glance with Alexi, feeling slightly uneasy, and took the call.

'Cas, what is it?' he asked, putting the call on speaker. It was important that Alexi didn't think he was hiding anything from her

'Nothing new yet, I just wondered if any of those numbers I gave you from the victim's phone meant anything.'

Alexi covered her mouth with her hand, presumably to prevent a snort of disgust from being audible.

'Nothing definitive as yet.' Jack made a mental note to check through the numbers more thoroughly. What with Diana's revelations, it had clean gone out of his mind. 'Any chance you can pop over?'

'To Lambourn?' Jack could hear the surprise in her voice.

'No, to New York.' He winked at Alexi. 'Of course to Lambourn. I'm on my own right now. Alexi's off somewhere with her delegates and to be honest, I'm struggling to make sense of this mess. Two heads are better than one.'

'Sure, if you need me, I'll be there within the hour.'

'I know what you just did there, clever clogs,' Alexi said, grinning when Jack hung up and shaking a finger at him in mock disapproval.

'Oh yes, and what might that be?' He returned her smile as he leaned towards her and kissed her lips.

'You knew she wouldn't be able to resist coming over here to be with you *and* that she wouldn't feel tempted to warn Patrick about it because she doesn't suspect that you have ulterior motives.'

'Guilty as charged, madam. I *always* have ulterior motives.' He straightened up, aware that time was of the essence, and that he couldn't afford to waste any. 'Let's look through this list of numbers while we wait for our guests and see if anything jumps out at us.'

It didn't take long. Foreman had made remarkably few calls. One or two to his bank, several here to the hotel once he'd been accepted on the course and one to a solicitor. They rang the number, got sent round in circles and finally got connected to the man who'd worked for Foreman who wouldn't reveal anything about the nature of his business with the dead man.

'Pompous prat!' Jack said, hanging up.

'That's one for Vickery,' Alexi said, smiling at Jack's frustration.

'Good luck to him with that one. Client confidentiality, my arse. His client is dead.'

'There are daily calls to Patrick's burner,' Alexi said, wrinkling her nose as she returned her attention to the list.

'And a couple to this number.'

Jack dialled it and heard a familiar nasal voice answer. He hung up immediately, feeling a buzz of excitement.

'What?' Alexi asked.

'That was Dawson. Amy's husband,' Jack replied. 'I'll stake my reputation on it. That irritating whine has stuck in my memory.'

'So Peter was in touch with him.' Alexi threw her head back as she absorbed the implications of that development. 'I suppose it's safe to assume then that Peter knew who Amy was with and told her loving husband where to find her.'

'Possibly,' Jack agreed. 'Probably.'

'But why, if he was working for Patrick? He would have been on a good earner if he had run the country's most wanted criminal to ground. That would be worth gold to the paper and Peter could have named his price.'

'We'll ask Vaughan about that when he gets here but if I had to guess then I'd say that Foreman knew what he'd stumbled upon and decided to sell to the highest bidder.'

'How long did the two calls last for?' Alexi asked.

'The first was for over three minutes. The second, less than a minute.'

'I wonder what Dawson did with that information, always supposing that Peter told him who his wife was getting up close and personal with, without disclosing their location.'

'You're thinking that Dawson killed the messenger.'

'The blackmailer, more like.'

Jack shrugged. 'Anything's possible.' He ran a hand through his hair. 'The deeper we delve into this case, the weirder it gets. To be honest, I'm not sure what to think.'

'If Peter did tell Dawson what he'd found then he would have broken his agreement with Patrick. If Patrick found out, then we both know that he isn't a man to accept disloyalty lying down. That *would* give Patrick a reason to bump Peter off *and* use the opportunity to get me back where he presumes to think I belong.'

'Yeah, but suspecting it and proving it are two entirely different animals.' Jack yawned and stretched his arms above his head. 'That's something else we need to share with Vickery later today.'

'Will you and I speak with Dawson about his links to Peter?' Alexi asked. 'You said after we saw him before that he wasn't telling us everything. And Cosmo and I have learned to trust your instincts.' She blew her cat a kiss. 'Isn't that right, baby?'

Cosmo yawned and returned to his slumbers.

'Oh yes, we'll talk to him after we've seen Vaughan and Cassie. Unless they throw up any new leads for us to chase down, I rather think that will be our next port of call.'

'Game on,' Alexi muttered, when the door opened. Cosmo was instantly alert again and hissed like a snake with a sore head as Vaughan strolled into the room.

'Hey, where's the fire, Alexi?' he asked, totally ignoring Jack.

Up until now, they had maintained a superficial politeness, despite the fact that Vaughan despised Jack and the feeling was entirely mutual. But by so rudely ignoring him, Jack felt no pressing need to go easy on the guy.

'Have a seat,' Jack said in a neutral tone, making sure to keep his animosity under wraps, at least for now.

Vaughan sat down, as far away from Jack as the width of the table permitted.

'Have you found something out that I need to know about?' Vaughan asked, glancing at his watch. 'We're running out of time.'

The arrival of Cassie saved Jack from answering the question.

'Jack?' Cassie paused in the open doorway. She glanced at the three occupants of the room, ignored Cosmo's growls, and focused her attention on Jack. 'I thought you needed my help.'

She looked pale and anxious, as well she might. She was no fool and must realise that she'd been found out. She studiously ignored Alexi, took the seat beside Jack and plonked her phone on the table in front of her.

'Care to tell us what you two have been colluding about?' Alexi asked venomously. Cosmo, ever intuitive, jumped onto her lap, arched his back and gave another hiss for good measure. Alexi kept her attention focused on Vaughan and Cassie but soothed Cosmo with gentle sweeps of one hand. The cat settled but remained alert, his piercing gaze burning into Vaughan and clearly unsettling him.

'I don't know what you—'

Jack held up a hand. 'Don't insult our intelligence,' he said, anger radiating through his tone. 'We know.'

Predictably, it was Vaughan who responded. A man accustomed to calling the shots, he wasn't about to be intimidated. He did however frequently glance at Alexi, either attempting to gauge her mood or hoping that old loyalties would surface in his hour of need. That, Jack thought, would be a pretty hopeless aspiration, given that she and Jack had jointly called him and Cassie to account for their behaviour. But then again, he thought a lot of himself and hadn't given up hope of forcing Alexi back into his particular fold.

'Cassie and I met accidentally in Newbury a few months back,' he said with a casual flap of one wrist. 'There's no law against two concerned parties sharing their worries as far as I'm aware.'

Alexi blew air through her lips. Cosmo growled. 'How dare you!' she said quietly but with so much venom that Cassie shivered and visibly paled.

Cassie must realise now that she'd make a grave error of judgement, Jack thought. She had allowed Vaughan to persuade her to do his dirty work, and it probably hadn't taken much persuasion. Vaughan was a plausible bastard, but probably hadn't needed to be at his most creative when recruiting Cassie to his cause because she would go to pretty much any lengths to get Alexi out of Jack's life.

Jack hadn't wanted to face up to the fact before now. Had his prevarication cost a man his life and left Alexi hanging in the wind as a murder suspect? Jack swallowed, afraid that might very well be the case.

'I make no apology for trying to keep you safe, Alexi,' Vaughan said, his voice low, persuasive, his expression full of utter devotion as he fixed her with an imploring look. 'You haven't been in your right mind since leaving London.'

'You patronising bastard!' Jack muttered, growling at Vaughan in a manner that should have made Cosmo weep with envy.

Vaughan ignored Jack and kept his attention focused on Alexi. Incredibly, he seemed to think that he would be able to talk her round, even now, after his grimy machinations had come to light and he couldn't justify them. The man's arrogance was truly stunning. 'Cassie knew it too,' he said, 'and in your heart of hearts, I think you do too. You're just being stubborn, but you've made your point. I didn't take your feelings into consideration, allowed the pressures of my position to make me forget what's really important in life, but I've seen the error of my ways and—'

'Stop it, Patrick. Just stop it!' Alexi let out a bitter little laugh. 'You're making a fool of yourself.'

'You should listen to him,' Cassie said. 'He means what he says.'

Alexi swung round to face her. 'You want rid of me so that you can get your claws into Jack. You knew that, Patrick,' she added, keeping her attention focused on Cassie, who couldn't look at her. 'You played upon her partiality for him and her dislike of me. Did you really think it would work?'

'I don't dislike you, Alexi,' Cassie said, lifting her chin in a defiant manner, 'but I do think you're wrong for Jack and that your skills are wasted here in Lambourn. I've heard the whispers in the village about you being bad luck.' Cassie waved a hand in the air. 'I know it's ridiculous but there *have* now been four murders in the area since you arrived and even you must admit that's odd. I can understand why people are suspicious about you.'

'Finished dissecting my life?' Alexi asked scathingly.

'Let's cut the bullshit, Cassie.' Jack's voice was harsh and uncompromising. Cassie visibly flinched and two spots of colour appeared high on her otherwise white cheekbones. 'We'll talk about this later but if there's any way out of this for our business partnership, which I somehow doubt, then you need to level with me.'

Cassie swallowed. 'What do you need to know?' she asked in a small voice.

'Why did you ask me to go to the Swan on the morning of the murder?'

'You know why.'

'I know what you told me, but I have no idea if it was the truth. I trusted you but feel as though I no longer know you.'

'Of course it was the truth.' Cassie puffed out her chest, but Jack's scathing look caused her to slump back in her chair again, her defiance fleeting. 'Amy's card was used there. I can show you if you don't believe me.'

'You could have checked it out yourself or simply told me and I would have but you wanted me there at that particular time for a reason. You knew Alexi would be there because you hacked into her phone and saw her diary.'

Cassie swelled up again, clearly about to protest her innocence. She glanced at Patrick, who studiously avoided catching her eye. Jack wasn't surprised that he'd be willing to push her under the bus. 'Yeah, but only because he asked me to.' She jerked a thumb in Vaughan's direction.

'Why?' Alexi asked, addressing the question to Vaughan. 'No, don't bother to answer that. I wouldn't believe a word of it even if you did.'

'Tell us why you got Diana Horton on the course,' Jack said to him in a deliberately abrupt change of subject. As Jack hoped would be the case, the question caught Vaughan completely off guard. He clearly hadn't realised that they were on to him in that respect and that gave Jack the edge.

'Come again.' Vaughan spread his hands. 'I don't know what...'

'Even now, you still have to lie.' Alexi shook her head, disgust forming the bedrock of her expression. 'We know what you did, Patrick. Did you really think that we're too dense to have found out? What we would like to know is why. You can either tell us or tell Vickery. Your choice.'

Vaughan took a very deep breath and fell silent. Jack knew he would be trying to decide how little he could get away with revealing. It must be obvious by now, even to a man with his disgusting level of self-assurance, that Alexi wouldn't be swayed by his coercive charm so he would have switched to self-preservation mode. And, unless Jack had misread him, he'd also find ways to blame Alexi for forcing him into doing what he'd done in an effort to make her doubt herself.

Narcissists seldom took responsibility for their own actions.

'Foreman has been working for me off the books for a couple of years now. He was a civilian researcher for GLAA. The Gangmasters and Labour Abuse Authority,' he explained, when blank faces stared back at him. 'It's an organisation that comes under the remit of the Home Office. They chase down traffickers and organised crime centred around those activities.'

Jack glanced at Alexi, who nodded. They were both thinking that setting an abusee to catch an abuser would be akin to letting a fox loose in a hen house.

'So how come he ended up doing your sleuthing for you?' Alexi asked, her tone of voice cold, distant.

'He got kicked out. He was a desk jockey, quite good with computers and chasing down leads. But he took matters into his own hands one day. Went after a particularly abusive gangmaster who'd trafficked young boys into the country. Blew a whole year's operation by revealing the government's hand too soon. The trafficker scarpered, the investigation collapsed at considerable cost to the taxpayer, and it was decided that Foreman was surplus to requirements.'

'How come you linked up with him?' Jack asked.

Vaughan shrugged. 'I have eyes and ears everywhere. I did my research on Foreman when I heard whispers about the collapsed case and discovered that he had a high IQ, no family commitments and a fierce desire to right a few of the world's wrongs. Idealistic is the word I'd used. Anyway, my research into his background sent up red flags.'

'Hang on a minute,' Alexi said, frowning. 'Wouldn't the Home Office have done vigorous checks of their own before employing him? They would have found out what you did so why take him on?'

'I asked him that question. He told them he'd changed his identity when he left the care home because of the horrendous things that had happened to him there. You know about that, I assume.'

'We know,' Jack replied, answering for them both.

'Foreman wanted to put the past behind him and make a fresh start.'

'But he couldn't leave it behind, not completely,' Alexi said softly. 'They shouldn't have put him in a department that would agitate his demons. What the hell were they thinking?'

'I don't suppose they cared much about the state of his mental health,' Vaughan replied. 'They just wanted a person who was motivated, willing to put in the hours and get results.'

Alexi rolled her eyes. 'Yeah, that sounds about right,' she said.

'But Foreman went off plan, the government could no longer control him and so they set him loose.' Jack knew the feeling. The Met had used him as a scapegoat to avoid adverse publicity. 'You found a use for him though, Vaughan. Tell us more.'

'I recognise damaged goods when I see them. I got curious about the home where he was raised, unearthed a few buried complaints about the treatment of the inmates and knew I was on to a story. The latest care scandal in which vulnerable kids had been used in the worst possible way, and yet no one did anything about it. It could have been a massive exposé.' Vaughan glanced intently at Alexi as he spoke, clearly assuming that her journalistic traits would overcome her disappointment in him personally. 'I found out that the principal had been murdered and that Foreman had adopted his name. I knew I was on to something and so tracked down Diana, who told me about her daughter.'

Vaughan paused, presumably to assimilate his thoughts. But Jack sensed that he had told them the complete truth, at least so far. 'Diana could have blown the lid off the entire scandal,' he pointed out.

'It was a calculated risk,' Vaughan replied.

'But Diana was unwilling to talk,' Alexi said, apparently drawn into Vaughan's account despite her reservations about his tactics.

'Oh, she'd talk all right. She'd wanted to for years. But she wasn't willing to do so without seeing Foreman first. She wanted him to meet his daughter. She felt that would help him and he then might agree to talk on record about what happened to him. The precise nature of the abuse he suffered. I wanted him to name names so that I could go after any of the perverts still living. Name and shame in other words.'

Alexi shook her head. 'He never would have agreed to it. Not if he really did kill his abuser.'

'It was worth a try. Diana said he'd probably blank her if she turned up on his doorstep unannounced. She needed to meet him accidentally in a situation that he couldn't walk away from. This was at about the time you mooted the idea of the course to me, Alexi, which just so happened to coincide with a possible sighting of Franklin in this area. That gave me a plausible reason to get Foreman to apply for a place on the course.' He spread his hands. 'And the rest you know.'

Jack believed him but that didn't mean he had to like it. 'So, who killed him?' he asked in a challenging tone. 'Presumably, you have a theory.'

'Actually, I don't have a clue. Unless Franklin really is in the area and got pissed off with Foreman's persistent questions. For the record, I never believed for a moment that he was hiding out here. If he's got a lick of sense, he'll have left the country long since and will be sipping cocktails on a beach somewhere, amused by accounts of the search that's being conducted.'

'Why should we believe that the two of you didn't arrange the murder and set Alexi up as a suspect?' Jack asked.

'Do you honestly think I'd do that?' Vaughan addressed the question to Alexi, who didn't deign to answer it.

'I can see how it must look,' Cassie said morosely, studying her fingernails, 'but it didn't happen that way. Delve all you like, you won't find any evidence because there's none to find.'

'Okay,' Jack replied with a weary sigh, acutely aware of the tension in the room. 'We'll leave it there for now, but you will have to talk to Vickery,' he added, sending Vaughan a hard look. 'Best coming from you.'

Vaughan gave a curt nod. 'I hear you.' He turned his attention to Alexi. 'We need to talk.'

'Nothing to say to you, Patrick. You've invaded my privacy and hurt me in ways that I didn't think even you would be capable of. I won't be submitting any further pieces for publication in the *Sentinel*. The trust is gone.'

Vaughan looked set to argue, glanced at Jack and stood up. Cosmo arched his back and bared his teeth. 'I'll give you some space. For now. We still have tonight's gala to get through.'

He nodded to Cassie and left the room.

'We need to talk too, Jack,' she said, glaring at Alexi as though willing her to leave the room.

'When this is over,' he said. 'In the meantime, I suggest you get back to the office.'

She opened her mouth and then closed it again with no sound emerging. There were tears in her eyes as she turned for the door.

'Well,' Alexi said, stretching her arms above her head, looking tired and disillusioned. 'That went well.'

Jack smiled at her. 'At least we now know a lot more about Foreman's background. I think it's safe to assume that no shadowy figure from our security services bumped him off. His position wasn't important enough.'

'True, but we still don't know who did the deed.'

'Have patience, darling. We need to talk to Diana again and get her to confirm what Vaughan just told us. I wonder why she didn't volunteer the information.'

'She would have signed an NDA, I expect,' Alexi replied. 'Patrick's big on secrecy. Peter would have signed one too but if we're right about his lack of morals then that wouldn't have stopped him going to Dawson with what he knew.'

'Right.' Jack stood up, ignored Cosmo's protest when he lifted him from Alexi's lap and pulled her into his arms. 'Go and root Diana out, sweetheart. Let's talk to her now. Immediately. Time's running out.'

15

Alexi let out a long breath as she wriggled out of Jack's arms, wishing she could remain cocooned in them for the next ten years. Or at least until this horrible business went away. But she was a pragmatist and believed in helping herself. She still felt shellshocked by the lengths that Patrick and Cassie had been prepared to go to in their attempt to separate her from Jack but saw little point in dwelling upon their duplicity. Their clumsy plot had backfired on them, and they must both now realise that they'd only succeeded in driving her and Jack closer.

She ran up the stairs to Sarah's room, hoping to find mother and daughter there together, feeling a great deal of sympathy for Peter Foreman. After his start in life, he really hadn't stood a chance. With the possible exception of Diana, no one had cared about him, unless he could be useful to them. Patrick excelled at exploiting people's weaknesses for the sake of breaking journalistic new ground and not so long ago, Alexi wouldn't have batted an eyelid at his tactics.

It seemed that she'd gotten out of the newspaper business at the right time, before she became hardened to the industry's lack of morality. Patrick's behaviour was typical, but she knew that Jack wouldn't have expected Cassie to get dragged down to his level. Their situation was now untenable; Jack couldn't stand disloyalty and Alexi couldn't see their partnership surviving the fallout.

Another reason to feel guilty.

Her relationship with Jack was definitely worth fighting for, so fight for it she would. She'd just publicly told Patrick to take a hike and had meant every word of it. He had crossed a line and she wanted no further contact with him. Jack would take the same tack with Cassie, even if Alexi told him after the dust had settled that there was no need. They worked well together and had spent a lot of time building up their agency's reputation. They needed one another, Alexi was secure in Jack's affections and hopefully, Cassie would now realise that her pursuit of him was a lost cause.

Anything was possible.

She paused outside of Sarah's room and could hear voices coming from within. Glad that Diana was still there and that she wouldn't have to haul her out of the annex in front of her other delegates, Alexi tapped at the door. Sarah answered and flashed a smile that appeared strained.

'Alexi,' she said, opening the door wider. 'Come in.'

Diana looked up from her chair in front of the window. 'Something else you need from us?' she asked in a defensive tone.

'A moment of your time please, Diana. Downstairs. There have been developments that you need to be aware of.'

'Do you know who killed my father?' There was something touching about Sarah's degree of anxiety over a man whom she had never met. A man who had fathered her whilst still a boy himself but reneged on his responsibilities as an adult.

'No, sorry, Sarah. We don't know. Not yet. But I hope we'll get to the bottom of things very soon.'

Diana looked disgruntled by the summons and set to argue

the point but something about Alexi's intransigent stance clearly made her reassess her options. With an irritated sigh, Diana pushed herself to her feet and smiled at her daughter. 'I'll see you again at the dinner,' she said.

'Sure,' Sarah replied, turning her attention to her laptop.

As they walked down the stairs together, Alexi waited for Diana to ask what this was all about. It seemed odd, not to say suspicious, that they reached the door to Cheryl's kitchen without Diana opening her mouth. Alexi hoped that Patrick hadn't called to forewarn her. She suspected not. When the going got tough, Patrick tended to put his own interests first and leave others to fend for themselves, much as he'd done with Cassie earlier.

'Diana.' Jack nodded as she entered the kitchen. Cosmo gave a guttural yowl of disapproval and stalked over to Alexi, tail aloft, wrapping himself around her legs as though protecting her from an imminent attack. 'Take a seat,' Jack added, ignoring Cosmo's theatrics but probably taking note of them. He had yet to admit it to Alexi, but he had long since come to trust Cosmo's character assessment.

Alexi tended to agree with her cat insofar as Diana was concerned. She felt great sympathy for the rocky start she'd had in life. She'd been lonely, confused and neglected as a child but at least she hadn't suffered the additional trauma of abuse. For that reason, Alexi tried to overlook Diana's hard edge and no-nonsense attitude but still found it hard to warm to the woman.

'What can I do for you?' Diana asked, hissing back at Cosmo as she took a seat and folded beefy arms across her torso in a defensive gesture.

'We've just had a frank exchange of views with Patrick Vaughan,' Jack said, matching her brisk tone. 'That being the case, perhaps you'd like to rethink what you told us about your reasons for being on this course.'

'I don't believe you actually asked me why I was here,' she shot back.

Jack thumped his clenched fist on the surface of the table, rattling the coffee mugs resting on it. 'A man's dead, Diana. A man you claim never to have stopped loving. A man who fathered your child. Now isn't the time for semantics.'

'Okay.' She held her hands up in a defensive gesture. 'Believe it or not, I do have my pride. Pride was about the only thing that got me through my childhood in that hellhole. I didn't want to admit the lengths I was prepared to go to in order to re-establish contact with John. Okay? Happy now?'

'It's not a case of one-upmanship,' Alexi said quietly. 'None of us are above suspicion until we resolve this matter.'

'Well then, you probably know that someone representing Patrick Vaughan got in touch with me about Parkside, the home where we grew up. The paper had gotten hold of complaints that had been lodged at the time and then swept under the carpet. I was very happy to talk to them about the general neglect. Not Vaughan at first but one of his underlings. They must have cottoned on to the fact that there was more to the story than I was willing to admit because the big man swept in, all charm and cheque book if you get my drift.'

Alexi nodded. She did, only too well. 'Go on.'

'He asked me straight away about John. I said he'd been my particular friend and that he'd suffered more than I had but that they would need to track him down if they wanted names and details.'

'Did you tell them about Sarah?'

'Not immediately, no. I hadn't told Sarah much about her father and didn't want her finding out all the lurid details in sensational headlines over her Sunday morning cornflakes.'

'You weren't aware that Vaughan was in contact with John long before he latched on to you?' Jack asked.

Diana's body jerked forward so fast that her chair wobbled. 'No, I was not.' She rolled her eyes and let out a long breath as a slow burn of anger crept up her cheeks.

'Patrick knew that John was the key to a sensational story,' Alexi said speculatively, 'but John, or Peter as we knew him, wasn't willing to dredge up a past that he'd done his best to bury. Besides, if he did kill his main tormentor, the last thing he would want was questions being raised about his death. It wouldn't take the brain of a rocket scientist to figure out who did it, even if it couldn't be proven. Anyway, I'm guessing that Patrick found out about Sarah, did the arithmetic and guessed who her father must be.'

Diana nodded. 'That's about the size of it. Vaughan offered me a large sum of money, more money than I've ever seen in one go before. This isn't about money though; that's what I couldn't make him understand. I raised Sarah on my own and never took a penny from the state.' She lifted her chin defiantly. 'But it was a struggle, I won't deny it. I had to go without in order to ensure that she didn't, and it would be lovely for once in my life not to have financial constraints.' She tapped the fingers of one hand on the arm of her chair, her expression distant. 'The payout would be for my recollections of my time in that prison and on condition that I persuaded John to name names. Of course, the only way I stood an earthly chance of achieving that ambition was to see him face to face.'

'So Patrick suggested my course,' Alexi said.

'He did, and I jumped at the opportunity. I'll confess that seeing John again took priority over a cash payout but... let's just say that the reality didn't live up to my expectations. Not only did he not recognise me, but he also didn't want to know about Sarah once I'd pointed out to him who I was.'

'I'm sorry,' Alexi said, reaching across the table to touch Diana's hand. 'That must have been hard to take.'

'It wasn't my finest hour. All those years of wondering, hoping, and for what? I lost it with him but not to the extent that I tracked him down and killed him the next day.'

'You saw your windfall going up in smoke,' Jack said.

Diana shrugged. 'What you've never had you don't miss. Frankly, I was more concerned about John, angry as I was with him. I don't know if he killed Foreman or not. What I do know, what I could tell from that one conversation I had alone with him, is that he still had a ton of suppressed anger simmering away just beneath the surface. I recognised the signs when I joined the course, and he came across as the life and soul of the party. It was all an act though and in private I'd bet what little I have in the bank that he went into real downers.'

'Did Patrick ask you to sign an NDA?' Alexi asked.

'Yes, which is why I didn't tell you any of this. But he obviously has so he's the one to have broken the agreement, not me.'

'Okay, Diana,' Jack said. 'Thanks for clearing that point up. We'll let you get on now. But you'd best tell the inspector this when he talks to you again, which he will. It could be relevant.'

'I don't see how,' she replied grumpily.

'Think about it,' Alexi said. 'If the *Sentinel*'s reporters have tracked other abuse victims down, they may want to let sleeping dogs lie too. It could have been one of them who killed the original Foreman, not your John. And if, say, they got wind of the fact from said reporters that John had been found and was willing to spill the beans, well... draw your own conclusions.'

'It could be that one of the abusers was contacted for a comment, panicked and permanently shut the man up who could see them jailed,' Jack reasoned.

'Point taken,' Diana said, hissing at Cosmo before the cat could get in first and leaving the room.

'That was a valid suggestion, about one of the abusers perhaps having taken Peter out,' Alexi said pensively, 'but unlikely. I don't think Patrick's reporter would have shown his hand before he had all the facts straight. That would give any surviving guilty parties time to construct a defence, or hide behind his lawyers, and that's not the way the press works. They like to sandbag people, even the *Sentinel*, that used to be above such tactics. But since I left the paper, it's all about sensationalism nowadays. Besides, I doubt if Peter named names. The one thing everyone seems to agree on is that he refused to talk about that episode of his life. Of course, someone else may have but it's a long shot, Jack.'

'I know, darling, but I wanted to put it out there. I feel sorry for Diana but still don't entirely trust her version of events. Only she and Foreman actually know what was said between them when they met here. Anyway, I wanted her to know that not everything is about her.'

Alexi inhaled sharply, filling her lungs with air and letting it out slowly. 'So, what now?' she asked.

'Now we tackle Dawson again.'

'What a fun life we lead.'

'Yeah, I hear you.'

'I don't mind going to see him but can't help wondering if it would be the best use of our time. What possible reason could he have to kill Peter?'

'Who knows?' Jack shrugged. 'That's the whole point of asking questions. We know that he lied to us, albeit by omission, by not telling us that he'd spoken to Foreman twice on the phone.'

'I guess.'

Jack's phone rang. 'Cassie,' he said, glancing at the display.

'Take it, Jack,' Alexi said when she sensed that Jack was about to decline the call. 'She might have something for us.'

Jack nodded and accepted the call. 'Yeah,' he said curtly.

'I thought you'd like to know that I've tracked down one of Peter Foreman's daughters,' Cassie said. 'The late unlamented Foreman as opposed to the murder victim.'

The call was on speaker and Jack glanced at Alexi. 'Where is she?' he asked.

'Her name is Sally. She never married and I've found an address for her in Winchester. I'll text it to you.'

'Thanks,' Jack said, cutting the call.

A few seconds later, Jack's phone pinged to indicate an incoming text. They glanced at the screen together as an image of Sally Foreman slowly took shape on the phone.

'I know her!' Alexi gasped. 'That's the woman we spoke to at the Swan.' Alexi bounced on the edge of her seat. 'She works there. She *has* to be connected to this mess, Jack, she just has to be.'

Jack felt that familiar buzz of adrenaline that he got when there was a significant break in a difficult case. He smiled at Alexi, delighted to see her energised now that they were finally getting somewhere.

'We'd best go to the Swan then,' he said, 'and see if she's on shift.'

Cosmo, seeming to catch on to the excitement, beat them both to the door and clearly had no intention of being left behind.

Jack drove swiftly towards their destination. Alexi had fallen silent and Jack saw no reason to interrupt her thoughts with idle speculation. He didn't remember much about the woman they were hoping to see and was even less sure what her role in the affair could have been. If she'd recognised Foreman and thought he'd killed her father that would give her a motive, but it all came back to a female's ability to strangle a grown man who was taller and a lot heavier than her.

And more to the point, his willingness to permit it.

They knew he'd been drugged but the chances of Sally just happening to have a syringe full of whatever incapacitated Foreman about her person when he called at the Swan were next to impossible.

'Ready?' Jack asked as they pulled into the pub's car park. Alexi looked pale but resolute, her earlier excitement having given way to a stern determination to get some answers.

'Absolutely,' she replied, leaving the car almost before the wheels had stopped turning.

'You're on guard duty,' Jack told Cosmo, cracking a window open for the cat's benefit.

The rain had been heavy again and they were obliged to dodge deep, muddy puddles as they made their way towards reception. For once, luck appeared to be on their side. They entered the foyer and the first person they saw was the one they'd come in the hope of tracking down. Sally's professional smile gave way to a resigned sigh of recognition.

'You again,' she said.

'Yeah, we need a word.'

'I'm working.'

'Well, Ms Foreman,' Jack said, with heavy emphasis on her surname, 'if you'd prefer for the police to come and talk to you then that's fine by us.' Jack glanced around. The lunchtime rush was over, and the place was almost empty. 'Is there somewhere we can chat in private?'

She seemed wary yet resigned. 'Just a minute.'

She walked away, had a quick word with the other woman on

duty and returned to them.

'This way.' She led them into a small staffroom off the bar area. 'Okay, what can I do for you?' she asked, perching her backside against a pile of wine cases as she pulled her phone from her pocket and glanced at the screen.

'You recognised the murder victim,' Jack said without preamble. 'Did you tell the police that he was known to you?'

'Known. How could I have known him? I was a kid when he was at Parkside.'

'By mentioning Parkside, you've just admitted that you did know him. And you must also have recognised the name he'd adopted.' Jack allowed a significant pause. 'Your late father's name.'

'Yeah, of course I did. The first time he breezed in here, a man of the world who seemed to think that charm would get him whatever he wanted. He told me his name and started asking questions about the Franklin sighting.'

'You say you knew him,' Alexi replied, 'but you also say you were very young at the time. He'd changed his name and is obviously a lot older. He was still a kid when you knew him so how did you recognise him?'

'He used to be kind to my sister and me. He had a way about him, even as a child. There was a heavy weight of sadness bearing him down.' She stared into the distance, clearly attempting to articulate her thoughts. 'Most of the kids in the home were like that. Well, they would be because they didn't have parents, or anyone else in their lives who gave a toss whether they lived or died. It must have been hard. But I do remember John making this massive attempt to overcome his feelings. That was unusual enough to stick in my mind, young as I was at the time. John was five years older than me but far too worldly for his age. Kids who grow up in care tend to wise up fast.'

'Did you confront him when he showed up here?'

'Of course I did but he denied being the John Bishop that I remembered. He was good at putting up a pretence and I would have believed that I'd made a mistake, but for the fact that his shocked expression momentarily gave him away. He got his features back under control so quickly that I might have imagined it, but I remembered that he had a distinctive mole on the side of his neck. No idea why it stuck in my mind, but my eye was drawn to it and I knew I was right.'

'Okay,' Jack said, believing her, at least insofar as things had gone. She had been open and honest, but the recollections hurt her. It was obvious that even she didn't have fond memories of the home that her late father had been responsible for. 'Do you think he killed your father?' he asked.

Jack expected an explosion, tears, ranting and recriminations. What he didn't expect was a casual shrug. 'Him or any one of the others. Take your pick. If I had to hazard a guess though, my money would be on John because he took Dad's name and because he was one of Dad's favourites.'

Alexi and Jack exchanged a glance. 'You knew about the abuse?'

'Not at the time, obviously, but since I've been old enough to understand these things, I remember the rumours, the tension. Looking back, I remember Dad having important men attending parties and pieced things together in my mind. Mum was having none of it when I tried to broach the subject with her, after Dad's death. She was very good at burying her head when he was still alive. Not that I blame her for that. My father was a sadistic bastard! There, I've said it,' she added defiantly. 'He didn't abuse my sister or me in the way that I suspect he did John and the others, but he was a firm believer in corporal punishment. Got off on it, I've subsequently thought. Our household was run like a military regime. Mum was petrified of putting a foot wrong. Now, if that's how he treated his own family, only imagine how much worse it would have been for the unfortunate kids in his care, who had no one to protect their interests.'

'You didn't mourn your father's death?' Alexi asked.

Sally grinned. 'My sister and I had a party. And now, years on, meeting John again, it seemed like fate. I wanted to shake his hand for doing us all a massive favour. Or would have, if he'd admitted to his identity. I wouldn't have wanted him to confess to killing Dad or to anything that might incriminate him, though.'

Jack nodded. 'A bit of a coincidence, you working here and him turning up.'

She shrugged. 'Stranger things happen every day.'

Jack thought of Alexi's story about the twins separated at birth and nodded. 'Fair enough.'

'Why do you work here?' Alexi asked. 'We found an address for you in Southampton.'

'If you'd dug a little deeper, you'd have found out that I've let my flat. I'm in a relationship with a guy in Lambourn and live at his now.'

'Okay.' Jack glanced at Alexi, who shook her head. Out of questions, they both stood. 'Thanks for your time, Sally, and for being so candid.'

'Not a problem. I'm really sorry that John was killed so brutally and trust me, if I had the first idea who did it then I would have told the police. I've thought about it a dozen times since it happened, but I can't think of a single person who seemed out of place, or furtive, or whatever it is that murderers are supposed to look like. We get all sorts in here and it's impossible to keep track of everyone.' She led the way from the room, smiling. 'Punters all look the same after a while.'

16

'Phew!' Alexi puffed out her cheeks. 'What did you make of that?' she asked as she and Jack puddle-dodged back to his car through a fresh downpour. Cosmo opened one eye, through which he regarded them with stoic indifference – his way of sulking when he was left behind – and returned to his slumbers.

'I don't think we can rule her out as a suspect,' Jack replied.

'Even though she hated her father?'

'She *says* she did, but people have been known to lie about such things, believe it or not. Foreman went to the Swan more than once. She recognised him, had time to concoct her revenge and took her opportunity?'

'If she did, we'll never be able to prove it.'

Jack started the engine. 'Nah, probably not but if nothing else, it's another avenue for Vickery to explore. Another person with potentially a genuine reason for wanting Foreman dead. Sally might not have grieved for her father, but I got the impression that her mother would have been devastated and has probably never gotten over her loss. Women who marry bullies are the type who make excuses for them and assume that if they're on the receiving end of a backhander, they did something to deserve it. The men in question can do no wrong in their eyes and are loved unconditionally by their wives.'

'So you're suggesting that Sally could have avenged her father's death because of what it did to her mother?' Alexi shook her head. 'I don't buy it. I mean, even if that was her motive, she could hardly tell her mother that her father's murderer had met his comeuppance, could she now?'

'It's more probable than you having knocked him off, darling,' Jack said, smiling at her as he indicated left, waited for a white van to pass and then pulled out onto the road, his windscreen wipes struggling to cope with the deluge.

Alexi knew that he was actively attempting to create doubt about her involvement by digging up alternative suspects with genuine motives. She appreciated the effort but would prefer to find the actual killer, to say nothing of unearthing some solid proof. A confession would be even better.

A girl could dream.

'What next?' Alexi asked. 'Actually,' she added, glancing at her watch and answering her own question. 'I have to see my delegates, take a look at their submissions and then get ready for the gala. Time's got away from us.'

'No problem,' Jack replied. 'I've got some stuff to do, then I'll join you.' He paused. 'It will be interesting to see what Vaughan does now to try and redeem himself in your eyes.'

Alexi snorted. 'Too late. That ship has well and truly sailed.'

'I know that, but he's too arrogant to take no for an answer and probably thinks that there's still a way back for him.'

'I could ask you the same question. About Cassie.'

Jack scowled as he shook his head. 'The trust is gone,' he said. 'I can't work with her any more.'

'I understand how betrayed you must feel. Even so, don't rush into decisions when feelings are still running high. Let the dust settle first, or at the very least, leave things until after we've dealt with this case, no matter what the outcome.'

'She tried to separate us,' Jack replied, grinding his jaw. 'She crossed a line, and I don't think I can get past that.'

'We both know she was manipulated by the hand of a master. Patrick would have found out about her obsession with you and played on it.' Alexi waved a hand in the air. 'She's never hidden the fact that she wants you and hates me, but she never would have done anything about it if Patrick hadn't latched onto her.'

Jack took his eyes off the road and glanced at her. 'I can't believe you're defending her.'

Alexi smiled. 'I know how Patrick operates. Once he gets an idea into his head, stopping him going through with it would be like trying to hold back a tidal wave. Cassie didn't stand a chance, especially because she'd convinced herself that I'm bad for you and that she was saving you from yourself.'

Jack took one hand off the wheel and waved it in the air. 'I still don't see—'

'No, and that's because you feel hurt and betrayed and it's too early for you to think rationally about the situation. Bear in mind though that you and she have built up a solid reputation and are turning work away. It would be a shame to break it up and start over. Besides, Cassie's had her fingers burned and probably knows that she's driven us closer together as a consequence.' Alexi touched his knee. 'She'd rather have you in her life as a friend than not have you at all.'

'You are a wise woman, Ms Ellis.'

Alexi grinned. 'You have no idea, Mr Maddox.'

They pulled into Hopgood Hall's car park and dashed through the rain into the kitchen, preceded by Cosmo. Drew and Cheryl were both there, providing Alexi with an opportunity to update them on developments. She said a silent prayer of thanks for two such loyal friends. She was indirectly responsible for this latest disruption to their business, and they had yet to issue a single word of censure.

'Blimey!' Drew scratched his head when Alexi ran out of words. 'What a tangled web and all that.'

'My money's on Diana being the culprit,' Cheryl said. 'There's a lot of suppressed anger in that one. Never underestimate the patience of a woman scorned. I mean, she's carried a torch for Peter all these years, and never looked at another man. Then, when they finally meet again, he not only doesn't recognise her but doesn't want to know her or his daughter when she tells him who she is. I'd be pretty miffed, to put it mildly.'

'My clever wife makes a good point,' Drew said. 'Diana has both anger issues and the physical strength to do the deed.'

'But for the fact that she has a rock-solid alibi,' Jack pointed out.

'Yeah well, I'm working on that part of my theory,' Cheryl said.

'At least you can rule out shadowy government assassins,' Drew pointed out. 'It doesn't sound as though Foreman's work tracking down gangmasters would have put a target on his back. Especially if he didn't work in the field.'

'You've been watching too much James Bond,' Cheryl said, punching her husband's arm. 'What do you know about field work?'

'Could Patrick have arranged it, Alexi?' Drew asked, his expression sobering. 'I don't trust the bastard, especially when it comes to you.'

Jack offered Drew a high five. 'We're agreed on that one and I haven't ruled out the possibility of his involvement,' Jack said, glancing at Alexi, who didn't respond.

'I need to get across to the annex,' she said. 'I've been neglecting my flock.'

'Don't worry about the dinner,' Cheryl said. 'Marcel is pulling out all the stops for you.'

Alexi gave her friend a little wave and left the kitchen. Cosmo growled when he wasn't permitted to follow her.

She took a deep breath before entering the annex, aware that she would have to behave as though everything was normal and that she wasn't facing the possibility of being branded a murderer. Despite her friends' best efforts to raise the possibility of others being culpable, as they had just done in Cheryl's kitchen, the fact remained that she'd been on the spot at the time of Peter's murder and was heard arguing with him. Powerful stuff, but for the fact that she had absolutely no motive.

Motives could be dreamed up, though. She'd made a lot of money writing about a couple of the murders that had already gone down in Lambourn, a source of income to replace her previous career on the *Sentinel*. The local populace's suspicions about her would add fuel to the fire of an ambitious detective, keen to get a good result. For that reason, she was thankful that Vickery was in charge of the case. He knew her, didn't listen to local speculation, was fair-minded and preferred to have solid evidence before making an arrest.

Even so, Alexi was worried about her future here in Lambourn. Even if the real murderer could be found, her situation could well become untenable in such a close-knit community. Polly Pearson, her nemesis, would make sure of that.

The conversation stopped and everyone turned to look at Alexi when she entered the communal lounge.

'Hi,' she said brightly. 'Sorry to have kept you.'

'Any news?' Grace asked. 'We were just talking about Peter's death and speculating. It seems so bizarre. Peter was loud and self-assured, but those traits are hardly motives for murder. And it's not as if he knew anyone down here.'

'Nothing so far but the police are following various leads, to coin a phrase.' Alexi sat at the table and placed her files in front of her. Each of them contained a detailed outline of her delegates' submissions. 'Right,' she said. 'To business. Who wants to go first?'

For the next hour, her delegates discussed their progress and read out parts of their final submissions for the others to critique. Patrick already had them and his decision would be final but Alexi knew it would be good for her team to receive feedback from their peers. She listened to their enthusiasm and praised their efforts, wishing she could enjoy the experience. The course would have been a success, the first of many, but for the spectre of murder hanging over it.

'So,' Archie said, when they'd all finished. 'Which of us do you think will get published in the *Sentinel*?'

Alexi put up her hands. 'If I had my way, you all would be. I'm not sitting on the fence here. You've all chosen different subjects and tackled them diligently. You have very different writing styles but have grasped the concept of short and sharp, getting the facts in order without boring the reader. I'm proud of you all for working so well under difficult circumstances.'

'Couldn't agree more.'

Patrick swanned into the room like he owned it, suave and disgustingly self-assured. A hundred times removed from the humbled individual who'd pleaded his case in Cheryl's kitchen a few hours previously. Alexi didn't know why she was so surprised. Patrick had always been a survivor.

He took a seat at the table and smiled at Ranya. 'I've decided,' he said, 'that your submissions were too innovative, too diverse, to choose between them so I intend to publish extracts from them all.' A gasp of appreciation went up. 'Along with brief bios and the reasons why you chose the subjects that you did. I'll be asking our readers to give feedback and let them decide which submission gets published in full.'

'We'll see our names in a national paper?' Grace asked.

'Absolutely. After everything that's happened, it's the least you deserve.'

Alexi would have been grateful – they all deserved their five minutes of fame – but for the fact that she knew it was a ploy to earn her appreciation. He hadn't once looked at her, but she knew him too well to be in any doubt about his end game.

Her delegates went off to their rooms to prepare for the gala once the debrief broke up, chatting excitedly about Patrick's decision. The man himself lingered in the lounge, still deliberately not looking at her but probably hoping to catch Alexi alone. She wasn't about to fall for that one, though. She had nothing to say to him that he'd want to hear and was immune to his toxic charm. So she gathered up her papers and left without so much as a glance in his direction.

Back in the main part of the hotel, Alexi made her way to the room that she and Jack would be occupying that night. Cosmo had already taken up occupation of the bed and gave her an imperious look when she walked in.

'Hey, big guy,' she said, smoothing his sleek back. 'Don't go overdoing it now.'

By the time she emerged from the shower, Jack was there.

'Hey,' he said, kissing her. 'How did it go?'

She told him about Patrick's latest ploy, and he simply pulled a face.

'My thoughts exactly,' she replied, discarding the towel she'd wrapped herself in and setting about moisturising her body.

'Need help with that?' Jack asked, grinning.

'Not if we're to stand any chance of making the gala on time,' she replied, leaning down to grab the end of her towel and flapping it at him. 'Get in that shower and get your mind out of the gutter, Maddox.'

He kissed her bare shoulder. 'Yes, ma'am.'

Alexi and Jack entered the hotel's bar a short time later and were impressed by the lengths that Cheryl and Drew had gone to. As well as the delegates and their invited guests, a number of local business owners who had agreed to answer her attendees' questions were present. Patrick was holding court and those surrounding him were hanging on his every word. He looked over their heads when he noticed Alexi but she ignored him.

'In that red dress, darling, he's finally got visual confirmation of what he gave up.' Jack squeezed her arm. 'Knock 'em dead!'

'You don't look so shabby yourself,' Alexi replied, revelling in Jack's admiring expression. For now, she'd forget about being a murder suspect. And the course had been a success, she reminded herself, if one forgot about Peter's death. 'Now go circulate, work your magic and let me chat to my delegates.'

The meal was superb – Marcel really had pulled out all the stops – and Alexi was glad for Drew and Cheryl's sake that she overheard so many complimentary comments. Speeches came and went, everyone applauded, and it was time to mingle.

Alexi and Jack and been separated during the meal and Patrick had somehow managed to wangle the seat next to her. But she'd mostly ignored him, giving her full attention to the mayor, seated on her opposite side.

She excused herself to visit the ladies and found Ranya already there, washing her hands.

'Did you enjoy the dinner, and the entire course, for that matter?' Alexi asked. 'We haven't had much time to talk, what with everything that's been going on. I had hoped to give you all more of my attention.'

Ranya nodded. 'I enjoyed it immensely and learned so much.' She frowned. 'It doesn't seem right to have enjoyed myself, though, not when Peter died.'

Alexi let out a protracted sigh. 'I know. It will haunt me for a long time.'

'About that.' Ranya chewed at her lower lip and frowned. 'I know there was something going on between Peter and Diana. She hasn't said a word about knowing him previously, but her daughter isn't so circumspect.' Ranya looked up at Alexi, her gaze wary. 'Peter was her father. Is that right?'

'Apparently so.'

'Well look, the thing is, I'm sure it's nothing, but Diana said we were together, doing our research, the entire time on the morning of Peter's death.'

'I saw you both,' Alexi reminded the girl.

'Yes well, when you left, Diana said there was something she had to do.' Ranya looked directly up at Alexi, clearly conflicted. 'She never said what or where she went but she was gone for over an hour.'

'I see.' Alexi's mind raced with possibilities. 'Can you remember how she seemed when she came back?'

'Did she look as though she'd just committed murder is, I suppose, what you're asking me. How does a murderer look?' Ranya paused. 'She was distracted, I guess. Her mind definitely wasn't on what various people had to say to us. I tried to update her on the facts I'd unearthed in her absence but could tell that she wasn't really listening. Do you think she went to see Peter? I mean, I don't know what their history is but obviously, they once knew one another well or Sarah wouldn't have existed. I assume that was the argument I overheard. I've thought about it a lot since then and wondered if Diana had gone to track Peter down in order to continue fighting with him.'

'It's possible,' Alexi said. 'I will have to pass this information on to Inspector Vickery. About Diana disappearing at the vital time, I mean.'

'Yes, I know.' She looked anxious. 'Will I get in trouble for not saying anything sooner?'

'The inspector will wonder about that. It could be relevant.' Alexi patted her shoulder. 'But don't worry. You haven't done anything wrong.'

'To be honest, I was too shocked about Peter's death to think straight at the time. When it did occur to me that Diana hadn't told the truth, I didn't know what to do.'

'Did you ask her about it?'

Ranya shook her head. 'Diana isn't the sort of person who I could stand up to. She sometimes terrifies me, truth to tell. I suppose I just convinced myself that she'd have no reason to kill Peter and would be incapable of it even if she did. Of course, I didn't know about her daughter or the fact that they'd once known each other until now. Once I met Sarah tonight and learned the truth... well, it changed everything.'

'You now think that she could have done it?'

Ranya paused to consider her response. 'It's hard for me to say. I don't know her very well. She's a hard person to get close to. But they do say that anyone is capable of murder, given sufficient provocation. But still, if Peter was strangled... that's what they're saying.' Ranya fixed Alexi with a significant look.

'He was strangled, that much I can confirm.' Ranya didn't know that he'd been drugged and that wasn't something that Alexi could reveal.

'Well, there you are then.' Ranya let out a pent-up breath and seemed more relaxed. 'Strangulation takes a lot of strength. A man must have done it.'

'More than likely,' Alexi agreed.

Ranya smiled timidly and left the cloakroom. Alexi used the facilities and made her way back to the bar, where the diners were now mingling and the noise level had gone up several decibels. She noticed Jack in the hallway, in conversation with Vickery.

'Hey,' Jack said, slipping an arm around her waist. 'I was about to send out a search party.'

Alexi smiled at Jack and then transferred that smile to Vickery, but she suspected that the gesture probably looked as strained as it felt. 'Any developments?' she asked.

'I just updated Mark on the machinations of your ex,' Jack said.

'It sounds as though he's a guy who doesn't like losing,' Vickery said.

'You're not wrong.'

'But he can't have done the deed. At least, not himself,' Vickery added. 'We've checked with the home where his mother now resides. He signed in before the murder was committed. We know that Foreman was still alive then. Vaughan's seen on the home's CCTV well after the body was discovered. If he hired someone to do the job for him, we'll likely never find out. We don't have any reason to speak with him under caution, which would allow us to search his records.'

'But not the paper's records,' Alexi said. 'Patrick often deals on the shady side of legal and knows how to cover his tracks.'

'I hear you,' Vickery replied glumly.

'Cheer up,' Alexi said. 'I've just heard something that might actually help.'

She proceeded to tell Jack and Vickery what Ranya had revealed. She watched the two men as they absorbed the implications and shared a knowing look.

'She's the one with the biggest motive,' Vickery said. 'We will, at the very least, have to ask her where she went for over an hour at the critical time. I shall also be interested to know why she failed to mention it to us.'

'I'd say she'd be capable of sticking a needle in his neck and then strangling the man who'd disappointed her so badly,' Jack added.

Alexi nodded. 'My thoughts exactly. It doesn't look good for her.' She glanced at Jack. 'Did you tell Mark that we tracked down the original Peter Foreman's daughter?'

'Jack just mentioned it,' Vickery replied. 'I'll talk to her. Do you really think that she celebrated her father's death?'

'Actually, I do,' Alexi replied without hesitation. 'But if Foreman didn't want to know Diana, he sure as hell wouldn't have wanted anything to do with the daughter of his tormentor. He really was trying to blot his childhood out of his memory, which makes sense if he actually killed Sally's father. She could have plotted her revenge, somehow found out what drug to use on him and managed to purchase it without raising suspicions.' Alexi frowned. 'But that still doesn't explain why Peter would have will-ingly gone into the men's room with her *and* obligingly turned his back so that she could strike.'

'So Diana remains our main suspect,' Jack said, sighing.

'Looks that way,' Vickery agreed. 'A woman twice scorned and all that.'

'Are you going to talk to her now?' Alexi asked. 'The evening's starting to break up so it would be as good a time as any. They're all staying for lunch tomorrow but will be gone after that, so...'

'Don't want to make a scene,' Vickery said. 'Innocent until proven guilty, as they say, so we'll give her the benefit of our discretion for now, even if she did lie to us. We'll go into the kitchen and keep Cosmo company if you get Diana to join us, Alexi.'

'I'm on it,' Alexi replied, taking herself back into the bar.

Diana was talking to Grace and Archie on the other side of the room. Alexi made her way towards the group but was intercepted by Patrick.

'A word,' he said, grasping her upper arm.

Alexi said nothing but fixed her gaze on his hand around her bicep until he released her. 'I have nothing to say to you, Patrick.'

'But I have to explain why—'

'Leave. Me. Alone.'

She enunciated each word with venom in her tone and then walked away, leaving him to stare after her. She caught sight of Jack in the periphery of her vision. He had noticed the exchange, and had been about to intercept. But he dropped back again when she turned away from Patrick, clearly appreciating that his interference was not necessary, nor would it be appreciated. She could fight her own battles.

Most of the time.

Her delegates greeted her with smiles.

'A great evening,' Grace said. 'Well done.'

'Yeah, a good bash,' Archie agreed.

Diana said nothing, her expression filled with suspicion.

'Need a brief word, Diana,' she said in a pleasant tone. 'Something's come up. It won't take a moment.'

'Don't mind me,' Archie said, yawning. 'I'm gonna have a quick nightcap then I'm for my bed. Can I get you one, Grace?'

'Why not,' Grace replied. 'It's not a school night.'

Alexi watched this most unlikely of couples stroll away from them, deep in conversation, laughing about something.

'They say opposites attract,' she remarked to Diana, 'but I really didn't see that one coming.'

Diana seemed disinterested. 'What do you need me for now?' she asked impatiently, following Alexi into Cheryl's kitchen. 'I've already bared my soul.'

Cosmo stalked up to Alexi and rubbed his head against her shins before lifting it again and hissing at Diana.

'That feline really doesn't like me,' Diana said, tutting, 'and I can assure you that the feeling is entirely mutual. I've never seen the point of domestic animals myself. They tend to take over people's lives.' She gave a weary sigh when she noticed Vickery looming large at the back of the room. 'A bit late for an inquisition, isn't it?' But Alexi could detect fear beneath the bluster.

'Sit down,' Vickery invited, waiting until she did so before sitting across from her. Alexi and Jack sat together at the end of the table, trying not to crowd the woman. Not that she would be easily intimidated, Alexi sensed, but because it was the polite thing to do. Cosmo jumped onto Jack's lap and started purring.

'You're right,' Vickery said, 'it is late, but this interview would not be necessary if you'd been honest with us about your whereabouts at the time of the murder.'

'Ah, so Ranya sneaked on me, did she?' Diana let out a long breath. 'I thought she might.'

'A bit unfair to expect a girl you barely know to lie for you,' Alexi said.

Diana shrugged. 'You can't get the staff nowadays.'

'This isn't a joke,' Vickery said in a hard tone. 'I'm talking to you here in the first instance as a courtesy, but if you'd prefer it, we can do it formally at the station.'

Diana dropped both her gaze and her attitude. 'Sorry, and you're right. I should have told you where I was and why but knew how it would look. I was hoping you'd find the murderer quickly and it wouldn't be necessary. Anyway, one of the few snippets of information that Peter did tell me was that he'd seen Sally Foreman. He remarked about buses coming along together, or some such nonsense. I suppose he meant her and me: two spectres, clearly repellent to him, from his past. He wouldn't tell me anything other than that Sally worked at the Swan and my curiosity was piqued. I wanted to get Sally's take on life at Parkside and find out if she'd known or heard rumours about the abuse.'

'What did she tell you?' Vickery asked.

'Nothing. I got there just after the body had been discovered. The car park was full of police vehicles, so I turned tail and went back to my research. I don't know if there are any cameras on the stretch of road I took but if there are, you'll be able to pick my car up on them.' She spread her hands. 'I didn't kill Peter, that's the God's honest truth, even though I was sorely tempted when he treated me like an unwanted surprise gift.' She stood up. 'You're barking up the wrong tree. Now, I'm beat so I'm going to bed. If you want to talk to me again, you can do so through my solicitor.'

17

'Vickery hasn't got enough to charge anyone, has he?' Alexi asked Jack as they slipped between rich cotton sheets in their room at the hotel that night.

'Nothing that jumps out at him, darling.' He pulled her into his arms. 'Least of all anything to do with you. There's no suggestion of his speaking with you under caution. He would have given me the heads up if that was his intention so try not to worry.'

'That won't change the fact that the local gossips will have a field day.'

Jack stroked her hair. 'Sticks and stones and all that. You worry too much about this place. The hotel's reputation hasn't suffered as a result of the previous deaths. Quite the opposite, in fact. And as to what the locals think of you... well, they have to gossip about something. It's human nature.'

'Even so, Polly is on a witch hunt and has me in her sights. She always has and mud eventually sticks. It's only a matter of time before she starts spouting off on social media, if she hasn't already.' Alexi let out a long breath. 'She wants me out of Lambourn, Jack. She feels threatened by me. I wish I knew why.'

Jack looked uncomfortable. 'Try not to think about her. You know what they say: the only thing worse than being talked about is not being talked about.'

'I guess.' Alexi knew he was trying to make her feel better. She also knew that Vickery had gone easy on her so far, but it was early days and that situation wouldn't continue if no new leads came to light. She curled her legs towards her belly and spooned against Jack. 'All I really care about is finding out who killed Peter, and why. I don't want it to remain unsolved. It will eat away at me, no one locally will ever believe that I wasn't involved and will assume that you persuaded Vickery to hold back with the thumb-screws. But this isn't just about me. It's the journalist in me, I guess. I always need to know why, how and who.'

'We may not get there this time. You need to be prepared for that,' Jack said softly. 'Foreman had a complex past and there are a lot of issues there that we'll probably never get to know about.'

'It doesn't look good for Diana,' Alexi said.

'Vickery knows she had a motive. Now that she's admitting to being at the Swan at the vital time, he can also put her at the scene. So yeah, he will want to talk to her under caution tomorrow, I imagine.'

Alexi drummed her fingers on Jack's bicep. 'My problem is that I believed her explanation.'

'Vickery will be fair and cover all the bases, you know that. At the very least he'll ask Sally if she saw her.'

Alexi leaned up on one elbow. 'But if Sally *did* feel the need to avenge her father's death all these years on, she will latch onto Diana being there and say that she *did* see her, thereby removing suspicion from herself.'

'Hush!' Jack leaned over and kissed her brow. 'Try not to think about it and get some sleep. All this speculation will get us nowhere.'

Alexi sighed and dutifully closed her eyes but knew that closing off her mind as well would be a damned sight harder. Jack was right to say that if anything, the hotel had benefited from being connected in various ways to four murders and that there was no evidence to suggest that she was in any way responsible for this latest one, other than having been there at the time of the murder and heard arguing with the victim. Even so, her reputation mattered to her, and it would remain tarnished until the culprit's identity was discovered. She cursed Patrick and Cassie for interfering in her relationship with Jack, intentionally or otherwise putting her name in the frame, and was determined to prove that she was an entirely innocent pawn in their manipulative games.

Somehow.

Alexi tossed and turned, finally falling into a troubled sleep what felt like ten minutes before it was time to get up again. Jack was already up and dressed, speaking in a quiet voice into his phone.

She sat up and yawned. A headache threatened and her brain felt sluggish; the result of too little sleep and too many thoughts jangling about inside her head like a washing machine on the spin cycle.

'Hey.' Jack finished his call and came over to the bed to give her a kiss. She could tell by his upbeat expression that the call had brought good news.

'What is it?' she asked. 'Tell me.'

'Good morning to you too,' Jack said, smiling. 'That was Cassie, who's been burning the midnight oil, obviously attempting to make up some lost ground.'

'What's she found? You look excited.'

'What she's found is my missing person.'

'Oh.' Alexi tried to hide her disappointment. 'Well, that's good. I know you dislike unsolved puzzles as much as I do.'

'Don't look so downhearted, darling. It's good news, not just because Amy's alive... I was starting to have doubts about that. But for our investigation too, I hope.' He paused. 'Well anyway, it might throw up some new leads.'

'Why?' Alexi blinked the sleep from her eyes, still feeling sluggish, her brain slow to keep up with Jack's line of thought. 'What has Amy Dawson's disappearance got to do with Peter's murder?'

'That's what I hope Amy will tell us. She's on her way here to the hotel now with Cassie. It seems she has something important to tell us about Foreman.'

Alexi jerked upright in the bed, suddenly wide awake. 'She knew him? She has a connection to him?'

'You know as much as I do,' Jack replied, spreading his hands. 'Cassie wants her to tell us her story face to face.'

Alexi leapt from the bed without another word and headed for the shower, a degree of cautious optimism filtering through her dwindling lethargy. Cosmo, who'd followed their exchange with one eye open, indulged in a feline stretch and Alexi noticed him trotting towards the door. Jack opened it for him, and she knew that her cat would find his way to Cheryl's kitchen, food and his friend Toby in that order.

Ten minutes later, Alexi was dressed and following in her cat's footsteps. She found Jack and Drew deep in conversation, and Cosmo tucking into a plate of salmon.

'He'll think it's his birthday,' she said. 'You really have to stop spoiling him, Drew, or he'll become as fat as a... well, as a smug overfed cat.'

'He knows how to intimidate me,' Drew said with a theatrical shudder.

Alexi laughed. 'Wimp!' she said, helping herself to coffee.

'I'm on breakfast duty,' Drew said, moving to the Aga and throwing bacon into a pan. 'Jack tells me you might have a break in the case, and you can't absorb good news on an empty stomach.'

'Let's hope it *is* good news and not just Cassie trying to redeem herself,' Jack said, echoing Alexi's earlier thoughts.

Alexi would do her best to ensure that Jack didn't end his business partnership with Cassie, for his sake. They brought different skills to the table and worked well as a team. But that didn't mean that Alexi had to like or trust the woman. Once the dust had settled, Alexi suspected that Cassie would again seize on any opportunity to drive a wedge between her and Jack. For that reason, she would never be comfortable in Cassie's company. In time, she would probably forgive Cassie for what she had done, if only because Patrick had been the driving force.

Forgive? Perhaps.

Forget? Never.

Cheryl and Verity joined them as Drew was dishing up. Alexi was distracted by Verity's antics in her highchair, from which she proceeded to bang a spoon against its tray, making herself laugh and covering herself in goo in the process.

With breakfast cleared away, Drew and Cheryl had only just gone off to kickstart their day when Cassie arrived with a tanned yet subdued Amy in her wake. One look at her was enough for Alexi to satisfy herself that Amy was the missing woman in question; she had seen her picture too often for there to be any doubt. She idly wondered where she'd been to acquire such a deep tan at that time of year. She was tall and strikingly attractive, but her expression was guarded, wary.

Cosmo stalked up to her. Alexi held her breath. If he took a dislike to her, there was no telling how he would react. But her cat seemed satisfied with Amy, swished his rigid tail at Cassie and returned to the basket he shared with Toby.

Alexi released her breath, grateful to her cat for reinforcing her own initially favourable impression of the woman. She sensed that Amy was worried about something and unsure whom to trust. Alexi sent her a reassuring smile, which Amy half-heartedly returned. She recalled that Amy was Cassie's friend and wondered what Cassie had said to her on the journey over to potentially poison Amy's mind against her.

'I'm sorry if I've created problems,' Amy said to Jack once Cassie had made the introductions. 'I gather you've been looking for me.'

'And I get the impression that you didn't want to be found,' Jack replied, shaking her outstretched hand. 'I'd about given up and I don't admit defeat easily.'

'Look, I'm going to leave you to it,' Cassie surprised Alexi by saying as she backed towards the door. 'I now know a little about where Amy has been but not so much of the why. I'm Neil's friend and if she has anything bad to say about him, it will be easier for her not to do it in front of me. Besides, we're all under suspicion in this case so it's better if I don't know more than I need to for now. I'm going to head back to the office, Jack. Call me if you need me.'

She didn't once meet Alexi's gaze but Alexi was cool with that, that's not to say a little suspicious about Cassie's sudden desire to do the right thing.

'It's nice to finally meet you, Amy,' Alexi said as their guest seated herself at the table and accepted Jack's offer of coffee. 'We were worried about you.'

Amy looked angry but whether that anger was generic or simply focused on Alexi, she could not have said. 'You don't know why I ran off, do you?'

'No,' Jack replied, as he placed her coffee in front of her and she nodded her thanks. 'We spoke to your husband, obviously. He's the one who called us in.'

'I'm sure he did.' A modicum of fear passed through Amy's expression. 'I hope you haven't called him to say that I'm here.'

Jack flashed a reassuring smile. 'Don't worry. He sacked me when I asked questions he didn't want to answer, so I owe him no loyalty. Cassie won't have done so either, despite their friendship.'

Alexi wasn't sure how Jack could be so... well, sure about that. Presumably, he assumed that professionalism would take priority over friendship.

'That I can well believe,' Amy said, snorting. 'Dismissing you for not toeing the line, I mean.'

'I got the impression that he's a controlling individual,' Alexi said into the ensuing silence. 'I mean, you have no children and yet you didn't have a career. I know not all women want to work but I also know from Jack's research that you have a degree so wondered why you didn't put yourself out there. Once I met your husband, the answer seemed obvious.'

'Very astute.' Amy paused, presumably to gather her thoughts. Alexi sensed her anxiety. She had run from something – or someone. It wasn't difficult for Alexi to guess who that someone must be. Her only question was why it had taken her so long to rid herself of his controlling influence.

'You're wondering why I married him, I expect.'

'Not really our business,' Jack replied.

'Sorry,' Alexi added, 'but I was wondering that very thing.'

'He hasn't always been a stuffed shirt, a pedant, or any of the other things that only came to light after I'd tied the knot. Believe it or not, he used to be fun. He was very good looking, and I make no apology for being shallow enough to be swayed by a handsome face. I mean, we're all influenced by aesthetics, aren't we?'

'Absolutely,' Alexi agreed, smiling at Jack. 'More doors open for the beautiful people. It might not be fair but that's the way the world works.'

'I went to university and gained a degree in history, but art was my passion. I had intended to combine the two and train as an art historian.' She let out a long breath. 'I did initially take a position with a small auction house in London, learning the trade. Then I met Neil, fell for his charm and the rest, as they say, is history.'

'You made a mistake,' Alexi said. 'It happens. What I don't understand is why you didn't cut and run. You're an intelligent woman. You could have made your own way.'

'I could but for the fact that my mother was in an expensive care home by then: the best money could buy. I grew up in a poor part of the country and when Mum got early onset Alzheimer's, she would have been shoved into so-called care wherever the local authority could find a place for her.'

She looked angry and Alexi knew why. She'd seen some of those places and although the staff did the best that they could, they were under-funded and overworked.

'Your husband got her the best,' Jack said, 'more or less buying your affection and keeping you tied to him.'

'Right. He'd gone along with my passion for art and encouraged my interest in becoming an art historian. He implied that he'd be the breadwinner whilst I learned the ropes but the moment we were married, everything changed almost overnight. He kept finding reasons for me not to go to work and in the end, I had to resign. He said they were exploiting me and that something better would come along. While I waited for that elusive something, he gently coerced me into doing things that didn't interest me. Like taking Cordon Bleu cooking courses, doing charitable works – things that frankly didn't rank high on my list of priorities. But he did it all so subtly that it took me months, years even, to realise that I was being played. I was grateful to him, you see, and *wanted* to win his approval.' She looked up from studying her fingernails. 'Pathetic or what?'

'Not pathetic at all,' Jack said. 'He's a control freak.'

'Yep, that he is. But he hides it so well. Ask Cassie. In social situations, he's the life and soul. We're the golden couple who have it all. But behind closed doors, it's a very different story.' She rubbed her upper arm and Alexi suspected that she was subconsciously nursing an old injury.

'Did he hit you?' she asked bluntly.

'Not often. He preferred to use words and they cut even deeper, because he was constantly undermining my self-confidence.'

'I've met the type,' Alexi said. 'They somehow manage to make you feel as though you're the one being unreasonable and have brought your punishments on yourself.'

Amy smiled. 'Spot on,' she replied with feeling. 'But by the time I worked that out for myself, I was trapped. He didn't care about my mother; she was simply a means to an end. I couldn't walk out on him all the time he was footing the bills, which is why he discouraged me from pursuing a career. He knew that I'd live in a single room and use the rest of my income to support my mother if I was in a position to do so.'

'Your mother's no longer with us, I take it,' Jack said.

'She died six months ago, and I can't say I'm sorry that her torment is over.' Amy shook her head and a single tear escaped. 'It had been a long time since she'd known who I was.' Amy sighed. 'Anyway, she's in a better place now and I know I did absolutely everything I could to make her final years comfortable.'

'By sacrificing your own life,' Alexi said.

Amy shrugged and said nothing.

'But you still felt trapped. Knew your husband would track you down and make your life difficult if you left him, no matter where you went,' Jack said. 'He wouldn't accept that your marriage wasn't working. I assume that's why you took six months to plot your disappearance.'

Amy impatiently tucked a long strand of dark-blonde hair behind her ear. 'I went to stay with a friend in Italy while I considered my options,' she replied, sharing a look of total transparency between them. 'I know you're wondering so I'll put you out of your misery.' She paused. 'I've heard what's being said but I wasn't with Paul Franklin. I've never met the man.'

Jack nodded. 'I'm glad to hear it.'

'Neil discouraged me from having close friends. He monitored my phone somehow and made it his business to push them away, but I didn't find that out until much later.'

Alexi thought of the ease with which Cassie had hacked her online diary and nodded. 'I hear you,' she said softly.

'But he knew nothing about Isobel, my Italian friend. We met at university and lost touch for a while. We met again, purely by coincidence about a year ago when she was at an art exhibition that I attended. We shared that passion, you see. Anyway, I didn't want Neil to know about her and so I got another email address and actually used the computer in the library to access it.' She waved a hand in the air. 'Ridiculous, I know, but that was the lengths I had to go to in order to be assured of privacy. Anyway, Isobel got the truth out of me about my marriage. She'd been in a similar situation herself and offered me sanctuary whenever I needed it.'

'A true friend,' Alexi said. 'So why did you come back?'

'A person can't stay on the run indefinitely,' Jack responded before Amy could.

'No, that isn't it. I was happy in Florence. All that art culture. It was like a drug overdose. I speak a little Italian. Isobel has connections in the art world and promised to try and get me work. My needs are simple and I'd work for next to nothing, just for the pleasure of having my freedom.' She paused. 'Then I read the local paper online. Peter Foreman's death is the reason why I'm sitting here now talking to you.'

'You knew him?' Alexi asked, sharing a bemused glance with Jack.

'Neil did. They worked together.'

'Good heavens!' Alexi said, recovering first. 'At the GLAA?'

'Yes. Neil was Peter's boss.'

'A fact that he failed to mention when we visited him,' Jack said, grinding his jaw, clearly as suspicious as Alexi herself felt.

'Neil was a lot more than that to him, it seems.'

The penny dropped. Alexi glanced at Jack and she could see that he'd understood too.

'They were lovers?' Jack asked.

'Apparently so, and I had absolutely no idea that Neil's tendencies ran in that direction. At least, not at first. Before we were married, he was flirtatious, appreciative of my appearance, and made me feel cherished. With the men, he'd share dirty jokes and raucous comments.'

'How soon did you realise?' Alexi asked.

'I should have had my suspicions before we married. He never tried it on, you see, but I was so wound up about Mum that the thought never crossed my mind. He said he knew I was preoccupied and would give me space. That he'd wait until we were married.'

Jack raised a brow. 'Why did he want to marry you at all if he knew he was gay?' he asked.

'He was in denial,' Alexi replied before Amy could. 'Even in this day and age when same-sex marriage is the norm, some people still feel... well, like it's a phase they'll grow out of, I suppose.'

'Spot on,' Amy replied. 'Neil and I had sex half a dozen times in the weeks after we married. It was always clumsy and unsatisfactory for us both, I think. I was relieved when it fizzled out and I didn't ask why. I soon learned not to ask questions of Neil that even smacked of criticism.'

'You guessed?' Alexi asked.

Amy nodded. 'Pretty much. But I didn't know, not for certain, until just before I left the country. Peter tracked me down and told me there was something that I needed to know. He said that Neil was in denial about his sexuality and that he'd gotten Peter fired from his position for trumped-up reasons when he insisted upon going public with their relationship.'

'Did your husband know that Peter had approached you?' Jack asked. 'Think carefully. It could be important.'

'I never told him. He'd have gone crazy at the mere suggestion. So I laid my plans, bided by time and then packed my bags and got on a flight to Italy.'

'How?' Jack asked. 'Your passport is still at your marital home. It's one of the first things I checked.'

Amy smiled. 'I learned to be devious. I told Isobel that Neil's job gave him access to all sorts of areas and that he'd be able to find me if I got on a plane. So, she arranged a forged passport for me.' She shrugged. 'Don't ask me how because I don't know. When I asked her, she said she knew people who know people...'

'So you were away and free of the man who tormented your life, but you came back when a man you barely knew was murdered?' Jack stared intently at her. 'Why?'

'Isn't it obvious?'

'I want to hear you say it.'

'I suspect that Peter told Neil what he'd done, which was to effectively break up his marriage. A marriage that was vitally important to Neil: his badge of respectability. No one got one over on Neil without bearing the consequences.' She shuddered. 'Take it from one who knows.'

'Which would account for the fact that he instigated a search when you left,' Jack said.

'I've wondered about that,' Amy replied. 'I have no relations, no close friends. No one was likely to miss me so why let the world know that I'd gone? Everyone knows that when a wife goes AWOL, the husband is always the prime suspect.'

'You think your husband killed Peter,' Alexi breathed, 'and he wanted to make sure that you didn't speak out of turn.'

18

'Yes,' Amy said in answer to Alexi's question. 'That's precisely what I do think.' Her expression remained resolute. 'By dismissing Peter from his work and from his bed, Neil must have subsequently realised that he'd miscalculated insofar as he could no longer control the man he'd once had feelings for. Losing control would have been anathema to him since he must be in total charge of everything he touches. He would simply have assumed that Peter would do as he was told and go quietly. Most people do as Neil tells them to, you see.'

Jack watched the young woman, impressed by her resilience, to say nothing of her strong moral compass. It must have taken a lot of courage to return to a place where her abusive and highly resourceful husband might find her.

And if he'd killed once…

But Amy had done it anyway. She'd done it because it was the right thing to do and perhaps because she wanted her freedom back. But she had not done it because she sought revenge, even though no one would blame her if she had.

'Thanks for your honesty,' Jack replied. 'I have one more question for you.' He paused, not wanting to pose it. Having to know. 'Did you use your credit card at the Swan a few days ago?'

Amy shook her head without hesitation. 'No,' she replied, 'I only returned from Italy yesterday. I stayed in a hotel in Winchester overnight, gathering my courage to ring Cassie. She's more Neil's friend than mine and I had to be sure that she wouldn't tell Neil that I was back before I was willing to even reveal I was in the country, much less come here.'

Jack nodded, his worst fears confirmed. Cassie had invented the credit card usage in order to get him to the Swan at a time when she knew Alexi would also be there. She had offered to show him the credit card entry on Amy's statement but Jack had trusted her and not taken her up on that offer. Now that he knew it was a lie, it begged the question: why? Unless Cassie, or more to the point Vaughan, had a hand in Foreman's murder, what purpose did it serve to have him and Alexi at the hotel at that precise time?

Despite everything, he didn't want to think that Cassie had been a-party to murder, albeit unintentionally. It *had* to be a coincidence. Even so, Cassie had lied to him, there was now no doubt about that, *and* she must have realised that lie would be uncovered when Jack spoke with Amy. He gave her reluctant credit for bringing Amy here anyway, but it was too little, too late and changed nothing.

The trust had gone from his business partnership with Cassie.

'You realise,' Jack said, leaning forward, 'that we will have to pass on what you've told us to the investigating officers. It could be vital.'

'Of course I know that.' Amy sat a little taller, a defiant expression gracing her features. 'But I would prefer it, much prefer it, if Neil doesn't get to hear of my return, at least until the police have spoken with him. After that, if I have to face him then I will. I'm through with hiding from him like a frightened mouse. I refuse to behave like the timid little wife, afraid of her own shadow.'

'Attagirl!' Alexi said, pride in her tone. 'What will you do now?'

'Oh, I intend to settle in Florence,' she said. 'I have a job that I love waiting for me there. But I want to do it openly, without constantly glancing over my shoulder, worried that Neil will find me.' She paused. 'I want my life back.'

'That I can understand,' Jack said.

'Would you like to stay here for now?' Alexi asked. 'It will be safe and I'm sure I can arrange it.'

Gratitude flashed across her features. 'Thank you,' she said with feeling. 'Cassie said it would be the safest bet.'

'Give me a moment,' Alexi said, standing. 'I'll sort it with Cheryl, the owner.'

Jack smiled at Amy when they were left alone. 'It feels good to fight back, doesn't it?' he remarked.

'You have no idea!'

'Have you thought what you will do if it can be proven that Neil is the murderer?'

'Either way, I shall go back to Italy and forget about him,' she replied emphatically. 'I'm known by a different name over there so no stigma will be attached to me.' She drummed her fingers on the surface of the table. 'My only concern is proving Neil's guilt. He's got a brain the size of a small planet and won't have left a trail. In fact, it will amuse him to think he's running rings round you all.'

'Let us worry about that,' Jack replied, with more confidence than he actually felt. 'There's usually something. Some small detail that catches even the cleverest person out.' But not always, he thought but didn't add. However, in this case, Jack would move heaven and earth to find that elusive something now that he was absolutely convinced of his guilt. Proving it would ease Alexi's mind and clear her name of all suspicion. Dawson's main error, he decided, was to cross a man as violently in love as Jack.

'Just so you're aware of his intellect: he speaks a different language to the rest of us and has knowledge about the most obscure subjects. Phytotoxicology was his latest obsession before I left.'

Jack blinked. 'Come again?'

Amy smiled. 'That's what I said when he first took an interest. It's the study of poisonous plants.' Her jaw dropped and her mouth fell open. 'He said there were a dozen different ways to use plants to kill a person and no one would ever know.' She allowed a long pause. 'Was the victim poisoned?'

'Not as far as I'm aware,' Jack said, prevaricating. 'He was strangled.'

'Oh, well that's different. Neil isn't a physical person.'

'All sorted,' Alexi said, reappearing. 'Come with me, Amy, and I'll show you the way. I'll have some brunch sent up. I don't suppose you've eaten. Then you can freshen up and I'll let you know what's happening as it happens.'

'You're very kind,' Amy said, standing and smiling at Alexi. 'Thank you. I love your cat, by the way,' she added, when Cosmo stalked up to her and graciously allowed her to pet him.

'You're highly honoured,' Alexi told her. 'Cosmo doesn't like many people.'

'Well, he knows that I like him. Animals are very intuitive.'

'That one's in a class of his own,' Jack said, laughing. 'By the way, does your husband have any hobbies that you've not mentioned?'

Amy looked surprised by the question. 'He doesn't get a lot of spare time but when he does, he's into trout fishing at Western Farm on the Lambourn river. Why?'

'Oh, no reason.'

Jack sat alone whilst Alexi settled Amy into her room, thinking about what their guest had revealed and how best to use that information to get a confession out of Dawson. Amy was right to say that he thought he was smarter than everyone else but clever people tended to be overconfident and were therefore often the easiest people to dupe. But for Jack, his interest in poisonous plants was the clincher.

He did it, and Jack would find a way to prove it.

If he and Foreman worked together then someone in that department must have known, or suspected, that the two of them were in a relationship, Jack reasoned. Just threatening to speak to his colleagues might be enough to force a confession.

But by no means certain.

'Well,' Alexi burst through the door, sporting a wide smile that gladdened Jack's heart. It was a smile that had been conspicuous by its absence since Foreman's death. 'I didn't see that one coming.'

'Is she okay?' Jack asked.

'She's fine. Cheryl and Verity are upstairs with her. Amy adores children, that much is obvious. It's such a shame that she doesn't have any of her own. Or then again, perhaps it isn't.' Alexi sat down beside Jack and stroked Cosmo when he leapt onto her lap. 'She really would have been tied to Dawson if that had been the case.'

'She's enjoying exerting herself again,' Jack replied.

'What now?' she asked. 'I guess a call to Vickery would be in order.'

'It would.' Jack smiled at her as he told her about Dawson's interest in poisonous plants.

'That's it!' Alexi bounced on the edge of her chair. 'We've got him!'

'Not yet, but at least we now have a motive and possible

means. But as things stand, we can't place him at the scene. It will be her word against his if Dawson protected his relationship with Foreman as closely as I suspect might be the case.'

'He really was conflicted about being gay, wasn't he?'

'He really was but they had to go somewhere to enjoy their trysts. If that somewhere was Foreman's flat in town then someone might have witnessed their comings and goings.'

'Jack, I...' Uncharacteristically lost for words, Alexi sent him a concerned look and clasped his hand. Jack knew what she was thinking and why she felt the need to offer him her sympathy.

'I get it,' he said softly. 'Cassie lied about the credit card use. I have no idea why she'd do that and what she hoped to gain from it but we'll sure as hell be asking her.'

Alexi squeezed his forearm. 'Don't beat yourself up over it. None of this is your fault.' She removed her hand from his arm and sat up straight, all business. 'Right, let's make that call.'

Jack picked up his phone and got through to Vickery's personal number. When Vickery picked up, Jack put it on speaker.

'What's occurring?' Vickery asked, his voice sounding strained, tired. 'Please tell me you've identified the guilty party. I have a life outside of this place that I'd like to live before I get much older.'

'Actually, we might well have done precisely that.'

Vickery didn't once interrupt as Jack gave him a succinct account of Amy's disclosures.

'Well well,' he said when Jack ran out of words. 'You really haven't lost your touch, have you?'

'Can't claim any credit for this one. At least not yet. Suspecting and proving those suspicions are very different beasts, as well you know. He's a tricky customer, Mark, and won't be easy to crack.'

'I hear you.' There was a momentary pause. 'I suppose you'd like to be in for the kill. You've certainly earned the right.'

Given that Alexi was still technically a person of interest, Jack knew that he was taking a massive risk and appreciated the gesture.

'We might be able to do a little arm-twisting,' Jack said. 'Presumably, you'll want to speak with Amy first. She's staying here until the matter's sorted.'

'That will be good.'

The door burst open and Cheryl stood there, looking fraught. 'There's a man called Dawson in the hall, demanding to see you, Jack,' she said anxiously. 'He's very rude and very annoyed. Is he the...' She pointed to the ceiling, clearly having connected the dots.

Before Jack could respond, Cheryl was propelled forward when the door was pushed further open with considerable force. Jack jumped up and caught hold of her before she lost her balance.

'He's here,' Jack said curtly, still clutching his phone in one hand. 'Get here yourself as soon as you can. I'll stall him.' Jack made another suggestion to his friend and then cut the call.

Dawson stood there, his face red with anger, breathing like a bull. All that was missing were flames shooting from flared nostrils. 'Where's my wife?' he demanded to know.

Alexi took charge of a winded Cheryl and helped her to sit down.

Jack stood to face Dawson, somehow managing to resist the urge to punch his lights out as he fixed him with a scathing look.

'An apology to Cheryl would be appreciated,' he said in a mordant tone.

'An apology?' He looked confused, as though apologising was an alien concept. For him, it very likely was. 'What the hell for? The woman was obstructing me. I know you know where my wife is. You work for me, damnit! I should have been the first to hear that she'd turned up.'

'For the record, you fired me, so I owe you no loyalty whatsoever.' Jack allowed a long pause. 'Anyway, what makes you suppose that I know where Amy is?'

'I... well, that is...' He rubbed the side of his nose, belatedly seeming to appreciate that his anger had made him incautious. Not something that happened very often, Jack suspected. Even so, that might be the way to trip him up, Jack thought. Rile him, refute everything he said and see where it led. The man wasn't accustomed to being challenged but now seemed like as good a time as any to alter that situation. 'A friend slipped me the word.'

Jack resisted the urge to glance at Alexi, aware that confusion and anger would be competing for dominance in her expression. She would assume that Cassie had told him. As a matter of course, Jack mentally sprang to his partner's defence. Then he recalled her recent behaviour and no longer knew what to think. There was, he reminded himself, a very good chance that Dawson had hacked into her phone like he'd hacked his wife's. For now at least, Jack would give Cassie the benefit of the doubt.

'I want to see my wife. I have the right,' Dawson said in a more moderate tone. 'Is she here?'

'She has absolutely no desire to see you,' Alexi told him, 'and I can perfectly understand why. You are a bully, Mr Dawson, and bullies always get their comeuppance eventually.'

'How dare you!' Dawson puffed out his chest, giving the impression of an offended bullfrog.

'She dares because it's the truth,' Jack responded calmly, 'and your performance here so far has backed up Alexi's assertion. But you might as well be aware that shouting and throwing your weight around will cut no ice with us, so I suggest that you lose the attitude and that we remain civilized.'

Dawson's face turned a darker shade of crimson as he folded his arms across his chest and sent Jack a look of stark defiance as he lowered himself onto the nearest chair. 'As you wish,' he replied curtly. 'Now, what must I do to gain access to my wife?'

'You could start by telling us why you didn't reveal your friendship with Peter Foreman.'

Jack watched the man closely as he spoke, unsurprised when the high colour drained from his cheeks and they turned chalk white. He hadn't expected that one, Jack knew, which made him wonder if he hadn't connected Amy's disappearance with Peter's revelation. He was so used to Amy doing as she was told that perhaps he'd refused to accept that she'd rebelled, much as he tried to dismiss his sexual tendencies as nothing more than a transient affair.

'I fail to understand you,' he said stiffly.

'Did you murder your lover?' Alexi asked into the ensuing silence.

'My lover?' Dawson half rose from his chair but at a look from Jack, quickly sank back into it. 'Are you mad? Who the hell gave you the right to—'

'The detective inspector in charge of his murder is on the way here,' Jack said. 'You can talk to us now, wait for him to get here and talk then, or accept Vickery's invitation to have this conversation under caution at the station.' Jack lifted one shoulder. 'Your choice. It makes no difference to me.'

'Foreman worked in the same department as me,' Dawson admitted after a long pause. Jack gauged his annoyance at being questioned but it was buried deep beneath an all-consuming layer of fear. He had never expected to answer any such questions and was severely rattled. 'I was his superior. He reported to me. Our work is... was, unconventional. No such thing as nine to five for us. We were always on the trail of ruthless individuals who manipulated the desperation of others.'

He ought to have recognised the signs, Jack thought. Set a thief to catch a thief, and all that.

'But you were seen socialising,' Alexi surprised Jack by remarking. 'Surely desperate criminals, keen to remain below the radar, don't frequent swanky restaurants so you wouldn't have been tracking them to those locations.'

Dawson sent her a sharp look. 'Who the hell told you that?' he demanded to know.

Jack admired the love of his life for her quick thinking. A man like Dawson would have entertained his lover, shown him off in public, but only in high-end places. The sort of places that he would imagine he deserved to frequent as a matter of course. The sort of places where he would almost certainly not be seen by colleagues, who wouldn't be able to afford the prices. Dawson, Jack knew, wouldn't be seen dead in a gay bar. That would be one admission too far.

'I don't know what you're trying to imply,' Dawson said stiffly.

'But you do know that Foreman revealed the true nature of your relationship to your wife.'

'Rubbish.' Dawson waved the suggestion aside with a casual flap of one wrist. On firmer ground now, he clearly realised that with Foreman dead, no one could confirm that assertion. 'He was a disgruntled employee out to make trouble. I dismissed him from his position because he was a loose cannon, pursuing his own agenda without telling me what he was doing. My department works as a team. Can't have individuals going off the radar.'

'You don't approve of homosexuality, do you?' Jack asked.

'What the hell...' He leaned back in his chair and a slow, confident smile spread across his features. 'Make up your mind,

Maddox. One minute, you have me romantically involved with another man, the next, you think I'm homophobic. Which is it?'

'Both,' Jack shot back.

Dawson shook his head. 'Where's your proof?'

'Languishing in a deep pool near Western Farm,' Vickery said, strolling through the door. 'You were right, Jack. We've just pulled Foreman's car out of the water.'

19

Alexi fixed her gaze upon Dawson, who visibly paled as that news was imparted. But he quickly rallied.

'How is that anything to do with me?' he asked with a supercilious sneer.

'Perhaps you'd care to tell me,' Vickery replied, taking a seat at the table. DC Hogan stood at the back of the room with her ever-present notebook to hand.

'Is this an interrogation?' Dawson asked. 'Am I being accused of something? If so, I'd like my solicitor present.'

'Which is your right. This is an informal interview,' Vickery replied, 'but we can take you to the station, caution you, wait for your solicitor and do things properly if that's what you would prefer.'

Dawson flapped a wrist negligently. 'Ask your questions,' he said. 'I have nothing to hide.'

'Let's start by discussing the nature of your friendship with Peter Foreman,' Vickery said. DC Hogan licked the end of her pencil and held it poised for action.

'We were work colleagues. I was his boss.'

'Were you aware that he'd signed onto a writing course at this hotel?' Vickery asked.

'Of course not. We did not discuss our activities outside of work. Besides, he'd been dismissed weeks back. I had no further contact with him.'

'Other than two phone conversations whilst he was here.'

'Other than those.' Dawson had clearly expected those calls to come to light and didn't miss a beat, an explanation already prepared. 'He wanted his job back, said he'd seen the error of his ways and wondered if we could meet as he was in the area to discuss the possibilities.'

'Give your private mobile number to all your employees, do you, sir?' Vickery asked, not buying Dawson's explanation any more than Alexi did.

'Some of them. It's necessary for out of hours communication.'

Vickery leaned forward and pinioned Dawson with a penetrating look. 'Are you absolutely sure that if we look into Foreman's online activities, we won't find any other communications between the two of you? Perhaps WhatsApp calls which won't show on his provider's records?'

'Of course you will!' Dawson gave an impatient tut. 'He reported to me. I've already told you that.'

'Ah yes, so you have. Make a note of that, Hogan. Our victim communicated with Mr Dawson on a regular basis.'

'Noted and underlined, sir.'

'Look, what is this all about?' Dawson rested his forearms on the table and scowled at Vickery. 'I don't like the nature of your suggestions. I don't know what nonsense my wife has been haranguing you with but it's all smoke and mirrors. She's being spiteful. We had a fight, she didn't get her way and so she took off in a strop in a deliberate attempt to make me worry.'

'You mentioned nothing about a fight when you asked me to investigate her disappearance,' Jack pointed out.

'Irrelevant!' Dawson snapped back.

'Fortunately for you, sir, she's turned up alive and well,' Vickery said in a droll tone.

'And I have yet to speak to her. We will undoubtedly kiss and make up.'

'I admire your optimism. My understanding is that she has no desire to talk to you. But that's your affair. I'm more interested in your association with Foreman. We have it on good authority that you and he were romantically involved.'

'Utter tosh!' Prepared for the suggestion, Dawson waved it aside. 'I am not homosexual. The mere thought of it disgusts me.'

Alexi glanced at Jack, wondering if he too thought that Dawson's protests were overdone. That he was denying who he really was.

'Were you aware that Foreman was brought up in care and that Foreman isn't his actual name?' Vickery asked.

'No,' Dawson said slowly, 'I did not know that.'

Alexi had been watching his reactions closely and reckoned it was the first honest, non-evasive answer he'd given.

'I was not responsible for his recruitment. You'll have to speak with HR if you want to know if they were aware of his background.'

'You fish the river close to where Foreman's car was found, I'm told,' Vickery remarked.

Dawson shrugged. 'So what? And before you ask, I know the stretch of river to which you refer. I'm not the only person who goes there on a regular basis, not by a long shot. And,' he added, looking more confident as he warmed to his theme, 'it's a good four miles from the Swan. If you imagine that I went there to murder Foreman, then took his car and dumped it in the river, how did I get there in the first place?'

Dawson sat back, looking pleased with his reasoning. He really did seem to think that he could run rings around their investigation; Amy had been right about his likely reaction to being interrogated. Fuming, Alexi wanted to wipe the smug expression off his face but knew better than to show a reaction.

'Do you own a bicycle, sir?'

'What?'

'It's a simple enough question.'

'No, I don't have a bike. My wife does. It's still in our garage.'

Alexi felt a jolt of excitement as she recalled the yellow mountain bike she'd seen at the Swan on the fateful day. Could it really be that simple? She glanced at Jack and could see that he was thinking along similar lines.

'Do you ever ride that bike?' Vickery asked.

'Good heavens, no! Why would I?'

'Would you object to our taking a look at it?'

'Why? It hasn't moved since she walked out.'

'Even so, if you have nothing to hide.'

Dawson grunted but didn't look happy. 'There's a keypad outside the garage and a code that will open the door.' He reeled the code off and Hogan made a note of it. 'Be my guest but nothing is to be touched other than the bike. Are we clear?'

'Crystal.'

Vickery nodded to Hogan, who briefly left the room. No one spoke until she returned.

Alexi reckoned that if Vickery was hoping to jolt Dawson out of his smug complacency by examining Amy's bike then he was barking up the wrong tree. Dawson was smarter than that. If he had used the bike to reach the hotel then he would have cleaned it to within an inch of its life when he got it home. There would be no lingering evidence. Alexi opened her mouth to ask if the bike was yellow but closed it again without speaking. A moment's thought made her realise that they would be showing their hand for no good reason. Dawson didn't know they were aware of the colour of the bike, that it had been seen at the hotel, and that's the way Vickery would want it to remain.

For now.

'So,' Vickery said, 'let's return to the subject of your relationship with Foreman. I don't believe what you've told me.'

'I can't help what you believe.' Dawson gave a conceited smile. 'It's up to you to prove your theory, for which you will require evidence. Let me save you the trouble. You won't find any because none exists.'

Alexi thought it interesting that he hadn't flat out denied that they'd been involved. He'd simply said that no evidence existed to support that supposition. Dawson was far too astute to have sent text messages or written anything down. When he and Peter worked together, they would have made their arrangements to meet in person. Once he left his position, presumably Dawson deleted any messages they had exchanged from his phone. Alexi wondered if they would be recoverable. Most things stayed in cyberspace indefinitely, didn't they, if one knew where to look?

'Now that we're aware of where Foreman worked,' Vickery said, 'we will, of course, be speaking to all his colleagues.'

Dawson looked irritated. 'Now you're just being petty, Inspector, hoping to goad me into making some sort of confession. Nice try but it won't work. Speak with whomsoever you like; I can't prevent it.'

'Why would your wife tell us that you were romantically involved with Foreman if that was not the case?' Jack asked. 'If you were as happily married as you told me was the case when you asked me to look for her, why would she be so spiteful?'

'I told you; we'd argued. All couples do. She just wanted to get her revenge.'

'It must have been some argument,' Vickery said. 'What did you disagree about?'

Dawson threw back his head, closed his eyes and yawned. 'What we always argued about. She wanted to work; I wanted her to stay at home. End of.'

'Why were you so opposed to her having a career?' Alexi asked. 'She's intelligent, has a lot to offer. Why hold her back?'

'That's personal. It has nothing to do with Foreman's death and I'm not prepared to discuss the matter unless... until the inspector here can prove its relevance to his investigation. *His* investigation, Ms Ellis. I will answer his questions, if I must, but not yours.'

Of course you won't, Alexi thought, because I'm a woman and you're a grade A misogynist.

'If your wife's career aspirations were a regular cause of conflict between you, what made her walk out on you on this occasion, do you suppose?' Vickery asked.

'That's a question you'd be better advised to ask her.' Dawson flicked at a speck of dust on his trousers, looking bored, disinterested. 'However, a letter came for her after her disappearance. I opened it, thinking it might shed some light on where she'd gone. It was from a fine art auction house in Winchester offering her the position she'd applied for. Perhaps that had some bearing on her decision.'

'She didn't take up the position?'

'Of course not, Inspector. It was the first place that I looked for her. She hadn't responded to their offer so they gave the position to another applicant.'

Vickery glanced at his watch. Alexi knew that Hogan would have asked the police situated closest to Dawson's house to check the bike out. Alexi didn't hold out much hope of their finding anything, in which case Dawson would saunter away, having got the better of them.

'Is there anything else I can help you with, Inspector?' Dawson tapped his fingers impatiently. 'If not, I have things to do, places and people to see. Most importantly, my wife. Where is she?'

'If she wants you to know, she will contact you,' Vickery replied curtly as he glanced at his phone.

As though willing it to ring through the power of his thoughts, the device chirped into life.

'Yes,' Vickery said, holding it to his ear so that none of his caller's words could be overheard. Everyone else in the room remained silent and still, all apparently realising that this was a defining moment.

'I see,' Vickery said, having listened for a short time. 'Thank you. Yes, do that.'

'I'll be off,' Dawson said, standing so abruptly that his chair toppled backwards.

'I think not.' Vickery spoke with quiet authority in his tone. 'Sit down, Mr Dawson. This conversation is not over.' Vickery paused. 'You tell me that you have never ridden your wife's mountain bike.'

'I have not,' he replied with an impatient sigh. 'How many more times?'

'Until we get the truth. How tall is your wife?'

'Five foot six. Why?'

'How tall are you?'

'Six two.'

'A constable your wife's height sat on the saddle of her bike and her feet didn't reach the peddles.' Alexi and Jack exchanged an exuberant glance. 'How do you explain that?'

'I can't. Perhaps she lent it to a friend.'

'She didn't have any friends,' Alexi said. 'You discouraged all her old friendships. And she certainly didn't have any men friends.'

'And it would have been a man riding the bike. A constable of your height tried it and it was exactly right for him.'

'Okay, so I rode it from time to time.' Dawson spread his hands, palms upward. 'What of it?'

'Why deny it then? I asked you the question twice, most specifically.'

'I rode it around the area when Amy first went missing. You can see more from a bike than you can from a car. I was worried about her. I thought she might have had an accident and be lying unconscious somewhere. My using the bike must have slipped my mind.'

'I see.' Alexi suspected that Vickery didn't believe it any more than she did. Dawson was over-explaining, a sure sign of guilt in Jack's manual of detection.

'Here's what I think happened,' Vickery said.

'This should be interesting,' Dawson muttered, but much of the bluster had gone from his attitude. He knew he'd made an error with the bike seat and that would be eating away at a perfectionist of his ilk.

'Peter Foreman and you were involved but Peter became demanding, wanting you to tell your wife. To leave her and set up home with him. But you were having none of it. Your reputation means a lot to you and although most people don't turn a hair at the thought of same-sex relationships any more, you're still in denial. But Peter kept on about it and you knew the affair had run its course. So you invented reasons to get him sacked, thinking you'd got rid of the problem.'

'An interesting theory, Inspector. Have you ever considered taking up fiction writing?'

'But you either didn't know about Peter's upbringing in that hellhole of a home, or else you disregarded it, which was a major error. Peter was abused in the worst possible manner, which toughened him up. Peter had decided never to be a victim again. He wasn't about to be thrown aside when he'd served his purpose either. When he couldn't persuade you to see reason, he took his revenge.' Vickery paused. 'By revealing your relationship to your wife. That's why she took off. It had absolutely nothing to do with her thwarted career.'

Dawson gave a slow, ironic round of applause. 'Gripping and highly plausible, but for one minor difficulty.' Dawson leaned towards Vickery and his voice turned hard. 'You don't have a scrap of evidence to back it up.'

'Your wife's mountain bike is yellow.'

'What of it?'

'A yellow mountain bike was seen at the Swan by a reliable witness at the time of Peter's murder.'

Dawson looked flummoxed – a rare sight – and Alexi revelled in his discomposure. 'So what?' He shrugged. 'There must be more than one in the area.'

'Possibly but most mountain bikes are splattered in mud because of the nature of their use. The one seen on that day was relatively clean by comparison. It's clean state and unusual colour got it noticed.' Vickery went in for the kill. 'You cannot abide dirt or disorder, can you, sir?'

'This is ridiculous!'

'The hotel was quiet that day and there are no cameras. So you put it in the back of Peter's car after killing him, drove to the stretch of water where you fished, which again would have been quiet at this time of year, and ditched the car. You then rode the bike home and cleaned it thoroughly. But you failed to take into account the fact that mountain bike tyres are fat, with a deep tread.' Alexi watched Dawson as he clapped an involuntary hand to his rapidly paling face. 'We've had a lot of rain recently and that section of the river has had input from the East Shefford sewage works as a consequence. Should evidence of that influx be found in the tread of the tyres then that will put you in the area. And trust me, sir, forensic science has come on leaps and bounds in recent years. There won't need to be much trace evidence for them to make the connection.'

Dawson turned sideways on his chair and refused to make eye contact with Vickery. He put Alexi in mind of a small child sulking because he hadn't gotten his way. But she knew that his mind would be churning away as he sought to come up with an explanation.

'You tried to wipe the tyre tracks and your footsteps from the mud,' Vickery continued, 'but you weren't thorough enough. Anyway, it didn't matter because heavy rain was forecast. Unfortunately for you, that rain didn't materialise and a partial footprint has been found, along with a few tyre tracks.'

'Which could have been left there by anyone,' Dawson replied in a disinterested tone.

'The tyre tracks could have been.' Vickery allowed a significant pause. 'Possibly. But if the shoe print matches any of your own footwear... well, we have you banged to rights, as they're inclined to say in TV shows. I've always wanted to use that phrase,' he added, speaking to Jack.

'Why did you take his car?' Alexi asked.

Dawson acted as though she hadn't spoken and so Jack answered the question for him. 'That's what comes of his thinking he's invincible, cleverer than the rest of us. He cycled to the Swan so he could cut across country and avoid being picked up by speed cameras. I'm guessing he realised that Foreman's tablet computer was in the car, probably containing intimate pictures of their relationship. He would have assumed that he'd have it on his person and it would have been easy enough for him to take after he'd murdered his lover. Dawson couldn't risk any evidence of their affair being found, so he took Foreman's phone for the same reason after he's strangled him, along with his keys. He hadn't planned to take the car and shouldn't have done it. We'd have likely never caught him if he'd stuck to the script.' Jack shrugged. 'But he knew the body could be found at any time.'

'Time is the issue here,' Vickery put in. 'The victim was seen alive fifteen minutes before his body was discovered.'

'Right,' Jack agreed, fixing Dawson with a sour look. 'You had to get away before he was found so couldn't waste precious time looking for that tablet and anything else of an incriminating nature that the victim had in his car. Anyway, Inspector,' he added, transferring his glance to Vickery, 'I expect you'll be able to pick the car up on camera now you know where it was taken and at roughly what time. And you'll be able to identify the driver. Like I say, arrogance has its downside.'

'So,' Vickery said, 'let's recap. We know you and Foreman worked together and are pretty sure you were romantically involved. Foreman wanted more than you were prepared to offer him, so you ended the affair and got him kicked out of his job. Foreman was a victim as a child and rejection wasn't an option. So he told your wife what you got up to in your spare time and she legged it.'

Dawson turned to face Vickery, his expression bored as he crossed one well-tailored leg over its twin. 'All very interesting, but pure conjecture. You can't prove a word of it.'

'We'll get to the proof in a moment but for the record, your wife has already confirmed to us that Foreman contacted her.'

Dawson looked a little less sure of himself. 'It's her word against mine.'

'Your wife's bike has been ridden by a man of approximately your height and our forensic team will place it at the site where you disposed of Foreman's car. We also know that you had two phone conversations with Foreman, indicating that you would have known where to find him on the morning in question. Perhaps you even arranged to meet him there, which would explain why he'd left his computer in the car. He wasn't there to further his research for his article. His only interest was in seeing you and trying to make you come to your senses.'

'And, Inspector,' Jack added, 'Dawson here takes a keen interest in phytotoxicology.'

Vickery raised a brow. 'Does he indeed.'

'When did hobbies become a crime?'

'When said hobby is used to commit one,' Jack shot back.

'If you say so.'

'Oh, I do.' It was Vickery who spoke. 'It's enough for us to charge you with first-degree murder, Mr Dawson, but if you continue to deny any involvement then we will have to delve into your life with a fine-tooth comb, looking for more evidence of an affair that you continue to deny *did* take place. Needless to say, we will also have to talk to all your work colleagues and—'

'Okay.' Dawson held up both hands. 'Enough. I did arrange to meet Peter at the Swan and have things out with him. His telling Amy about us brought me to my senses and made me realise what's really important to me. The tendencies that Peter brought out in me aren't who I am but it was... I don't know, like a drug. I couldn't keep away from him. So I tried to cool it but Peter was having none of it. He said I was in denial and would never be happy if I continued to live a lie. Our relationship turned toxic and I had to get him out of my workspace. It was the only way that I stood a chance of resisting the allure.' He ran a hand though his hair. 'God help me, I've never known anything like it. I just couldn't stay away.'

'Before you go any further, Mr Dawson,' Vickery said. 'If you're admitting to murder then this needs to be done formally under caution at the station.'

Dawson shrugged. 'Doesn't much matter where I bare my soul, does it? I've lost everything that matters to me, most especially my reputation. I agreed to meet Peter that last time and knew we'd finish up... well, you know. I seem to lose all resistance when with him. We went to the men's room. He laughed at me and said he knew what I wanted, that I'd never be able to let him go. He was right. I saw then a future of denial, of tearing myself in two and something inside of me snapped. I strangled him.'

'What with?' Jack asked.

'A length of cord that Amy kept on her bike. God alone knows what for, or why I took it with me for that matter.'

Premeditation, Alexi thought. He'd planned to silence Peter all along and was now trying to pass it off as a spur of the moment decision. *I snapped. I didn't mean to kill him.* But he absolutely did mean to. He'd gone there with a drug to subdue the man he both loved and hated. The only part of the operation that such a meticulous man hadn't planned was the taking of Peter's car and that had proven to be his downfall.

'What was on the laptop that you went to so much trouble to get your hands on?' Jack asked.

Dawson shrugged. 'I suppose it doesn't matter now. Photos,' he said. 'Peter took photos of us in compromising positions and was threatening to email them to my department. I had to stop him. I should have just taken the tablet from his car but I couldn't be sure that he hadn't printed off the pictures. He'd put one through my door, you see. That's why I agreed to meet with him. I couldn't risk anyone finding them so dumped the car in the river, knowing that they'd be unrecognisable if they existed and were subsequently found.'

Vickery motioned to DC Hogan, who read Dawson his rights. A uniformed officer, stationed outside the door, was summoned and his handcuffs were put to the use they were intended for.

'I assume by admitting to my momentary lapse that this won't all have to come out in court,' he said to Vickery.

Alexi and Jack exchanged a glance. Even now, when he'd lost everything, his primary thought was for his reputation. She shook her head in stark disbelief as she watched a ruthless killer being led away.

'It's over, darling,' Jack said, slipping an arm around her shoulders, 'and not one iota of blame can be attached to you.'

'I know. I ought to feel relieved but... I don't know. I just feel tired.'

'Do you want to put Amy out of her misery?'

'Yeah, I'll do that right now.'

'You realise there's one more loose end to tie up?'

Alexi nodded. 'Yes,' she replied with a grimace. 'I do.'

20

'I'm not surprised,' Amy said, taking the news with commendable calm. 'He'll go to prison for a long time, won't he?'

'Yep. A life sentence, I imagine. It wasn't a crime of passion, as he will doubtless try to imply. He went armed with a ligature and a poison to subdue Peter with. I dare say a search of his internet history will prove where that drug came from but since you've told us of his interest in that subject then he can't worm he way out of it.'

'I'm still surprised that he confessed.'

'He knew he'd made an error with the bike and was clever enough to realise that admitting what he'd done would prevent a sensational trial in which all his activities would come to light,' Alexi explained. 'Besides, if Peter did have pictures of them stored somewhere online then they would come out too. He wouldn't risk that.'

'No, he most emphatically would not.' Amy sighed. 'Poor Neil. I almost feel sorry for him.'

'It is a tragedy all round,' Alexi replied.

'Well, that's it then. I can collect the things I want from the house and return to my life in Italy. I won't be needed here, will I?'

'The police will want to talk to you but since your husband has confessed then no, you shouldn't be needed.'

'Thank you,' Amy said, impulsively hugging Alexi. 'I'm afraid I feel nothing other than relief to be shot of him finally. And if that sounds heartless then I make no apology. He's made my life a living hell, forcing me to live the life he wanted for me. It was stifling.' She gave a little laugh. 'I sometimes wonder how I resisted the urge to kill *him*. I thought about it more than once in my more desperate moments.'

'It's entirely understandable,' Alexi assured her. 'Send me your address when you get settled in Italy and Jack and I will come and visit.'

'You'll always be welcome.'

Alexi paused on the stairs as she made her way back down them, aware that Jack would have summoned Cassie. She had a lot of explaining to do and that explanation would be make or break for her business partnership with Jack. *If* that partnership was not already broken beyond repair and that, Alexi knew, was a very big if.

She entered the kitchen to find Cassie there with Jack. She had clearly hung around after dropping Amy off, despite intimating that she was returning to the office. At least she wasn't a coward and was prepared to face the music that she had to know would be coming.

'Hey.' Jack looked up and smiled at Alexi as she walked in: that soft, intimate smile that never failed to melt her insides.

'I'm so sorry,' Cassie said to Alexi, sounding sincere.

'We were waiting for you so that Cassie can tell us together what the hell she was playing at.' Jack's tone was brisk, emotionless. His expression cast in stone. Alexi knew that he was furious and struggling to contain his anger. Jack valued loyalty over almost any other human trait. He had been made a scapegoat and driven out of the Met through a campaign of lies and half-truths. Little or no support had been forthcoming from the organisation that had employed him for so long and had a duty of care. Jack's scars ran deep and so Alexi could understand why his resentment at his partner's duplicity had hurt him so badly.

'Amy didn't use her card at the Swan,' Cassie said, swallowing and looking deathly pale. 'It was a ruse to get Jack there at the same time as you, Alexi. I knew he wouldn't question my findings, you see.'

'Why?' Alexi asked. 'What did you hope to get out of it?'

'It was Patrick who persuaded me.'

Alexi nodded, unsurprised to hear it. She had sensed his manipulating hand behind things from the first. 'Go on,' she said.

'He told me that you had a roving eye, enjoyed the high life and rubbing shoulders with the rich and famous, which you had done during your years in London. He said you'd soon grow tired of Lambourn and would leave, breaking Jack's heart.'

Jack looked ready to commit a few murders of his own. Alexi though wasn't surprised to hear what Cassie had told them. She indicated to Jack that he should keep quiet and not interrupt Cassie's flow.

'I believed it because I wanted to,' Cassie said, biting her lower lip. 'Anyway, Patrick said that Peter Foreman worked for him. He'd commissioned him to come on to Alexi publicly during the course. The idea was for you to catch them together in a compromising position at the Swan, Jack.' She shook her head. 'I'm so sorry. I don't know what I was thinking, going along with it.'

'Patrick can be very persuasive,' Alexi said, shaking her head in disgust. 'But I didn't think that even he would stoop that low. I blew your plans by arriving early and having a public argument with Peter about his tactics at the Swan. An argument that no one could interpret as intimate. Then I left. As for Peter, he had his own agenda that Patrick knew nothing about. His mind would have been full of his anticipated reunion with Dawson and so he didn't even try to seduce me.'

'I got held up in traffic and arrived later than anticipated,' Jack said.

'It was a stupid idea anyway,' Cassie said. 'I never felt comfortable with it.' She threw up her hands. 'When will I learn? I'm going back to the office, Jack. I guess you will want to break our partnership up after this. Call me when you've had a chance to think about it and we'll decide how to go about it.'

She left with a quiet dignity that Alexi admired. She knew that her feelings for Jack ran as deep as ever and that she would realise there was definitely no hope for her getting together with him now, even if Alexi's relationship with him didn't bear up under the strain. Alexi, despite all the trouble Cassie had caused, felt sorry for her.

'Don't be hard on her, Jack,' she said. 'She was played by the hand of a master.'

'I know, but still...'

'Let's take a few days off, you, me and Cosmo. Go somewhere and have a complete break.' Alexi grinned. 'Away from Polly Pearson and her gossiping, which will go into overdrive when the results of this murder investigation break. What's the betting that she still tries to implicate me somehow? Away from my agent, who's pushing for the first draft of the book I've committed to writing. Away from everything. We need to put what's happened into perspective and we can't do that here.'

Cosmo looked up and meowed.

'Seems I'm outnumbered,' Jack said, smiling. 'How about Cornwall?'

Alexi slipped onto his lap and wrapped her arms around his neck. 'Sounds perfect,' she said, 'providing we can find a cat-friendly hotel.'

ACKNOWLEDGMENTS

My thanks as always to the wonderful Boldwood team and in particular, to my talented editor, Emily Ruston.

ABOUT THE AUTHOR

E.V. Hunter has written a great many successful regency romances as Wendy Soliman and revenge thrillers as Evie Hunter. She is now redirecting her talents to produce cosy murder mysteries. For the past twenty years she has lived the life of a nomad, roaming the world on interesting forms of transport, but has now settled back in the UK.

Sign up to E.V. Hunter's mailing list here for news, competitions and updates on future books.

Follow E.V. Hunter on social media:

x.com/wendyswriter

facebook.com/wendy.soliman.author

bookbub.com/authors/wendy-soliman

ALSO BY E.V. HUNTER

The Hopgood Hall Murder Mysteries

A Date To Die For

A Contest To Kill For

A Marriage To Murder For

A Story to Strangle For

Revenge Thrillers

The Sting

The Trap

The Chase

The Scam

The Kill

The Alibi

Poison & Pens

POISON & PENS IS THE HOME OF
COZY MYSTERIES SO POUR YOURSELF
A CUP OF TEA & GET SLEUTHING!

DISCOVER PAGE-TURNING NOVELS FROM
YOUR FAVOURITE AUTHORS &
MEET NEW FRIENDS

JOIN OUR
FACEBOOK GROUP

BIT.LYPOISONANDPENSFB

SIGN UP TO OUR
NEWSLETTER

BIT.LY/POISONANDPENSNEWS

Boldwood

Boldwood Books is an award-winning fiction publishing company seeking out the best stories from around the world.

Find out more at www.boldwoodbooks.com

Join our reader community for brilliant books, competitions and offers!

Follow us

@BoldwoodBooks

@TheBoldBookClub

Sign up to our weekly deals newsletter

https://bit.ly/BoldwoodBNewsletter

Printed in Great Britain
by Amazon

36339201R00149